ROWING HOME

ROWING HOME

Sybil Terres Gilmar

Wising Up Press

Wising Up Press
P.O. Box 2122
Decatur, GA 30031-2122
www.universaltable.org

ISBN: 978-1-7376940-5-2

Catalogue-in-Publication data is on file with the Library of Congress.
LCCN: 2022948319

For my family
who made me a better and wiser woman

For my rowing community
who expanded my horizons

Chapter 1

George Grossinger turned from his position in the number two seat to catch the eye of his friend, Arthur Schwartz, in the number four seat of the wooden eight that had just glided toward the far end of the dock, leaving precisely enough room to tilt starboard oars perfectly in place. Both young men knew there would be an acknowledgment of friendship and trust—it had been that way ever since they first met as freshmen at Berlin University and found their way as two German Jews who enthusiastically rowed with fellow university students at the Germania Club. Coming in from practice early evening, the eight rowers stood up in the boat, planting a left leg on the dock, then at the command of the coxswain, pulling the port oar in with a motion that settled four long oars nearly simultaneously on the dock. George turned to see the last vestiges of sunlight glint off the slight waves of the Spree River as he grabbed his shoes.

"Don't linger," shouted Henry, the nineteen-year-old coxswain, who spoke with authority despite his slight 5'6" frame and weight of 120 pounds. George returned quickly to the boat, ready to join the others to hoist it on his shoulder, knowing full well that Henry, although diminutive, could use his role as coxswain and newfound Aryan ideology to make life difficult for both him and Arthur. The coxswain wasn't the coach, but still, he had eyes on the crew at all times and seemed to want to let people know that although small in stature, he held power. He was also responsible for getting boats deftly in and out of the water.

"Hands on!" cried Henry, as tall and spare young men spread out among eight aluminum riggers, kneeled slightly, and each placed a left hand on starboard and right on port.

"Overhead," came the following command, and eight young men, each at least six feet tall, stood from kneeling position and raised the boat overhead with a deftness that indicated ease and authority despite the grueling hour-workout just completed on the water. Although their coach, Conrad Messinger, philosophized that more challenging drills paid off at races, sometimes he would have the rowers complete a steady-state row at a lower pace with longer strokes. For some reason, George found those more tiring.

With four men on either side, each easily holding his portion of the weight with raised arms, they moved the boat up the ramp and into the boathouse, where, in unison, they hoisted it onto the third-highest rack.

"George," called Henry. "You stay and wipe down the boat's insides too. I don't think you need a reminder that seawater is not good for boats."

George started to protest because he had already had his turn, and according to the roster, it was Johan's responsibility tonight to wipe the boat clear of excess water and dirt. George decided not to argue when he saw that Coach Messinger was not yet at the dock. George knew Henry would have avoided his unnecessary directions if the coach was within earshot.

Arthur passed by. "I can help."

"No. Your friend, George, he can do it himself." Henry stood with folded hands, seemingly ready to supervise.

"I'll wait," said Arthur, and he walked back to the dock, still able to see, lining the river, the outlines of the goods promised to the populace by the new German leader, Hitler. Although only a sliver of the moon shone, tugboats streamed, and trawlers and freighters lingered. The early-evening sky was filled with a few stars that shone down on the river, which had grown calm as winds died down at dusk.

George grabbed a towel and wiped the boat in a fury, although he was bone tired. Henry grinned a crooked smile.

Coach Messinger slowed his motorboat as he approached the dock, lifted his eyebrows slightly to acknowledge Arthur.

"You still here," he asked. Not exactly a question.

Even in the dusk, Arthur could see the tightness of his coach's cheekbones, his strong jawline with his dark blond hair cut close to his head. A light jacket covered a spare, muscular, six-foot frame. He stepped onto the dock with grace and reached for the rope to tie the launch securely to a metal S-hook fixed to the dock. He quickly ripped off his safety vest and tossed it back into the launch as though it was an unnecessary annoyance.

"Just waiting for Georgie Grossie to finish cleaning the boat," Arthur said comfortably, using the family nickname for his friend. Arthur had watched the simmering confrontation between George and Henry, who had expressed his admiration of Hitler. Even at rowing practice, it was hard to avoid the quietly looming political tensions. Although never stated aloud, Arthur knew coach Messinger was unhappy with the pronouncements by Goebbels about the superiority of Aryans. The boathouse now had a radio like so many households in Germany, and if Goebbels came on, Messinger would immediately shut it down, muttering and shaking his head. "Not my Germany." He never took down the photos with the medals awarded to Hans Goldfarb and Jonathan Golden in 1924. Nor had Messinger ever commented about the Jewish blood of the medalists.

Neither George nor Arthur knew that Messinger suspected that one of his ancestors might have been Jewish somewhere back in his past, beyond his great grandfather. What they did was trust him to be fair and dedicated to the sport.

"Go home," Messinger said. "And eat. You need to be ready for tomorrow's practice."

Outside the boathouse, where only streetlights shone, Arthur and George grabbed a tram to their homes in the Charlottenburg section of Berlin. Headlines from the passengers' newspapers practically roared at them: "Adolf Hitler to Be Leader and Chancellor—Fuhrer, and Reichskanzler."

"Do you see?" Arthur whispered. "Ninety percent approval rating."

George averted his eyes.

"All right. Bury your head in the sand," Arthur said.

"Just shush."

Arthur lowered his gaze to avoid the eyes of the newspaper reader, who had looked up at the whispered conversation.

George turned toward the window, looked fleetingly at Werthheim's map store, which seemed to have the courage to hang a map of the world in the window. The message from politicians of late had been that they needed to look to the motherland for their dreams and strengthen her. But George knew that behind that map stood colorful globes that could be spun around to demonstrate the plentitude of the earth with all its mysteries. He wondered, considering the day's news spewing venom toward "outsiders," if he could find another spot for himself in the world with less uncertainty and pain. He drew images in his mind of beautiful rivers and lakes and imagined himself rowing with a comfortable and powerful connection to the water.

George got off the next stop with his customary good-by to Arthur. "See you tomorrow at practice" and hurried to his home, looking forward to the dinner he knew would be waiting for him.

Arthur stared after his friend through the departing trolley window and saw George deliberately walk away from a man standing on a corner and reading the newspaper with headlines that blared about Hitler.

"Mom, "George called at the entrance door

"Come, sit. We're waiting for you." She greeted him with a hug

"Don't ask too many questions," she warned him, her black hair with slivers of gray, neatly coiffed in a short hairstyle and parted on the side. Her pearl necklace hung over the heart-shaped neckline of the navy-blue silk dress decorated with shipboard anchors. She had always adored the ocean and sometimes bought clothes as a testament to this love. At times, he thought, that's where he got his love of connecting with the water in a boat. Rowing was his own and totally his own.

His father, Werner, sat at the head of the table set with a white linen tablecloth and sparkling glasses and china. Folding back his newspaper and peering over his reading glasses, he appeared grim.

As Werner looked up to see his wife, Frieda, push through the swinging door of the dining room to the kitchen, he thought she had not changed all that much from the girl who loved music so much that she forgot to eat, to the woman who now took care of the family's nutritional needs, and yet still managed to display that fiery joy for her violin. When he observed her students who came to her for lessons, he noted there were those who picked up her passion and others who just drilled away.

He knew she was disappointed that George didn't follow her interest in music, that he was content with his passion for art and his rowing. Recently George had managed to get copies of Thomas Eakins paintings, and he would work for hours trying to copy *Max Weiner in a Scull* as though that act would transmit the skills necessary to become a fierce rower. At least, Werner reflected, there's that passion in both of them. I'm sure he gets it from her because, at least, I know when to let something go.

But do I, he wondered? Right now, the newspaper was being besieged by the Minister of Propaganda and even its readers, to print nothing but good stories about what was happening—especially the service of the brown shirts and those committed to seeing Germany the way it was before 1918—before it was so miserably treated by the Treaty of Versailles. This was the story that Hitler and his ministers wanted to see. This was what "The Day of the Awakening Nation" was all about, and Werner could see that more and more people were buying into it even though it promoted the demise of the labor unions. Not his Frieda—she was too bright for that. He loved her intelligence, her ardor, traits that translated well in the bedroom, and though he hardly ever told her, he was eternally grateful for her unabashed displays of passion. These helped to smooth the edges of his rough world—there was no hint of musicality in printing a newspaper now.

Folding the newspaper, he said quietly, "We need to leave Germany. This news is not good. It keeps getting worse. All these conversations about maybe it will be getting better are evaporating with time."

Frieda looked up from her plate. "Listen. It's your newspaper. Change the news. After we eat, we will talk. The stuffed cabbage will not wait."

George looked up from his plate of food. "I'm with mother. We cannot leave. Besides, our boat is going to win in the next regatta. I need to be in that boat with Arthur."

"Maybe, you'll win," said his father, "and maybe you'll lose. You have to be realistic."

"Your classes are important, too," said his mother, ladling stuffed cabbage onto plates. "You can't leave in the middle of a semester." She felt that this was not the time to say anything about the difficulty of leaving her orchestra and music students. Let George and his rowing have the headline today.

"Turn on the radio," Werner Grossinger demanded.

"But we are eating," his wife said.

"The world is crumbling," he said. "We can eat and listen at the same time."

"You think you're going to get the truth?" George eagerly ate the stuffed cabbage. He knew he must have consumed 6000 calories in that practice. "With Goebbels in power?"

They stopped eating when they heard the commentator say, "Don't shop at any business run by a Jew." He added, "Yes, that is what we need to do."

"See," said his father. "The commentator—the idiot whose name I can never remember, is supporting this idea that the German people need to retaliate against the German Jews who are saying bad things about Hitler." He drew a sharp breath. "It's utter nonsense—that's all it is."

"But Hitler might consider restarting the Olympics, and our crew would have a shot." George tried to minimize the pleading tone; he knew his father hated it.

"Please, no more talk with his name in it," said his mother.

"You will see," said his father. "The handwriting is on the wall. Do you think they will let you and Arthur row in the Olympics if they are not letting the Jews own businesses?".

Frieda Grossinger offered her son a piece of black rye bread that appeared like a peace offering. Her eyes implored him. "No more dissension. Change the subject."

"No thanks, Mom. I have to maintain weight. I plan to row lightweight in a double with Arthur."

Acknowledging her son's request, Frieda put the bread back on the plate. She wished she understood more about her son's passion for rowing. She was a violinist, and it was with music she could explain everything: rhythm, shading, dynamics, the joy of a composer. In those wistful moments of conversation with her son, he had tried to explain to her that rhythm in rowing is equally important.

She sighed. 'You have such blisters on your hands. I could never play the violin with such hands."

George grinned. "I could never play with or without the blisters. But you can understand my desire. I understand yours. After all, I listen to hours and hours of practice, and I've learned to love *Mozart Symphony Number Forty in G Minor*." He hummed the first few bars off-key.

His mother smiled and waved her hand. "Enough. I understand. Just finish your dinner and bring your plate into the kitchen."

Before going to sleep, George lingered over a rowing magazine advertising Empacher boats; these were being built somewhere east of Berlin. If he won in the double with Arthur, perhaps a company would be willing to sponsor them for future events. George drifted off to sleep dreaming of the sleekness of a wooden shell crafted especially for a seat that slid effortlessly—and the veneer that caught light that emanated from both sky and water.

He dreamed of his ability to take in the eight liters of oxygen needed to maintain the stroke rate and output to race his boat past his opponents. He saw Coach Messinger beside him, urging him on with a shorter layback and demanding he sit straighter at the end of the stroke, thus being more prepared to begin the slide efficiently. He saw himself having a brief conversation about the possibility of changing the design of the long oars and realized, when he woke, that painting them from white to blue would not make one bit of difference in speed. He awoke in a sweat because, in the dream, he had caught a crab—the oar had entered the water too deeply, had become stuck, and although the boat would keep going, the oar would not. For some reason, the dream did not have him tumbling into the water after this mistake. But upon awakening, he thought this little dream episode should serve as a reminder of the need to pay attention.

CHAPTER 2

After dinner, Frieda gathered the music she had strewn on a coffee table in the living room, and a glance at the first few bars prompted the ordering in her mind of what she thought to be tonight's orchestra rehearsal. Beethoven's *Fifth* would be first and then Mendelssohn's *Italian Symphony*, which they might not have time to complete. Then again, they might not get to it because his grandfather was named Moses Mendelssohn. Respect and rehearsal time for composers of Jewish heritage were becoming more and more limited.

She slung the music knapsack over her shoulder. *I need to spend less time listening to the radio and talking to my parents*, she thought. And more time practicing. But recently, during their daily calls, her parents voiced more and more concerns about the crackdowns on Jewish businesses. They could no longer open their jewelry store on Langerstrasse without fear of graffiti on Jewish storefronts.

She had spent extra time practicing today even though she had played Beethoven's *Fifth Symphony* so many times, she could practically play her violin part without music.

At the last rehearsal Hans Friedrich, the conductor, had warned them that Goebbels, the Reich Minister of Propaganda, might be in the audience. Her stand partner, Paul Fuchs, had also suggested that she be prepared with the "Horst Wessel Song."

"Why are you telling me this? Why didn't Friedrich give me the music?"

"You know," he had said with his eyes cast down, handing her a copy.

"That is just nonsense," Frieda had retorted. "My Jewishness can't be the issue. Besides, we haven't stepped foot in a synagogue in years, and my grandmother said the last synagogue we went to was more like a church—an organ. We had an organ," she repeated with emphasis. "And he can't expect me to play that song without music. The idiot wanted me to look like a fool."

"I can share my copy of the "Horst Wessel Song." Unless you know it from memory," Paul said.

"Memory? Why would I know that song from memory? Musically, it's terrible." Reluctantly, she had taken a copy of the song and practiced the violin part, trying hard not to hear the words in her head about raising the flag and how millions were looking upon the swastika with hope. These words did not define her Germany—her father had served in The Great War. Beethoven, Bach, Mendelssohn, Wagner—some of the most brilliant musicians in history were German. Yes, Germany had struggled after the war, but music had gotten them through. The Berlin Symphony still counted as one of the greatest orchestras in the world. And so did the Kroll Opera, with Otto Klemperer as conductor. And wasn't Klemperer Jewish someplace along the line? She saw the display of the swastika as a false promise of hope to some and worry to others in the population.

Also, at the last rehearsal, Frieda had noticed that Morton Goldberg from the cello section was no longer there, but she assumed he had gone on to take another job somewhere else. Or maybe he had just returned to teaching full time. *I don't know. I should be in touch with him,* she mused. *I do not want to think the worst.*

With the music already in her knapsack, Frieda lovingly placed the violin in its case along with the handkerchief used to tuck under her chin for comfort and the rosin she needed for her bow. She clicked the case closed with some measure of defiance. *Let's see what anybody dares to do after tonight's rehearsal. Let's see if they think there's a better first violinist.*

"Werner? George?" she called out with the door open. "There's mandel bread cookies in the bin. Don't leave a mess for Ingrid. Get some of the dishes washed. Also, if any of my students call, take a number. I will call back."

Ever since the order that only Aryans could acquire civil service status, she noted that Elsa and Johann—both excellent violin students and Johann, a prodigy—had not been back for a lesson. But the mother in her always commingled with her thoughts about family. Almost simultaneously, she worried about George consuming more than a modest proportion of the mandel bread. His practices on the river made him ravenous at mealtime. She would ask Ingrid to make some more. Baking had never been her strength, nor was anything connected to kitchen duties.

On the trolley, Frieda saw most passengers staring glumly out the windows, some reading newspapers with headlines blaring "Watch Your Neighbor." Several passengers wore coats frayed at the collar and cuffs; men's hair that needed to be cut stuck out beneath dirty caps. *It's a blessing that we have a concert,* she thought. *People want to come to hear music, not watch their neighbor. Maybe that's the good that has come with Fuhrer. People have money to pay for tickets.*

Werner had told her that President Hindenburg was too frail to continue to fight the rise of Hitler's National Socialist Party; he would capitulate, and it would be a disaster for Germany. Her head told her maybe; her heart told her no because she wanted to go on with her music. She also wanted Werner to continue to be the fierce newspaper editor she adored. Editing was his core. So was putting finishing touches on stories he hoped would touch his readers. He would say, "I want to make the readers smarter. We have too much stupid." She would wrap her arms around him and say, "Stupidity. We have stupidity." He would say, "In this case, I can say stupid," smile gleefully, scoop her into his arms, and pick her up, saying, "Stupidity, stupid. What's the difference? I love you, but we still have a lot of stupid."

She pulled the bell cord to alert the conductor for her stop, descended in the street lit by one lamp, and quickly passed beggars lying on the sidewalk. There were fewer now; maybe that was another good thing that came from the Third Reich. *But where had the others gone,* Frieda wondered? She entered the music hall through the stage door, dropped her coat, and rushed to take her seat as she heard musicians tuning up. When she sat down, she gasped; a large Nazi flag hung at the back of the stage. *Thank goodness she would not see it while she played*—but Friedrich, the conductor, would. *Only when he looked up from his music,* she thought. *Yes, the music keeps one sane and focused on the beautiful possibility of making all the sounds of the instruments blend to offer just the right tone. That sound allowed people to feel that beauty is a prospect in everyday existence.* She looked out at the audience, startled to see what looked like a brown wave every few rows. *Were young men buying into this nonsense of trying to act like authoritarian soldiers? They were just kids,* she thought, but they apparently liked being bullies. *Thank goodness George had his rowing and his university studies. Universities with their bright minds would not tolerate such nonsense.*

She shook her head, trying to shake the thought away, and started to put the "Horst Wessel" music on the stand when her eye caught the piece of paper with the writing, "Let the Jews moan and bloat, the Nazi list is what we vote." She quickly turned, and Simon, a second violinist behind her, averted his eyes and shrugged.

The lights dimmed, and a rustling emanated from the audience. Heads turned to see black-booted members of the SA come down the aisle and take their seats. Frieda watched conductor, Hans Friedrich raise his baton.

Instead of giving the downbeat for the first note, he mouthed the words to the orchestra "Stand, Heil Hitler" and raised his hands. Everyone stood because that gesture from conductor to orchestra members always meant stand; and then take your bow with him. But this time, after they stood, Friedrich immediately raised his right hand, waited a beat, and after a moment's hesitation, all orchestra members raised right hands. When Friedrich turned to face the audience and said, "Heil Hitler," several orchestra members said the two defining words along with him, some with more energy than others.

Frieda was so stunned that she could not remember what she did other than stand. She must have raised her right hand because she knew that, if she hadn't, she would have been reprimanded—if not by Hans, by Simon, who, as orchestra organizer, had recently joined the National Socialist Party and made it known to everyone. Frieda had surmised that keeping her job as first violinist meant complying with insidious practices.

"We will begin with the "Horst Wessel Song," Friedrich said to his audience. A sporadic round of applause followed. "We can do better than that," Friedrich said to the audience, striving for a pleasant tone. This second round of applause also gave his orchestra members time to find the music. As the first few bars of the "Horst Wessel Song" played, the audience stood immediately following the lead of the SA members.

⟶

As she opened the door to the apartment, Frieda looked at her watch; it read 10:30, and she was wide awake. Performances always did that to her, but tonight's agitation was the instigator.

"George, Werner," she called, throwing the knapsack on the coffee table. It landed with a thud.

"Sh," said Werner, opening the bedroom door, reading glasses in one hand and a cigarette in the other. "George is asleep. He has early morning rowing practice tomorrow."

"All right. Werner, then. Just you."

"Then, what?"

"We are not leaving. We will stay and fight this . . . this . . . this," Frieda sputtered. "This puny dictator. This thug. You, with your newspaper! Me, with my music." She pulled the kitchen chair out and collapsed in its seat, elbows on the table, head in hands.

"Darling, throwing your knapsack won't help. The people don't think this dictator is so puny or a thug. France likes the idea of a dictator so much, she has two parties embracing fascism."

Frieda slumped in the kitchen chair and started to cry. "My parents. My music. My country. We've got to do something."

He gently tousled the hair on her bent head. "We will. Without being trite, let me say tomorrow is another day." He took her hand and gently led her to the bedroom. He had thought to himself that leaving might be the only solution for us. He didn't think this was the right time to share that thought.

"For George, too," she continued. "We have to do something for George. For his future. What we see now cannot be his future."

Chapter 3

Captain Ben Leicester, of the British Army, stripped off his khaki uniform pants—he had worn his athletic shorts underneath to save time—quickly unbuttoned his shirt and kicked off his sandals, grateful that army boots were not regulation. He threw the excess clothes in a heap on the stone floor of the warehouse. The hastily improvised structure was bare of everything but two wooden single sculls and oars leaning up against a wall of corrugated tin. He walked to the side of the makeshift building to relieve himself even though no one else was around at this ungodly hour of 6:00 a.m.

Given the possibility of soaring temperatures as the sun rose higher, Ben knew this was the best time to do the hard rowing that so energized him. He would start with a pace of about twenty-two on the slide, gradually move up to what he imagined would be about a thirty-eight, and then cool off with about ten minutes of steady-state back to twenty-two.

Leicester knew he desperately needed time to reconnect with the river and disengage from the relentless boredom and dissatisfaction of his British army assignment in Haifa. The briefing before his arrival was short. We've been here (the British, of course) since 1918, and Haifa is becoming a busy port, maybe even an airport and a British hospital in the works. It's ours— but it is such a complicated history, and no one wants to hear it

Early morning was the only time Lieutenant Colonel Harry Markham would allow Leicester time off from his unsavory duty of keeping Arabs and Jews from killing each other. Markham's daily briefings with his troop of British soldiers tried to emphasize the critical importance of their mission. Still, his soldiers seemed uncomfortable not only with the heat but with these unruly and somewhat exotic people. The khaki shorts and short-sleeved uniforms exposed the recruits' muscled, sweating appearance. With rifles slung over their shoulders, they stood guard at various intersections, trying to exert a presence that symbolized "keeping the peace." It barely worked. British command knew that the Jews had gone underground with their fight to establish Palestine as their homeland. Leicester thought that, after all these years, they would have given up. After all, what did the desert have to offer?

It was now 1933, but the Balfour Declaration of 1917, giving Jews a homeland, had been met with enormous resistance by the Arabs, who had lived under the Turks in the Ottoman Empire for hundreds of years. Palestine had long been part of Ottoman Syria. Yes, Jews had lived there as well, and it was simply a territory, not recognized as its own country with a functioning government. Jews would be the last people the Arabs would want to rule over them. They would prefer the meandering limited current rule of the British governing under a League of Nations mandate, or better yet, their sovereignty. But many Jews had memorized the words of Balfour's letter of declaration: "His Majesty's Government view with favor the establishment in Palestine of a national home for the Jewish people."

Both Ben and his Lieutenant Colonel, Harry Markham, had done their rowing on the Henley before this unforgiving assignment in Palestine. Rowing and being an officer in the British Army seemed to go together. From its raw beginnings in the boats of slave galleys, rowing had managed to evolve into a gentleman's sport. How does something go from utilitarian roots to become an intensively followed sport, he had often wondered?

Ben did know that the camaraderie engendered by rowing in an eight had been memorable, but that could not be duplicated in this desert and violence-ridden stretch of land that seemed to consume and produce passions at an equal rate. Desert heat and extreme temperatures only slightly slowed down daily conflicts.

The single scull was where he had left it the last time he rowed—hull side up with two slings supporting it on either end. Ben hoisted the single scull onto his shoulder, shifting its weight somewhat under its heft. He was accustomed to the weight being evenly distributed among eight rowers. Fortunately, the walk was less than ten feet from the warehouse to the Kishon River. The oars already rested along the shoreline. From his shoulder, he swung the boat in a narrow arc and placed it gently and deep enough into the water so the skeg would not get caught in the sediment. With quiet reverence, he slid the oars into the oarlocks, grabbed the right and left oar handles to align with his right hand, then gracefully placed his right foot on the boat deck and gently lowered his torso, putting first his left foot and then right into the straps affixed to the boat footplate. He put on his cap and sunglasses and took a small breath, digging the starboard oar into the river bottom to push off. He clasped both oar handles, adjusting his grip to leave the fewest blisters, although he knew some would appear on his palms after so much time away from rowing.

Would the villagers ever think of putting a dock here? he wondered. *Doubt it*, he answered himself. *They're too busy fighting one another—they'll never get to the pleasures of the sport of rowing—you had to have some degree of stability and civilization in your country, and none of that seemed to be going on here.*

Ben focused on getting himself on the right path on the water to avoid being stuck on an embankment and started the row with a slow continuous slide for about ten minutes. Occasionally, he looked at the land alongside, and after a half-hour of rowing, he saw the remains of a quarantine camp for Jews. Mostly immigrants from Poland, these Jews, inspired by Theodor Herzl's plea to establish a homeland, had fled in a desperate attempt to escape pogroms. Who could blame them? But here? Malaria ruled without an easy cure because mosquitoes reigned and governing required baksheesh—the Arab word for "bribe." No, he thought going back to his days as a divinity student, this river flowing to the Mediterranean and its shores has been forsaken by God even though according to the Old Testament, Deborah praised the Kishon River for washing away the Canaanite army.

Ben paused and grabbed the two oar handles with one hand so he could use the other to slap away the mosquitoes buzzing around his head close to his ear. He stopped to look around, thought he had done about 10,000 meters, decided it was time to turn back. The sun was now significantly higher when the zing of a bullet zipped right past his ear, interrupting the buzzing of mosquitoes. Instinctively, he crouched down his head toward the stern of the boat. Then quiet. Dare he get up and start to row? He had to. Staying down huddled this way was not an option. He peered up and saw along the shoreline what appeared to him a young man with unkempt, ragged garments, a black handkerchief covering his nose and mouth, and another wrapped around his forehead that didn't entirely hide his mass of dark, curly hair. A rifle that should have been slung over his shoulder was held dangling by his side in his left hand.

"You should not be here," shouted the young man in Arabic. Ben was grateful that the British Army required that he study the language for this assignment. He understood the words perfectly despite the young man's heavy accent.

Ben saw the rifle being raised again and began a process of rowing hard and ducking. *Row and duck*, he thought. *They never taught me this at Oxford.*

The young man stopped shooting long enough to shout, "This land belongs to Iraqi Petroleum."

I'm not going to stop and let him know that I'm here to protect the interests of Iraqi Petroleum. Great Britain, since Colonel Lawrence had set foot, thought of Palestine as being rich in petroleum. Ben, with heart pounding, breath racing, and pain in his quads so severe, knew he was over his maximal aerobic capacity, and he was producing lactate. The last time he had felt such pain was in his senior year, May 1930, at Oxford when he rowed against Cambridge's Tad Phillips. Leicester recalled that this level of pain gave him the two-second win over Tad, who had been his nemesis for many years. He prayed it was going to get him safely back now.

The next two shots sounded as though they had been fired into the air. Ben turned and saw the corrugated metal wall of the warehouse coming into view. He was slowing the pace of the oars to give him some breathing relief when he heard more voices in Hebrew. He knew enough to hear them shout "leave him alone" in authoritative voices. His attacker was now nowhere in sight. His "rescuers" must have waited close by or spread out along the shoreline.

Ben looked for a spot to rest the boat close enough to shore where he could get out without injuring the skeg now that he was under some sort of protection. He stood up slowly in the boat and carefully placed his left foot in the shallow water while pulling the port oar in. He was grateful to put his aching feet in cool water before he reached the hot sand.

In front of the warehouse stood two young people, maybe darkened by the sun, each attired in khaki shirts and shorts. To his surprise, he saw one with a casually slung rifle was a young woman. Both had sweat-soaked kerchiefs around their necks. The boy's was blue; the girl's was pink.

Ben sighed and thought. Are we in a world of under-age armed soldiers? Although they look much different from the brownshirts in Germany. There they don't have dark curly hair and certainly no young women.

"We will take the boat in for you," said the one with the blue kerchief. The young boy proffered his hand. "I'm Ethan, and this is Nurit."

Ben stood silent for a moment, his hands resting together on his chin, and offered, "Shalom?"

They both grinned simultaneously. "Shalom, definitely," said Ethan and eagerly shook Ben's hand. Nurit smiled and said, "Me, too." Ben knelt to put on his sandals. "Do you know how to carry a boat and place it securely inside?"

"No, but you will show us. We have been watching you, and in Poland, not many Jews rowed. And now that we saved your life, you will show us how to carry the boat, and then we can talk about how we can do what you're doing."

Ben decided to remain silent and not respond to the "we" in the sentence. Who knows what could happen in the crazy small strip of land where he thought he had found a quiet, peaceful spot to row? *I guess*, he thought, *unpredictability is the order of the day.*

CHAPTER 4

George sat on a bench, pulled his physics text out of his bookbag, smashed it into the locker, opened his book to a page, and immediately began banging his fist against his forehead. *I've got to get this concept into my head. If I can understand the dynamics of a better blade stroke—water and body power and wooden oar strength—surely, I can get the relationship between electricity and magnetism.*

The moon reflected on the Spree River, and the dock was slick from accumulated frost. It was the type of 6:00 a.m. morning that made most people linger under the bed covers at least until a hint of light shone through a window. But George loved to get to the water early, to see the river coming into view as the trolley brought him closer to the boathouse. He also relished a few minutes of concentrated studying in the locker room—to finally understand a physics concept he couldn't get late at night because he was bone tired.

He hadn't noticed Hans hovering nearby. Hans usually rowed six-seat in the eight and, of late, also came to practices early.

"What do you want to study for? Don't you see what's coming? You shouldn't even be here."

George kept his eyes focused on the book. The last thing he wanted to do was get into a discussion with Hans, who had taken on the role of the harassing police. He had recently been seen wandering the university campus in a brownshirt uniform. Fortunately, none of the "brownies," as George called them, were in George's regular classes—they all seemed to be part of the agriculture and animal husbandry classes—areas of study considered important in the university. But his father, Werner, had pushed him toward the sciences. As a newspaper editor, his father had told him that the world was going in a different direction—study the sciences. Albert Einstein had been making a name for himself in the world. "And," his father had said, "we definitely need science to help people be smarter about their dumb choices in leadership." So far, George hadn't seen any connection between students studying physics and their ability to know the difference between good and bad leaders.

His mother, who noticed his love of both Van Gogh and Vermeer, had suggested he pursue art history as well as history, saying those studies would help with his understanding of the world. Maybe her advice is a bit wiser than Dad's, he thought as he put his physics book away, slammed the locker room door, and followed the boys on their way to the weight room. He anxiously looked around. Where was Arthur? He depended on him for companionship and sound advice.

George grinned broadly when Arthur entered, followed by coach Messinger. Lately, he needed both of them for some level of comfort to reduce the anxiety he felt by the hostile remarks of Hans and Henry and the seeming indifference of the other rowers. He wasn't sure if the indifference was toward him or toward winning, but either thought was disturbing. Maybe they are having a hard time focusing because of all the disturbances at the university, he thought. Unruly political discussions seemed to permeate the atmosphere, but George knew rowers needed to pull together and work as a team to be competitive. The outcome of any race was going to prove who was best in order to thrive in the Olympics. Weight training needed attention.

Arthur leaned over as he hoisted thirty-pound weights in each hand above his head. "Are you going to the Red Guard meeting—third-period class?"

"Sh," said George struggling to lift his weights over his head. "Someone could hear you. Besides, my father says it's too extremist."

"Here, we're all friends," said Arthur. He put the weights down on the floor, breathing hard and looking intently at his teammates. "Aren't we all friends?"

Unfortunately, the plea for quiet conversation was too late. An unwelcome voice interrupted the conversation. "Either you support the Fuhrer—the man who has made us proud to be Germans, or you will not last on this team, let alone in Germany." It was Henry. He started for the door. "Better forget about the Red Guard if you want a place on the boat." The coxswain spoke out of earshot of coach Messinger but close enough to other teammates, who suddenly became very busy with a flurry of exercises.

George shot back at him, surprising himself with his vehemence. "No, Messinger said it's going to be the best of us who qualify for the boat and that it has nothing to do with the madman, Hitler, or Goering with his fat body and big mouth." He resisted the urge to push him. "And you, little man,"

Arthur said, drawing close to Henry, "could be the first to go. Small men like you can be easily replaced." Then, as though to emphasize his point, Arthur shoved Henry, who fell backward against a metal locker door. George smiled nervously and wondered why he didn't or couldn't act on the urge to fight back against Henry's arrogance with more than words.

The thud brought Messinger to see the coxswain sitting on the floor rubbing the back of his head. "Everything all right, here?"

Silence and averted eyes greeted the coach.

"Just tripped," said Henry. He reached up to take George's proffered hand, avoiding his eyes.

"Good," said Messinger. "Everyone out to the dock with the boats. We've got two eights practicing. Small race at the end. We're ready to start eliminating, so we have only the best." He patted Henry's back. "Go get yourself set up in the boat. Otto Cornish will be the coxswain in the other eight. See if you can teach him a thing or two. "

Henry got up rapidly and saluted with his arm raised in the air, stopping short of saying anything.

"No need to do that here," Messinger said. "This is about rowing—the best will be picked. No need to choose sides. Just support your teammates," he said cryptically.

~~~

Back at university, through the windows of his history classroom, George could see students in brown shirts marching in military formation with members of the university band, playing marching music he couldn't recognize. The professor was droning on about the revolutions of 1848. There is a revolution now, George thought, and Professor Saybolt says nothing. He's probably afraid to say anything. This sixtyish professor of history was well dressed in a navy-blue bespoke suit, white shirt, and impeccably knotted blue and red tie. George had been surprised that Saybolt had expressed Communist sympathies at the beginning of the semester. Back then, Saybolt had spoken with enthusiasm about how working classes in 1848 had sought freedom of assembly and freedom of the press as they rose against royal regimes. But history revealed that tens of thousands had been killed by the conservative aristocracy in the German States, who had crushed the revolution. Lately, though, Saybolt's lectures had turned from fiery and interesting to bland and boring.

"But isn't there a possibility for such a renewal for equality? After all, it is now 1933, not 1848," George asked, hoping to bring some animated discussion to the class. Instead, Saybolt waved a dismissive hand.

That didn't deter him from trying to talk with Professor Saybolt after class about the situation on campus. Could he help the professor start a political science group to support neither the Communists nor the National Socialists? Something that recognized the importance of the Bill of Rights to the American constitution? Something that promoted individual rights? Freedom of the press and assembly? Saybolt had been so excited when he taught the American Revolution. Yes, he had said, America was a slave-holding country, but eventually, there was a Lincoln. Governments need to evolve toward democracy, he had also said, but he did not see that in the near future for Germany considering the rise of the Third Reich.

George was shaken from his reverie by persistent and loud band music. He peered out the window again to see the afternoon sun glinting off the windows across the quad, illuminating the harsh Gothic Revival stonework. He was surprised to see his friend from physics class, Siggy Heinz, playing his tuba with clarinetists and trumpeters and brownshirts marching around the quad of the campus. George recognized the tune as the "Alte Kameraden;" he had vaguely heard something around the dinner table when his mother said that the orchestra brass section was brushing up on its marching music under Goebbels' orders. Still, he could not believe he was hearing it on campus. It was 1890's music about a regiment of soldiers being attacked and winning. He had thought that with the Treaty of Versailles, militarization was not to be promoted on college campuses. But he heard the words clearly.

> During the attack, things happen fast,
> Victory will bring us glory and honor,
> Come, comrades, we shall reload,
> This is our marching music.

As the musical marchers came closer, three of his classmates, ignoring Saybolt's lecture, rushed to the window, opened it, and screamed, "Heil Hitler!" George reddened and waited for the reprimand from his professor. But Saybolt, with bent head, just stared at his notes on the desk. The music faded, and grinning students went back to their seats and gave each other hand slaps.

"What's the matter, George?"

George didn't even know the name of the student who had dared to call out.

"Your father's going to have something to say about this in the evening newspaper? Hope it's good."

"Professor Saybolt," George said. "You were saying that the conservatives in Germany pushed the liberals into exile, and the revolution didn't succeed." Saybolt gave him a look of gratitude.

The anonymous student shot back. "And they will be pushed back again. The Reds don't stand a chance anymore. It's a new Germany." He stood and shot his right hand in the air with his three comrades joining him, shouting "Heil Hitler."

Saybolt slammed a large book down on the desk. "Class is dismissed."

"Tomorrow, you'll be dismissed," one of the followers said to Saybolt, and the three left the classroom in unison while some twenty other students kept their eyes down and only looked up when they heard the door slam to see their professor standing hunched over his desk. George thought he saw the man's body shaking slightly.

Saybolt raised his voice. "I said you are dismissed."

The students arose, slowly gathering their books and papers. George lingered and approached his professor. "I will talk to my father. The newspaper will write something about the infringement of politics on university classes."

Professor Saybolt shrugged his shoulders and gathered his papers to be placed in his briefcase. He wiped the lenses of his glasses. "No, this terror can't be stopped. It's impossible. You will see. This is a different Germany. All I want to do is teach and publish a book about the French Revolution." He sighed. "As I said, it's impossible. You stay strong, George, and help your father."

Watching his tired and crestfallen professor walk out of the classroom, George realized he had absolutely no idea of the right thing to do. He just hoped that nothing would interfere with his rowing at the Germania Club.

CHAPTER 5

From their apartment bedroom, Werner caught aromas of French toast frying and strips of bacon simmering in what he knew would be his mother's old cast iron pan. The pan had been a gift from her, and she would have done a 180-degree turn in her grave if she knew bacon crisped in it now but marrying Frieda and keeping kosher was not an option. "It's the twentieth century," Frieda had said, "and I will not be bound by a tradition with a 2000-year-old nonscientific history written in a book. I don't care if it's a bestseller." She had gone on as though she needed to bolster the argument. "And it's Germany. People have eaten pork sandwiches, bratwurst, schweinenebraten, and kohl. You don't see them dying. Besides, it's what Ingrid likes to cook." Ingrid had been with them since their marriage twenty years ago.

When we married in 1913, Germans thriving on pork may have been true, he thought, but today we Germans are dying, not thriving. He sat on the edge of the bed to affix his sock garters and then hoisted his suspenders, already attached to his pants, over his shirt. He grabbed his jacket hanging on the chair, checked his receding hairline in the mirror, planted his hands on the dresser, and whispered dramatically to his image. "There is no moral fiber against the grab of Hitler. The people and von Hindenburg must stand up to him and his gangsters. They HAVE eaten pork, and it HAS corrupted them." He grinned. He could hear his mother's voice in his ear with its stern inflection.

"Breakfast is ready." He heard the musical lilt of words that he had loved because they came from her. Somehow, she had translated her talent at playing violin to her voice and managed to make them both breathtakingly beautiful.

He realized that the aroma of Ingrid's breakfast might be the only good thing that would happen in the course of his day at the newspaper—*Der Tagblatt.*

"Can't sit today for breakfast," he said as he grabbed a piece of French toast directly from the pan, put it in a paper bag to be tossed in his backpack, and kissed Frieda on the cheek as she sat sipping her coffee, looking expectantly at him.

"Be careful on the moto and watch out for the thugs," she said, half hoping that remark would engage him in conversation. He kissed her again, knowing that she would have liked him to linger at the table. "Not today. The crises at the office await my charms." She frowned but quickly kissed him back. "It will take more than charms."

He hopped on the motorcycle outside the house, grateful that he had enough petrol. Sometimes George used up the petrol when he rode the bike down to the clubhouse to row—an obsession he was trying to understand. *Why not writing*, he thought? *There's got to be a gene in one of George's cells for writing. After all, I know we are a family of obsessives: Frieda and her music, me and my newspaper, George and his rowing. But we have other passions, I think.*

He parked the motorcycle in front of the six-story building on Meinekestrasse that housed the newspaper offices. Rumors had circulated that one of its many floors also housed a Zionist organization. If so, he needed to do a story about them soon to alert his readers that organizations exist to help with the possibility of emigration.

He anticipated going right to his office and looking at the overnight ticker for international news but stopped when he saw the publisher, Rupert Adler, in the newsroom surrounded by reporters and editors. One did not have to be a clairvoyant to sense something dark was happening. It was the kind of "you could cut through the atmosphere with a knife" moment.

"We're waiting for you," said Adler. Adler, now in his seventies, had always maintained a cordial but distancing relationship with his many editors and reporters. Rupert Adler had rarely shown up at the office during Werner's tenure. Instead, he had left much of the running and management of the newspaper to his longtime friend, Theodore Wolff.

"Sorry," muttered Werner. "My moto was a bit sluggish this morning. Also, more traffic than usual." He gestured "helpless and hapless" with both hands in the air and a shrug of his shoulders. "Business must be getting better for the Third Reich. Traffic means the economy is picking up." The irony was not lost on the publisher, who frowned at his editor's attempt at humor.

Rupert Adler's father, Rudolf, had started *The Berliner Tagblatt* as an advertising newspaper but had managed to convince his many business advertisers that promoting democracy was good and developed the newspaper into a thriving liberal journal. Rupert had continued that tradition, hiring the best of reporters in music and the arts as well as those who covered news of the world.

"Now that everyone is here, I will begin," Adler said. Werner thought that his usually commanding voice was softer than usual. "You'll notice," Adler continued, "that Wolff is not with us today. Unfortunately, I had to decide to protect the newspaper. The government has been unhappy with his constant criticism of the Nazi government."

Silence reigned until a small voice called out. Werner thought it was the reporter who covered the Berlin city news, but he was not sure until he heard, "And his grandmother was Jewish." It was Simon Levy.

Another voice. "We are supposed to be critical of the government to protect the people. People have fought revolutions for freedom of the press."

In that small dramatic instance, Werner was enormously proud of those who used their voices to protest.

"Look, do you want jobs or not?" Adler tried to squelch the irritation in his voice. "Do you want the Third Reich to take over the press? Right now, I think I can get Goebbels to release us from the obligation to print Nazi propaganda. He wants to tell the world that Germany has a free press." He slammed his hand on the table. "We need to survive. You need jobs." No one jumped at the noise. Reporters and editors had gotten used to his tirades, which they realized came from frustration at dealing with the uncertainty of the Third Reich and its various new laws. What would Hitler do with the Enabling Act that said he could bypass the Reichstag? He could now pass laws without its approval. Even though the Reichstag knew the act would make the body powerless, it passed with an overwhelming vote of 441 to 91. At the time of the vote, SS thugs dominated the visitors' section.

Werner decided it was time for him to speak. "I bet we can keep our current status if we continue critical reporting on Russia's five-year plan and the Ukraine famine." Russia relations and sports were his specialties, but he was known for fierce writing and editing skills. As a result, many reporters sought him out on the best way to shape a story when they got stuck.

"Put me on the Ukraine story," said Marvin Belsky. Belsky usually reported on the theater and had received a reprimand from Adler that the latest review was not flattering enough to the writer, whose play was espousing the idyllic virtues of a Germany that he wasn't sure ever existed—bucolic, peaceful, and thriving, with every woman in an apron in the kitchen and every man working away at something practical to make Germany as significant as it had been before 1914.

"How about the story of New York Jews protesting Germany's policies in Madison Square Garden?" asked Werner. "They want to boycott German goods. Imagine that!" When Werner saw the anger in Adler's face, he immediately said, "I was manifesting irony with that comment. Don't worry. I want to keep this paper alive as long as possible. We will figure out the stories that work to keep truth alive and this newspaper going." He muttered under his breath, "Before I'm gone."

"You are thinking of leaving?" Belsky asked.

"No. You misheard me." Werner looked around quickly to see if anyone else heard. "Besides, didn't you hear Goebbels ensure freedom of the press in his latest proclamation?"

Adler interrupted. "Time to get to work. Let's see how much of the truth we can bring to the German people," With a wave of his hand, he abruptly dismissed the group, who filed slowly back to their offices or cubicles.

Before Werner could settle in at his desk, the copy boy came into his office without knocking. "Come see the ticker tape." In a newspaper office, no one questioned interruptions as rudeness if it meant they would have headlines before their rival newspaper *Volkischer Beobachter* got access to them.

"Listen, the only news that'll get me to the ticker is if you tell me we are going to have the Olympics—you know, the Olympics that the sportswriters want, but Hitler and his gang don't because they're afraid they'll get beaten by a couple of Jews." Werner started rolling up his sleeves, indicating he was about to do something else.

"You'll want to see this. It's about the Olympics and the American, Avery Brundage," the young man persisted. Werner continued rolling up his shirtsleeves while walking rapidly to the ticker tape room. Avery Brundage and the Olympics and Germany in one sentence would make news. He read the tape carefully. Brundage doesn't care that Hitler's a dictator. Germany has defeated Communism, and that's a greater evil. Yes, it said that and also that Brundage admires Hitler's ability to restore prosperity and order to Germany. Brundage concluded Germany should be a perfect place for the Olympics in 1936.

Werner reread the ticker tape and picked up the thread of paper to take back to his office. For a moment, he was pleased to see that Belsky was still there so he would not be seen as muttering to himself.

"I suppose that's good news. The sports lovers will have stuff to cover.

Better start thinking of assignments. What sports would you like, Belsky?"

Belsky was staring out the office window. Before he could even answer, Werner said, "Don't think about rowing. That's going to go to George."

"No question," said Belsky. "Besides, I prefer cross-country."

CHAPTER 6

This time Ben Leicester came down to the warehouse with his rifle slung over his shoulder and an extra round of ammunition in his pouch. Rowing was important, but so was his life. He thought about a hand grenade, but if he were in his single scull, would he be able to hold on to the oars with one hand and throw the grenade with the other—and how far would it reach? He would have to be stable and spectacularly close to his target.

An order had recently come down from British high command that soldiers could take a harsher tone with the Arabs now that the Mufti was supporting Hitler's Third Reich—and a historic transfer agreement had gone into effect. Palestine would receive 60,000 German Jews who could come but with limited assets. Germany was keeping some of the emigrant's holdings through a complicated agreement that involved assets and a substantial reduction of their unwanted population. Zionists and Nazis had agreed to the initiative proposed by Sam Cohen, owner of the Hanotea citrus-export company in Netanya. Probably the Arabs were left out of the agreement, which would mean god-knows-what, Leicester thought. It could go from rock-throwing to bold assassinations. Guns and ammunition were rife in the area—especially around the port of Haifa.

His commander had warned him. "You are not to do anything that will start a flare-up between Arabs and Jews. The race riots we had in 1929 were hard enough to contain. Such stupidity started by people who are convinced they won't be able to pray at their special wall."

Leicester hadn't commented, deciding that it was not the time to argue that much of religion was about holy places. After all, didn't people make pilgrimages to walk along Jesus' route, the Via Dolorosa in Jerusalem, and what about trips to Mecca and Camino de Santiago in Spain?

"So, you have a boat for us?" It was Ethan with Nurit at his side, grinning. He was not surprised that they showed up again on his watch.

He had noted a restlessness in them that he thought just being a pioneer in this god-forsaken land would satisfy. No. These kids wanted more. This was not the time to explain that learning to row here would be difficult and, furthermore, women don't row.

"There is no 'us' in boating here. There are only two ancient single boats. For an 'us,' you need a double," Ben said, hoisting his rifle sling on his shoulder and drawing on his cigarette. His mother disapproved of his smoking, but somehow a carton of Dunhills arrived monthly. For some reason, Ben felt the need to explain. "I guess my mother knew I needed something to keep me going in a land that bore no resemblance to England . . . and it was cigarettes."

"You don't need your rifle," said Nurit. "Put it away. We come in peace. We have made peace with the Arab settlement near us. They leave us alone, and we don't bother them."

"You are not taking any of their lands?" Ben flicked his cigarette butt into the river. He didn't see any particular harm since it was already dreadfully contaminated with toxic waste and sewage.

"Anything we built on was deserted," said Ethan. His quick response told Ben that Ethan had heard this argument before and had developed a reflexive response.

"Yeah, tell that to the Grand Mufti. Why do you think we British are here? I got shot at the other day by one of your now peace-loving Arabs. Remember?"

"You know we have 60,000 Germans coming. They're going to come with money, and maybe they'll know how to row," said Nurit. Ben could tell that she was the patient and determined one. She was going to learn to row no matter the obstacles. He started to light another cigarette.

She took advantage of Ben's silence. "You should know that Jews didn't row in Poland. My parents told me they weren't allowed. So maybe we can start a tradition. You can teach us. Right?"

Ben thought the only way to get rid of them was to show them how difficult the sport was to conquer. Learning to row was not an overnight process, and it had taken him about 4,000 miles of practice to get comfortable in his single scull. He remembered with joy the moment he began to feel that the boat and the water were under his control. He could make it race, turn, stay still at his will.

"All right," he said. "If you're going to learn, you have to follow my directions exactly. The last thing I want to do is have a couple of young Jews die on me. And this has got to be between us. My commander would be very unhappy if he learned that I was teaching when I was supposed to be guarding. No one else knows. Right?" he smiled. "No one in whatever forsaken village you're living in."

Nurit snapped back. Ethan and I . . . we're not forsaken. We will make wherever we settle grow and thrive and people will know that they're safe."

Ben sighed. "The heat's coming up. We better get started. Just get the oars out first, then one boat. I'll teach one at a time. The other can watch, and the next time will get in the boat on the water." He paused. "The second one will be a faster learner just from observing."

Ethan started toward the warehouse.

"No, the first time, two of you will need to carry the boat. Hoist it to your shoulders, hull side up, and then bring it to the water. One of you at the stern, one at the bow. You will have to go into the water to your knees to make sure the skeg is not hitting bottom."

"Stern? Skeg?" said Ethan. The sun was high enough to show sweat at his armpits and the back of his dirty T-shirt. Ben noted that it even had holes in it. Nurit crossed her arms with bemused patience.

"Stern—what you see in front of you. Skeg—that piece that lets you decide if the boat goes port or starboard."

"Port? Starboard?" Ben wasn't sure who said those words. "Just get the damn boat. One of you in the front and the other in the back. Wait, get the oars first."

Ethan jumped up with a military salute—fingers to his forehead. "Yes, sir."

Ben turned his face away so he wouldn't demonstrate his annoyance at what seemed to him amused mockery. What didn't these kids get? That they were unwanted in a land that barely provided sustenance for those already here? That it was won from a war that turned the losers into vengeful perpetrators of war? Yet these two playing at soldiers wanted to learn to row. So be it.

"Walk into the water until it's about a foot high and gently place the boat in hull side down." He clarified, "That's the bottom of the boat."

Ben was amazed at how slowly and carefully they placed the boat in the water. "Like Moses was lifted out of the water . . . gently and with tenderness," said Nurit.

"Nurit, you're first. Ethan and I are going to hold the boat for you. You are going to place one oar on the left—your starboard side—lock it in the rigger—and then place the other on port—your right side." Ben demonstrated on the starboard side and then handed her the other oar. Looking briefly at the starboard placement, she carefully and correctly locked in the port side oar while Ben and Ethan steadied the boat for her in the slowly moving water.

The three stood side by side in the water, intently looking at the wooden boat that floated and moved ever so slowly with a light ripple in the current.

Ben directed. "Now you're going to turn sideways to grasp the handles of the oars in your right hand. Make sure that port oar blade," he said, pointing to the other side, "is flat on the water."

Nurit started to grab the oars.

"Wait," Ben said. "You need to do a couple of things at the same time. First, you're going to step in with your right foot on the deck and then your left foot while we hold the boat. Normally there is a dock, and you would be able to do this while keeping one foot on the dock."

Nurit held on to the oars and did exactly as directed and somehow figured out that as she sat down, she needed to get her left foot into the foot holder and then the right.

"Now, sit straight," Ben ordered. "And definitely, don't move to the left or the right. Don't wiggle, and don't try to turn around. Not yet. Not until you've figured out how to be stable in a scull. Being stable in a scull is the goal. This is not a rowboat. Say those last two sentences every night before you go to sleep and when you get in the boat."

"Now, square the blade, so it is perpendicular to the water, and you move your body forward on the slide," Ben directed. He started to say more but saw the quizzical look on Nurit's face. She doesn't have a clue—not a clue—as to what I mean, he thought. "All right. Now get out. I'll show you." I should have demonstrated first, he thought.

"Ethan, hold the boat with me while Nurit gets out. I'll get in and . . ." Ben didn't finish the sentence. A sharp, loud crack of a gunshot interrupted. Ethan slumped into the water; blood began to pool around his chest. Nurit let go of the oars and tumbled into the foot-high water while Ben, who quickly took his rifle off his shoulder, pointed it and shot at what appeared to be a young boy fleeing on the other bank of the river. The boy stumbled, fell, and picked himself up again, grabbing his thigh and dropping his gun on the ground.

Ben steadied the boat and, with rapid, practiced movements, quickly settled himself into the boat, started to row while yelling at Nurit. "Take care of Ethan. Stem the bleeding. Call for ambulance service. There's a walkie-talkie in the warehouse."

He raced to the other side of the river with what must have been a split of 1:40 and 500 meters more, all at the same speed. "Good thing, I've raced Henley," he thought. "That little bastard is not going to get away with this. The Arab chieftain promised me peace."

In five minutes, he pulled up alongside the kid who was limping along the shoreline. "Want to get shot again? Just stop right where you are." Somehow that threat did immobilize the boy. Ben could not quite see his face. Just his dark eyes and heavy eyebrows showed above a dirty green bandana. And tears. Ben pulled his oars in as he got close to the bank, thinking, *How the hell am I supposed to do this? There's nothing in the manuals about taking down a terrified, stupid Palestinian kid from a single rowing shell.*

"What is your name?" Ben yelled.

"Omar Khalidi." The boy answered through sobs.

Ben sighed. "Is Safid Khalidi your father?"

"My uncle."

"Then you should know better. You stay here. I'm going to send an ambulance for you. You're going to stay, aren't you?" The British officer used the sternest voice he could evoke. Getting law into an uncivilized country— not even a country—was not supposed to be impossible. After all, isn't that why we British are here? But no one had ever written the manual on how to overcome tribal law ruling this land.

Omar, tears continuing to stream, nodded and threw up his hands in a gesture of defeat.

Ben pushed his port oar into the side of the bank to give him some paddling space while feathering his starboard oar so he could turn the boat. Again, he rowed at a Henley race pace to get back to the sandy spot where he could get out of the boat and store it.

With gratitude, he saw a jeep awaiting with two privates in command.

"They've taken the two Jews to the hospital," one said while they both saluted.

Ben grabbed the two oar handles in his left hand and barely saluted while stepping out of the boat, again, into a foot of water.

He grabbed the sandals he had left on the shore. "You. Get the boat and oars in. I'm going to take your jeep to go to Wadi Ara and talk to Khalidi. He's got to help us bring some peace to this land."

Chapter 7

The dark of evening was no friend to Sigfried Messinger. He nursed his nightcap of Pilsner beer—something that he would not recommend for any of his rowers. One beer stein helped him start the process of drowsiness that eventually led to sleep. He desperately needed to stop ruminating nightly about choices he had to make. At the same time, he knew that forces beyond his control influenced those decisions—every law signed recently by the Third Reich seemed to wreak havoc on his decision-making. Who the best rowers were, what seats they should be in, and whether they could row a single in the Diamond Sculls plagued him, daily. Since 1844 this event was the world's most glorious competition for single scullers. Few countries could even begin to dream about developing the sort of rowing legends that England had already produced. Knowing he had Diamond Sculls champions in George and Arthur brought worry and joy to him at the same time. The Third Reich was invoking the Volkist Principles of Racial Equality, purporting that the Aryan race needed to be supreme to make Germany great again. That theory excluded Jews, Romani, and Jehovah's Witnesses, and he sensed the board members of the Germania Rowing Club would support this particular nonsense.

At times, when Messinger struggled to fall asleep, he would lie on his back in his bed without a pillow and visualize himself as an eighteen-year-old, sitting ready and upright in his boat, beginning the row with a steady-state of continuous strokes, each one exactly like the one before as though he were a brilliant musician able to maintain a conductor's firm beat of two-four time. He visualized pools of rippling water left by the precise fall of a squared blade on either side of the boat. The space between each pool indicated the strength of each stroke determined by the power in the legs. He frequently told his rowers that an equidistant area between pools in the water was a good sign.

This near dream usually worked as a sleep inducer, and when he tried to explain it to friends who didn't row, they vaguely nodded in polite acknowledgment, but he knew they could not comprehend.

Messinger would tell the rowers tomorrow that the Germania Rowing

Club had agreed to sponsor the best eight boat to row at Henley, and the team would be flying Deutsche Lufthansa airlines. He would reserve the news that they would not be rowing their own Empacher, to which they had become accustomed. Arrangements had been made for the men to row a Stampfli while practicing and competing. Somehow, The English Rowing Federation had acquired one from Switzerland, and Messinger hoped it was already there downloaded from the ship's cargo load. He loved imagining a ship hold filled with cedar shells and spruce oars. Sheer rapture.

In his sleeplessness, he continued to ponder the problem of the "final eight." Who would be rowing in the boat? Cutting nine men was not easy. He dared not share with anyone the challenges he had in making the final decision. That would not be in keeping with his stoic demeanor. Even when his wife was alive, he was reluctant to share anything that would worry her. In today's climate of playing Aryan favorites, talk was even more unnerving. One did not know who an informer to the government might be, eager to tell anyone what they perceived as misdeeds against the Fuhrer.

Freud came to his mind suddenly. Messinger had been an avid reader of the psychoanalyst's books. His first was *Beyond the Pleasure Principle*, and he eventually read *The Interpretation of Dreams*. What would this famous psychiatrist say about his soul searching? Messinger was on a college campus in May 1933 when he watched the famous doctor's books burned in the courtyard. Freud had dared to write, "In the Middle Ages, they would have burned me. Now they're just burning my books." He wondered if a session with Freud, himself a Jew, would give him any more insight into dealing with those who would be unhappy with his choice of the final eight, who would probably include two Jews.

Messinger thought, *I didn't utter one word of protest when I saw the books of Alfred Adler, Bertolt Brecht, Albert Einstein, Franz Kafka, H.G. Wells being burned. Instead, I stood by and watched. Would Freud even want to talk to me, considering my ignominious passivity? Tomorrow I must decide on the final nine.*

He waved his hand as though to rid himself of the thought and finally began to doze.

⸺⸺

The next day eighteen young men sat silently still on the club locker room benches, trying to contain excitement and competitive spirits. If they were tired from their early ten-mile training on the water, it only showed in slumped shoulders and a slight weariness in their eyes.

"You have all worked hard these nine months for what will be ten minutes of competition. I must remind you that we can only win if we row in unison, as a team, in the eight." Messinger paused. "And we must respect one another."

Messinger had rarely felt comfortable talking about team spirit. He was much better at teaching the techniques of rowing that brought about the surge of power in the boat. But he also understood that power came when the eight rowed together as one and how hard that was to achieve. And right now, sixteen young men and their coxswains wanted to compete, and only eight had the possibility of being sponsored and supported in the upcoming race on the Thames.

"And what about the Diamond Sculls?" All eyes turned toward George Grossinger, who was practically seated at Messinger's feet. That moment seemed to stretch into lingering minutes filling the air with anxiety. Why was he talking about Diamond Sculls for single rowers? It was the crew of the eight that was important.

Messinger hesitated. He understood the passion of the rower of a single. "Rowing singles will be decided after we have chosen the crew of eight." The Diamond Sculls singles events were the last thing he wanted to discuss openly with the rowers in a group. He knew that the two single rowers had to be George and Arthur, who had demonstrated they could compete even better in singles than in eights. Maybe it was the freedom of not having to be dependent on anyone, but he noticed their bodies just gave more in the single. Messinger remembered that luxury and demand of just relying on yourself to produce a win.

He continued. "And it will be decided based on their rowing ability. Nothing else. After all, don't we want to do what's best for Germany?"

The hand of Ned Holstein suddenly sprung up. He did not wait for acknowledgment. "Will Germania sponsor a Jew even if his splits and times are the best?"

George and Arthur exchanged glances while most of the others chose to stare at the floor. They weren't sure about Holstein's loyalties. George looked over to see Hans sit up with interest at Holstein's question. George put a finger to his lips to signal "quiet." It was as though Ned Holstein read Coach Messinger's fears and wanted to confront them for all to see.

"Time to go home and rest up for tomorrow's early practice. We will race and then the decision. We leave next week." Messinger looked to see Holstein's face. He was relieved to see him focusing on getting his backpack together, but then he saw him greet Hans with the Nazi salute as he walked by.

Before the coach got to the locker room exit, he turned to address the rowers. "And that's all you need to think about. Doing your best. By the way, we are a club where everyone gets equal treatment. Please remember that. We are going to be racing against Oxford—a university with a great rowing tradition."

He hoped that comment would squelch any discussion of the two Jewish men on the team. He needed them—they made a difference, and he didn't want to lose. He prayed that they and the team could convince Hans that these two rowers were critical to their success.

⟶⟶

That had been the third week of May. George and Arthur had made the final eight despite Henry calling out each of them to either shorten or lengthen their strokes at precisely the wrong time. When that happened during practice rows, their teammates were with them and adjusted strokes accordingly. Franz Hauptfurhrer, Benedikt Roth, Abraham Schwarz, Ulrich Scheuer, Klaus Fleming, Willi Eichel all valued the precision of rowing. Their strict practices had given them an appreciation of the strength, endurance, and persistence of each rower. They valued that more than one's religion and allegiance to the Nazi party.

Ned Holstein was not even selected as an alternate.

When the rowers boarded the plane at the Berlin Templehof airport, each gave a gracious, thankful wave to a loved one who had come to see them off. George noted that not one of them thought it was important to say goodbye by thrusting their arm in a Nazi salute, despite the flags lining the airport entrance. Maybe this is an observation I'll keep for an article I'm supposed to write for the newspaper, he mused.

"When you land at Gatwick Airport and go to your hotel, I expect complete comportment, and that means no stupidity on display." George thought Messinger had directed that to Henry—at least he hoped so. He and Arthur had recognized and were grateful for the coach's quiet support.

George had brought along his assigned reading of *Madame Bovary* in French to keep him challenged on the long plane ride. He also had a notepad to write down thoughts that might interest him and others. This notepad was now becoming something important to him. He was beginning to realize how much his father's lectures on "observing" were critical to becoming a writer.

He had managed to get a seat next to Arthur and immediately began to read his book, for which a homework assignment was due when he got back to class. "Does it really say this?" He referred to the book and pointed at the passage. "That you must pull hard at the oar and get calluses on your hands if you want to accomplish something? Would Flaubert know anything about rowing?" Arthur leaned over trying to peek out the tiny plane window.

"Don't you want to be looking out the window now? After all, we're in a plane for the first time in our lives," Arthur said, realizing that he should have taken the seat next to the window, considering George's need always to be reading. And now, he was always carrying around a notebook and writing down esoteric thoughts. "I'm sure it had something to do with Emma not working hard enough. But definitely not at rowing. Women don't row."

Franz, who usually sat in seat six in the eight and was in George's physics' class at university, leaned over the small airline seat that overflowed with the young men's arms and legs. "Rowing even in Flaubert's time was a challenging sport."

Ulrich, seated next to him, added, "And we are the best of Germany; we are going to demolish their eight." He paused. "Do not think for a moment that we will have traditional Edwardian calm—you know gentlemen in their frock coats and ladies in their fancy hats. No, think Brunhilde and Sigfried." He smiled broadly. "Yes, Goering loves our Wagner. Do you not love our Wagner, George?"

George turned, taking his eyes off his book.

"Yes, of course," said George. "My mother is a violinist for the Berlin Symphony. She talks about her love for Wagner all the time."

Arthur lowered his head, hoping to hide his grin.

"Ah, you Jews. So talented. You row. Your mother's a violinist. I bet your father is a doctor."

"No. Newspaper editor."

"I hope he writes good things about our Fuhrer," said Ulrich

"Look, we're about to land." This time George looked out the window. Arthur leaned closer. "Is that fog?" "Yes, it's fog," said George. "But you can still see the lush green that everyone talks about because of all the rain." He took out his notebook.

"And beautiful buildings." Arthur could not contain the excitement in his voice. "And such history. Kings, queens, Henry VIII."

George thought, *We're rowing and competing in England. It's going to be memorable. If I do write an article, I'll need to come up with a better word than "memorable."* He gripped the armrests tightly as the landing wheels came down.

Chapter 8

George tried to contain his joy as he flipped through dials on the three-by-three-foot mahogany console radio sitting atop a four-drawer dresser that held clothing they brought for the competition: extra shorts, T-shirts, and underwear. He had not been sure what the washing facilities would be at the assigned dorm rooms, although he supposed he could always rinse out a pair of underwear and an undershirt in the bathroom sink. His father had told him stories of being out on the road as a newspaper reporter, which meant he sometimes had to be prepared to rinse socks and underwear in a sink the night before and hope they would be dry enough to wear the next day.

"Remember," his father had said. "'Dry enough' are the operative words. Better that than the body smelling too much. A little dampness never hurt anyone. Foul body odor is offensive."

George kept switching radio dials, finding it hard to settle on one station. It was his first time in a university dorm room, first time in another country, and the excitement made him a bit unsettled.

Arthur lay on the bottom bunk bed leafing through a magazine—*Gentleman's Guide to Playing Cricket*. "Look," he said. "They play this game with clean white clothes, and wooden balls, and bats that look like small paddles—you know, a little like the blade of an oar. Everyone looks so fancy, and the grass is so green." British history was a mandatory course at their German university. The syllabus covered kings, queens, and wars, while common cultural mores, including the history and prevalence of the game cricket, were never discussed. These facts would have been considered frivolous and unnecessary material.

George continued to roam through radio dials. "Listen, you can go from classical music to Shakespeare sonnets to Prime Minister Ramsay McDonald. Apparently, he just came back from the United States after meeting with Roosevelt. I bet this guy Winston Churchill is going to have something to say about our fabulous Fuhrer, Adolf Hitler." He paused. "I could use this as background when I write about the regatta. Would inform the public, wouldn't it?"

"Churchill's not in government anymore, so it doesn't matter, and you need to watch your sarcasm with your 'fabulous Fuhrer' especially around Henry," said Arthur tossing the magazine on a small nightstand. "Let's go out to the quad and maybe we can find a soccer ball to kick around."

George chortled. "Never saw you with a soccer ball before." He grabbed a sweatshirt. "Race you down the steps." They ran down the hallway steps jostling to keep the other from getting ahead. Arriving breathless outside to a deserted university quad, they didn't see four men in black suits and fedoras come out of dark shadows of the buildings and slowly approach them.

"You need to come with us." The sentence came from the tallest of the group. As he spoke, the four broke into two who stepped to either side of George and Arthur.

"But . . . but . . ." George seemed unable to formulate a sentence. The men spoke in perfect German about what sounded like the intention of kidnapping them from a British university quad where he and Arthur had been looking for a soccer ball to kick around. What was the best response to something so unfathomable? Do you yell? Do you try to fight your way out?

"No," said Arthur, starting to pull away from the two who stood incredibly close to him. Without hesitation, the two men dragged him back, grabbing his elbows.

"Don't resist and be silly. We are here to take you to Zionist headquarters."

"What for?" said George, trying to sound as authoritative as possible. Unfortunately, nothing in his brain was clicking about the two of them in a University of London college courtyard and "Zionist headquarters."

"For a bit of a discussion about how you can help the Zionist cause."

By this time, his legs were forced to move because the two men were carrying him along by his elbows.

"The Zionist cause?" George did not try to hide the incredulity in his voice. "I'm here to row for Germany in a college regatta. We," he said nodding toward Arthur, "did not come here for a Zionist cause . . . whatever that might be."

"He's right, and our coach told us not to leave campus," Arthur said, his voice rising. He gasped. He could feel the outline of a revolver through the jacket of the man closest to him; he could also smell his cigar breath. He looked over at George, who appeared to have his head down in submission.

The tallest one attempted a reassuring smile.

"We will keep you just an hour. After the hour, we will return you to campus—better equipped and more enlightened to help you win the race."

George looked up and nodded toward Arthur. The gesture was made to signify acquiescence. He had looked around. No one was there to help. The "Zionist cause" men had staked out the time and the area well. Arthur, in turn, gave a slight shrug of his shoulders.

The car was an Austin Twenty, clearly large enough to hold all six. George looked around frantically while they drove, trying to record the route should they have to walk back. *Landmarks? What could possibly be considered a landmark when you don't know the city? Damn. He should have done some studying ahead of time. Just look at a map of London as his father had suggested. Know something of the history, not just the vagaries of the river, his father had also recommended. All that would have been helpful at this critical time. Unless, of course, they were just going to be killed.*

The ride lasted only twenty minutes, with the driver deftly turning when they reached Ballard Lane. George made a mental note of the street before they entered the building that had a plaque with the letters ZOGB. *Thank goodness, it's an office building on a busy street.*

The elevator took them to the fifth floor. Walking single file, they entered a narrow door with a glass panel that looked like all the other doors except this one also had the letters ZOGB.

"Sit," said one of the men. The office was overflowing with metal filing cabinets. Again, George took in the surroundings. *I need background to write about in case I get out alive.* Cabinets were labeled with names of countries—Ireland, Australia, United States—those were the only ones he could take in quickly. He wondered if Germany had a file. He also hoped that Arthur was trying to take in details. They would need them for future reference if they ever got out of this.

Three office desks and a large conference table dominated the rest of the room. Maps filled every wall except where three huge photos each captured a man dressed in a three-piece business suit. One of their captors pulled out the chairs at the conference table and motioned everyone to take a seat. By this time, the men had taken off their fedoras, placed them on hooks, and loosened their ties.

"And who are these men on the walls, let alone who are you?" Arthur had found his steady voice, and curiosity surfaced a bit now that abject terror had subsided. They were in an office and not in some underground cell.

George became acutely aware of the sudden bravery in Arthur's voice.

"Yes," he said. "Who are you? What is this all about?" *Bravery and courage. Where was his? Wasn't that what we find at our best in rowing? We forge ahead through the pain of lactic acid building up in our bodies. We forge ahead.*

Before anyone answered, one of the men brought out glasses filled with hot tea—even though it was the middle of summer—and sugar cubes on a small china plate.

"You deserve an introduction and an apology for the way we brought you here. We saw no other option. I'm Chaim Halevi—sometimes known as the tall one." He then pointed to the other three. "Abraham Felder, Joshua Greenberg, and Ron Schwartzman at your service." The men nodded.

"At my service?" Arthur questioned sarcastically.

"And on the wall?" George asked.

"You don't know?" Halevi asked gently. "Abraham, could you enlighten them?"

Abraham stood and walked to each photo and said briskly, pointing at each one. "Theodor Herzl, founder of Zionism, Chaim Weizmann, president of our Zionist Organization, and Lord Lionel Walter Rothschild. He was presented with the Balfour Declaration. They are our heroes."

George wanted to say that he needed a reminder of the Balfour Declaration, quickly passed over in his history classes. He was four years old when it was signed in 1917, stating British support for a homeland for Jews in Palestine. Important to many, it didn't precisely shape his world of assimilated Judaism. He remained silent, waiting to hear more.

"And you can be our heroes, too." This comment came from the man identified as Joshua Greenberg and drew approving nods from the others.

George and Arthur sat rigidly, staring at the glasses of tea set before them. If George was glad about anything, he was happy that Arthur was stuck here with him. Arthur's steadfastness, his trustworthiness, his ability to see the rationale in any situation made him not only a perfect teammate but, he guessed, someone who could make the critical moves to get them out of this situation safely. A problem that seemed less terrifying but did not guarantee a beneficial ending. George finally picked up the glass of tea and took a sip.

"So, you know nothing about what we are trying to do in Palestine?" asked Abraham Felder. Without waiting for an answer, he added quickly, "Let me give you an introduction." He drew a breath. "Current events indicate it will not be good for the Jews in Germany under Hitler. Yes, I know. The Olympics are coming up, and you want to represent Germany. Good. We want you to represent Germany. But . . . come to Palestine and bring your knowledge and help us to start rowing here."

Chaim Halevi interrupted. "We need more people. It's true. We need people to grow the land, but we need examples of courage and strength. No more the Jew who just sits with the Talmud all day. You will show our citizens what strength and persistence can do to build a strong body."

George started to protest. Arthur put his hand on George's elbow, but George pushed it aside.

"Is that what this is about? Couldn't you have written us? You knew where to find us, so you must know where we go to school." George stood up.

"You wouldn't have come to meet us," Greenberg said.

"How do you know?" Arthur asked.

"Are you involved with the Zionist cause in Germany? What are you doing to save the Jews from Hitler? You are so busy being assimilated." The rising color in Halevi's face supported the irritation in his voice.

"We are Jews who are going to row for Germany. Take us back now so we can row for Germany. That's what we are going to do," George protested.

Arthur pulled his friend's arm, indicating he should sit down.

"We will contact the Zionists in Germany. I can assure you we will help the best way we can," Arthur said quietly. He wasn't sure it could be done, but he decided this was the only way they could comfortably quit the situation.

George didn't quite believe what he heard, but he couldn't come up with another option. He surmised that Arthur had thought this was the best way out. "Yes, just take us back and let us compete. We will contact the Zionists in Germany."

The men looked at each other. "Compete your hearts out," said Halevi. "But know that we will be in touch."

CHAPTER 9

With time on his hands before the race at Henley-on-Thames, George trained his reporter's eye on lawn chairs, rowers sweeping down the docks, some handshaking, but no brotherly hugs, the casual wiping down of boats on slings and at the same time, an industriousness; quick words to each other rather than long sentences. With his limited English, he couldn't be sure of what they were saying; he had to depend on his observational skills. His father had taught him that interview questions were important, and one must listen carefully to the answers. "Are they specifically answering your question?" was his father's cautionary advice. But words went only so far. You had to look at behaviors. What were people doing with their eyes and their bodies when they were talking to you? And here? How did rowers carry the boat to the dock? Lockstep? In absolute unison? How will they sit in the boat while waiting for the signal to begin? How will they express nervousness? Will they be able to sit still while waiting for the instruction to start the race? Where will their eyes be focused in anticipation?

Finally, eight boats were at starting position. George sat in his four-seat anticipating the start of the race and was not surprised that everyone in the boat sat tall with quiet intensity, eyes centered on the rower in front of him. Talk would not be welcome. At the same time, he hoped his teammates had remembered the coach's words. "Relax. Your muscles. Your nerves. Your breathing. Relax."

George was surprised that so many eights were able to show up. There was a worldwide financial depression, and it cost money to participate. Rowers from Australia, Sweden, France, Spain, Austria, Italy, New Zealand, the United States, and British teams were their competitors. Maybe he wouldn't understand them if they spoke, but he knew they all understood the language of rowing. Again, he could see it in their upright bodies, the tenseness in their muscles. The crowds lining the river were primarily British, but some in the enthusiastic mass were waving flags of other countries. Again, he was grateful to see no Nazi flags because he was sure the crowd would meet them with some act of hostility. Or maybe not. His father had taught him to think that somewhere in every country, a fascist element existed, and the best way to keep it underground was a lack of a welcome by the majority population. The fascist component needed to know it was an unwelcome minority. "The goal of civilization," Werner would say, "is not to let the worms crawl above ground." He had repeated that expression so often, George had it memorized.

He continued his observations despite the anticipation of the race. Some spectators, many of them women in chiffon dresses, stood with delicate umbrellas at the water's edge. Others sat in chairs, wearing big hats broad enough to diminish the heat of the sun. In addition, men and women in Sunday best outfits sat in huge rowboats that lined the riverbank. George noted that they tried to stay in the shade of the large trees overhanging the water. In his mind, it made for an idyllic scene fit for being captured in a painting.

Henry, along with other coxswains, couldn't enjoy the rowers' lightweight white T-shirt and shorts. George smiled as he saw him and other coxswains outfitted in a colorful coat jacket, long pants, and a jaunty cap. Each coxswain, nattily outfitted, had a hand on the rudder ready to make sure the skeg remained steady in the direction of the call. Each rower, lost in thought, remained expectant for the drop of the red flag to start the race, as demonstrated by the tension in their bodies. Observers could see them practicing rapid air intake to fill lungs and body with needed oxygen to complete the race, perhaps as a winner.

Henry shouted the ready question. Beginning with the eight-seat, each rower shouted a quick "Ready!" The same could be heard indistinctly from the other boats while all eyes focused on the starter holding a red flag aloft. Down it swiftly came. The words then came loud and clear from the referee. "Ready. All. Row." George wasn't sure if it was "Ready all. Row! or "Ready! All Row!" in order to write it correctly, but no matter the written punctuation, the rowers understood and waited expectantly. With this signal to start, eight rowers and one coxswain propelled their boats into motion against a mild roar from attendees. Rowing enthusiasts were distinctly different from those at soccer stadiums because the venues were so unalike. At stadiums, individuals in a crowd sat in one seat to watch a soccer spectacle, cheering, or solemnly watching. Whereas, at a rowing regatta, not many spectators could run along the riverbank to keep up with the boats, but along the Thames, some bicyclists accepted the challenge of riding along the bank to cheer on a particular boat.

Rowers were accustomed to the lack of cheering, preferring to hear the call of the coxswain when they needed to speed up or slow down on the slide. Right now, Henry had the boat at 52 strokes per minute. Rowers could not last long at that rate. Their bodies would produce too much lactic acid. Henry brought it down to 46, the rate they had practiced and anticipated. They knew they would have to deal with the searing pain at that pace to beat the English boat. Messinger's daily practices had readied them. He had also reminded them that morning that their daily 6:00 a.m. rows, regardless of weather, fog, or rain, built endurance, discipline, and comradeship to prepare them not to let each other down. Today, the weather honored them with a mild 70 degrees and a wind of barely four miles an hour. Weather conditions couldn't be better for success.

Their boat covered the first 500 meters in less than a minute and a half, but they were not leading. Although George tried to keep his focus on the motion of Franz's enormous back right in front of him, he saw the English and Swedish boats moving ahead.

"Endure the pain," he whispered out to the air, trying to breathe at the same time. He appreciated Henry's constant shouting of the numbers indicating either the strokes per minute or the number of meters the British boat was ahead because those numbers helped him focus on something other than his endurance.

"Endure the pain!" shouted the rower in the number one seat. The cry passed from rower to rower. Those words of team play seemed to give the boat an extraordinary surge as it pulled into second place with the British boat only two meters ahead.

Each rower gasped at the air, hoping to fill his lungs with the necessary oxygen to keep his body going.

"Remember, an inch is all it takes!" shouted Henry.

"Just always be inching! Just always be inching!" George kept saying to himself as he felt the boat moving like a symphony with oars feathered and squared in unison. He barely heard the splash of the water as they passed the 1,500-meter mark. Somehow Sweden had managed to overtake them again. He had to give Henry credit for keeping them in their lane with his commands of "more on port" or "less on starboard."

"Power ten," came the call from the coxswain. That command meant that rowers in this very moment should forget about technique. Instead, focus on the legs and all the power possible. The pain will not be forever.

The horn sounded; they had crossed the finish line after five minutes and 240 strokes. Three rowers collapsed breathless, bending over their oar handle. Five turned to see that they had come in third. They raised one hand in triumph while holding on to the oar with the other, lifting their eyes to the sky. If they had looked forward, they would have seen Henry raise his hand in the "Heil Hitler" salute.

CHAPTER 10

Frieda stood at the kitchen sink, grateful that the apartment window looked out on the mid-morning sky, not the alley wall as did those of many of her neighbors. This morning it was a cloudy blue with occasional bits of sunshine peering through. She mindlessly let the water run as she ran a dirty plate under the faucet. My mother's dishes, she thought, given to me with the hope that I would duplicate her greatness as a cook. Never worked. There's no way I'm ever going to be great with stuffed cabbage and roasted chicken and sauerkraut and pickles, which she recalled constantly fermenting in vats under the kitchen sink during her childhood.

She dried the dish slowly, her mind returning to today's reality. She had a student coming in the next hour. She needed to practice more today, teach—although the number of students seemed to be on the wane. I need to touch that instrument at least several times a day, she mused. Like a child that you simply want to hug because of its innocent presence. That's what music was to her—innocent in its attempt to beautify the world. One kept at it to get notes in proper order and maintain correct position of fingers on the instrument to produce something beautiful to rest the soul and restore the spirit. It took practice. Practice that Frieda never minded.

The phone ring startled her. She waited to answer because they had a party line. She had heard that if you swore allegiance to the National Socialist Party, a family could be wait-listed for a private phone line. Still, she and Werner would never align themselves with the party promoting a dictatorship. In the meantime, Frieda waited for the three consecutive rings that indicated the call was for her family. No, the ringing continued, which meant it was for someone else—someone she did not know—but who could be listening in on telephone calls and decide to report the family to the authorities on something real or untrue. It didn't matter that she was playing for the Berlin Symphony, or that her husband was an editor at a "good" newspaper, or that her son might be rowing for the German Olympic team in 1936. If she hinted at a negative thought about the current regime, she might receive a call to report to the police station. And sometimes those who went never came back.

This was what the country had become, and the only moments that gave her solace were with her music and her family. The rest of life just couldn't be trusted or turned to for comfort.

She could hardly wait for George to return from England to hear about the regatta. She and Werner had already heard through teletype news that the British had won the gold medal for the eight, and *Der Tagblatt* had run the story touting the German boat's third place. The article noted that Italy and Norway, countries that always produced great competitive rowers, lost to Germany. Frieda realized it was the best the sportswriter could do, knowing that the Minister of Propaganda was reading this newspaper daily. Somewhere, buried at the end of the story, was the fact that the British had taken the gold medal. The half-page photo showed the German rowers smiling and raising the bronze medal that hung around their necks. George and Arthur looked particularly happy, Werner had said.

The phone rang again. This time Frieda heard the three-ring family signal. She hurried to pick up the receiver. Maybe the call would be news of a place for her in a quartet for which she had auditioned last week. The cellist had commented on her blue eyes; maybe that was a good sign, but the blue eyes went with dark brown, almost black wavy hair. The other violinist told her that he liked the "story" in her playing of Bach's *Partita #2*. She wasn't sure what he meant by that as she always enjoyed playing Bach for its precision and repeat of its motifs. Aha! Maybe that's what he meant by "story," since motifs were like the repetition of a theme in a story.

"Frieda?" It was her mother. For some reason, she always had to question if it were her daughter answering the phone, although Frieda was the only woman in the household, and she knew her daughter's voice. Frieda recognized it as symbolic of an underlying anxiety.

"Frieda," she repeated loudly. "They've taken him away. He spent one night in a cell. Do something."

Frieda heard hysteria in her mother's voice.

"Who?"

"Your father. Who else?" She shouted even louder.

Frieda knew that she had to be the calm one in this situation but hiding the terror in her voice was a struggle. *I need to take the word "invincible" out of my vocabulary as applied to my family.* Usually, her mother's years revealed themselves in wise sayings. One of her favorites to calm her daughter was,

"It's not a problem if money can fix it. Real problems are only those that money cannot fix." But unfortunately, Frieda had felt that with the rise of the Third Reich, these "money couldn't fix problems" were increasing.

"What was the charge?" Her quiet voice belied her anxiety.

"Something he said in his French class about Karl Marx."

"Was he talking about the time Karl Marx lived in France with his family?"

"Are you going to help, or are we going to have the Spanish Inquisition here on the phone? Your father is sitting in a jail cell, and he could be sent away to a concentration camp. It happened to one of our neighbors. And yes, he probably talked about the radical newspaper *Forward*, but it was all about utopian socialists—nothing real. And it was written in German. Please, no more Spanish Inquisition."

Frieda knew that the caustic remark came from real fear and desperation. Her parents, both in their seventies, had recently discussed her father's retirement from his university professorship as a teacher of French literature—a subject her father loved. He felt that language nurtured the romance in souls. She knew her father had complained that his classes were not filling, and that the current German regime was maligning the French government, discouraging students from taking his class even though he often discussed German authors like Goethe in connection with Victor Hugo, Alexander Dumas, and Jean Jacques Rousseau. He watched in anguish as Italian classes filled while his class rosters languished. But whenever his wife had suggested retirement, he stubbornly disagreed.

"They're going to have to carry me out on a stretcher. We cannot ignore German history and its connection to French literature." He was adamant that he was not going to retire willingly.

Frieda looked at the clock on the wall as her mother continued her words of concern. She had students coming.

Her mother continued as though she read her daughter's mind. "Cancel your students. Go use your charm and influence with the commandant in the jail." This woman knew about her daughter's devotion to music, and if there were students who could be captivated by music, Frieda would nurture them like newborn babies. Instead, today she would have to nurture her father. Her mother ended the call with, "And bring some good chocolates." And hung up.

Frieda immediately knew what she had to do. She left a hurried note pasted to the door. "Be back soon. Practice while you wait for me." She grabbed her coat and handbag and stopped at the corner store for a box of chocolate truffles. She practically ran all the way to the police station.

A young man in police uniform greeted her with "Heil Hitler" when she arrived. She recognized him as the young boy who grew up in the neighborhood of Langer Strasse and went to gymnasium—the state maintained secondary school—with George. She recalled he had not expressed much interest in university, but she remembered him as polite. So instead of returning the salute, she reached out and gently touched him on his arm.

"No need to do that with me, Henrik," she smiled. "Remember me? I'm George Grossinger's mother. I understand you have my father here, Professor Schwartz."

He blushed. "I don't have him. It's not me."

"Do you know why exactly he's here?"

"They have no idea why I'm here, and it's because they are stupid and don't know history." Her father was shouting from his jail cell. He had heard his daughter's voice.

"I'll get the commandant for you," the young policeman said hurriedly.

The commandant came out of the office with worried eyes that brightened as soon as he saw Frieda.

"I recognize you from the symphony. You play such a beautiful violin."

"Thank you." She decided to take a polite approach. "I'm sure you can help me with my father."

"This professor is your father?"

The young man suddenly had a voice. "Herr Commandant, I tried to explain to you that I knew them from my neighborhood. I had seen Herr and Frau Schwartz visit the Grossingers in their apartment."

The commandant approached her with authority. "The complaint was that your father was teaching about Communism. We now have Hitler as Fuhrer and the Third Reich. Thankfully most of the Communists are gone. We want to avoid any students thinking that there's good in Communism." He clicked his heels and added, "My name is Leo Fuchs."

"I was teaching history, you idiot." This time the voice from the cell was slightly hoarse.

"He has been shouting all morning," said the guard.

"You do know that Karl Marx was living in Paris and Emile Zola quoted Marx?" She tried to make the question as gentle and nonthreatening as possible. "I'm sure he was just trying to explain the history of the 1840s, which led to the revolution of 1848." She paused to let the information be absorbed. "I think our Fuhrer has even praised revolutions that got rid of kings." She had no idea if this was true, but she was also sure Leo Fuchs didn't know either. She reached into her handbag. "By the way, my mother suggested you might like these chocolates—even though they are French truffles."

"Maybe the student who reported him didn't understand what your father . . . Professor Schwartz . . . was trying to say," Fuchs said sheepishly, taking the box wrapped with a bright red ribbon.

"I'm sure the student didn't understand. Henrik will tell you that we are a good family," she said lightly, planting a kiss on Henrik's peach fuzz cheek. He blushed a deep pink.

"Yes," said Henrik. "Your mother was an excellent cook, too."

"May I just have a word with him?" Frieda said gently.

"Just go right up to the cell," said the guard, taking off the ribbon and opening the box of candy.

She whispered to her father. "Tell him you will clear up any misunderstanding with the student. Tell him you support the Third Reich."

Her father, who was still immaculately groomed in his blue slacks and tweed jacket with a shining white shirt and striped tie to match, quietly said, "Let me talk to him."

Frieda never knew what her father had said to him. She felt she owed him the respect of authority and ability. She never knew if the box of candy influenced the decision. As the daughter of a father she dearly loved, she was thankful they released him and allowed him to walk out with her in dignity, as though this was simply a polite visit to a police station for academic research.

CHAPTER 11

Ben Leicester tried to maintain standing at attention in front of his commanding officer, Henry Markham. This was even more difficult considering the fact that his clothing could no longer absorb the sweat, pouring down his back and backside. Thighs, too, he thought. The ceiling fan circulated hot air and a buzzing which made conversational sentences sound like shouted orders. Today, the hills of Haifa provided no respite. It was as though relief offered by high altitudes and breezes had departed the universe.

"And you could not avoid this happening? You're supposed to be protecting the country, not teaching Jews how to row, let alone a teenage girl?" Markham barked while furiously tapping a pencil on a worn mahogany desk—a left-over from what once had been a piece of elegant furniture in a home. Whose home, Ben wondered? He took a breath.

"It's okay," Leicester reassured Markham. "The newly arrived Jews, they consider themselves pioneers and expect their women to do something over here other than bake bread and wash clothes. The Zionists will not take up arms because I'm teaching a girl how to row. They may even give me a medal. And they've come to Palestine to escape whatever ugly antisemitism they were dealing with in their country. They're here, not Uganda. Remember? We were taught this history before we came here. Remember our Lord Balfour, the British foreign secretary writing a letter to a Rothschild and promising a homeland for his Jewish brethren? Besides, we like them because they supported us against the Turks. So, we welcome them with their fifth aliyah." Ben wiped his brow with the back of his hand and hoped he had not overstepped his bounds with all the words. "Is it all right if I sit down?"

He wasn't sure why he needed to remind Markham about the number of migration waves of Jews coming to Palestine. They were clearly in the middle of a new wave with the rise of Hitler in Germany. The British had better figure out which side they wanted to be on.

Markham waved a hand in the direction of a swivel chair with only two wheels. He had once attempted an investigation to find the other two, but he gave up after two months of dealing with the bureaucracy. Maybe if he had been comfortable with baksheesh, he thought, but bribery was just not in his nature even though it seemed to work in Middle Eastern countries to get things done.

"The Arabs will lob grenades if they think you are supporting these people who are taking over their land—driving their farmers out. And the Zionists will take up arms to retaliate," Markham retorted with his standard argument.

"Listen, if the farmers are willing to sell their land that hasn't been producing much, having no land might be an incentive to try something else." Ben knew he was repeating the war of words that Markham probably had heard many times before—not from newspapers or radios, but the zeitgeist—or the repeated village gossip.

Markham sighed. "Or it could be a disaster if it's all that you're used to—all you've been taught to do is cultivate land. Instead of soldiering, we should probably be helping people go from the Middles Ages to modern times."

"People need to help themselves." At this moment, all Ben could think of were the catchphrases that his rowing coaches had taught him. Show up to practice ready to participate, with focus and energy. Follow the directions and instructions of the coach. Cooperate and value each other. Respect the strongest rowers. Those same coaching words, he thought, could be taught to the Palestinians who were going to have to consider what they would do without land and work. If you were going to sell your land for what you thought would be opportunities, cooperate with others to find ways to test your skills and work on those you need to improve.

Markham swiveled around in his chair and pointed to a massive map that he now faced. "See that little spot here," he said, putting his finger on Palestine so that it was almost entirely covered. "Look how small it is next to Syria, Egypt, Saudi Arabia. A spot that in 1919 was almost entirely Arab and about 70,000 people. A handful of Jews—mostly the very religious ones. You know."

"And backward until the Jews came and brought citrus fruit production. The Arabs could have joined in to become the commercial center of the Middle East," Leicester retorted. Somehow, he had found an authoritative voice.

"Where do you think the Jews got the idea of selling the Jaffa orange? From the Arabs, of course." Markham pulled one out of his desk drawer and held it up as though it were a special prize. "Doesn't matter," he said dismissively. "Ancient history. Go to the village and talk to Safid Khalidi to get his kids under control and then to the kibbutz and tell them their kids learning to row disturbs the peace."

Ben thought, *I could stand and salute smartly and say, "Yes, sir," or I could sit here and describe why that is an impossible mission. These people want nothing more than that no one else should be on what they see as their land. Neighborliness is not in their vocabulary.*

He stood slowly and gave a half-hearted salute. "I will do my best. After my morning row. Okay?"

Markham pretending to read a report with his head down, ignored Leicester.

~~~

His 10,000-meter row gave him some measure of resolve. He pulled into the territory of Wadi Ara near Rosh Pinna. That's precisely what it was—Arab territory. Land with an equal measure of olive trees and swamps, with mud hut houses scattered around twenty-five acres. Families toiled in olive orchards and looked for work in Jewish villages nearby. They helped pick citrus fruits, plow the land and clear it for roads. Ben suspected that Arabs were building the new white-washed houses with red-tiled roofs for Jews. He knew that some even worked in an oil and soap factory that Jews had constructed. Some Arab villagers looked askance, but others looked in wonder and awe to see what the fifth aliyah, another wave, had brought in. He wondered if the Arab villagers understood that worldwide Jewry was supporting this wave of immigrants.

The Zionists were helping not only to pay for passage to help threatened Jews flee the pogroms of Europe but supporting them with tractors, lessons in farming, grains, and housing supplies. Suddenly the names of Rothschild, DeHirsch, and DeSchumann were on the lips of every Jew fleeing a country, coming to settle in what they were hoping would be a safe homeland.

The road, barely wide enough for his army jeep, led to the largest dwelling in the compound where many pigs and donkeys roamed the property. As he pulled closer to the door, children ranging from ages five to eighteen came out to greet him, and he saw Omar Khalidi with his arm in a sling. He waved to Ben with his other arm. His older brother, Ahmad, came from behind, scowling and pushed down the welcoming arm.

"They take good care of you at the hospital?" Ben asked, smiling at Omar. He hoped they appreciated that they now had a hospital thanks to efforts of recent arrivals and the Rothschilds, of course. He ignored the gun slung over the shoulder of the oldest sibling.

The boy nodded. "My father is inside with Moses Goodman."

Ben tried to hide his surprise. "That's nice. Will you take me inside?" He was planning to call on Goodman as well. This should be interesting, he thought.

Ben's eyes adjusted to the darkness inside the house and made out Safid Khalidi and Moses Goodman seated on a low sofa, both smoking hashish.

"Welcome," said Safid, waving to Ben to take a seat on the low sofa. Then, with another wave of his hand, he dismissed his children. "Get your mother to bring in some tea."

The British army officer knew enough not to say that it was too hot for tea. You accepted whatever generosity, whatever courtesy your host offered. It was the obligation of the guest. "Thank you, Effendi," he said, hoping that Safid recognized that with the use of his title, he was coming to negotiate, not to dictate. Animosity between the British and Arabs had been seething ever since the Arab revolt, beginning in 1916 against the Ottomans, had failed. Of course, the Balfour Declaration furthered the animosity. The British soldiers were expected to learn how to help these people live with one another. But suspicion and mistrust seemed to dominate whatever situation the British tried to negotiate.

"Maybe we don't need you here anymore," said Safid Khalidi slowly and precisely. Ben realized this was directed toward him.

Khalidi continued. "Moses here and his kibbutz now have . . ." He turned toward him. "What are you called?"

Moses smiled. "Hashomer . . . means the guard. We Jews have finally figured out that we must build ourselves up. Get muscles, if you will, and learn how to use a gun. It seems to have worked. We now can live in peace with our neighbor here. We ourselves protect our land and our property."

Ben thought this was not the time to divulge that more money was being brought in from Zionist organizations to buy up more land from Haifa to Megiddo and the Eshel Valley. Some of that land could very well be what they were sitting on right now, where pigs and donkeys roamed and olives were starting to grow on trees.

Ben wondered when the subject of Khalidi's coming to shoot at him, and the rowers on the Kishon could be introduced. The polite rules of this society were that guests did not bring up unpleasant topics. It was the obligation of the host to do so. He sipped his tea and was strangely gratified for the sweet heat that ran down his throat. It also gave him waiting time that turned out to be an advantage. "I'd like to talk with you about rowing on the Kishon," he said. The preliminaries of cordiality had been done. Safid understood.

"He will not do it again, I promise," said Safid. "Omar, come here," he called, and the boy immediately came in. He had been waiting right outside the door.

"Tell the British soldier here that you will not be bothering him or anyone else on the river. That what you did the other day was done out of youthful ignorance."

Before Omar could open his mouth, Moses said, "We have conditions. My kibbutz, Ben Shemen, has sent me with conditions."

Safid Khalidi paused, looking directly at Leicester. "Yes, we have conditions. Conditions are necessary to bring an agreement."

"And what are they?" Ben set down his glass of tea, not being able to imagine that they both agreed on anything significant to a British soldier.

Khalidi shrugged and looked at Goodman.

Goodman spoke in rapid Hebrew. "That you teach Ahmad here and Nurit and Ethan how to row. Omar, when his arm gets better. How to row like the British. We want to be ready for those who come from Germany and row. We don't want them to think of us like peasants; or people who spend all the time reading Torah. We want them to know we want to be strong, settle the land and work the land. Rowing will make us stronger. The pious with their davening have been here long enough studying. We do not need more praying now." He took a breath. "Khalidi and I have agreed to put down arms. Rowing together will eliminate the need for arms."

Ben didn't know what to make of this torrent of words, simultaneously grateful that he had studied Hebrew and Arabic. Safid Khalidi sat silently throughout, occasionally nodding. Omar and Ahmad just grinned. They were going to learn to row.

Ben thought. I'm going to need more boats. German or British? And how do I get them here? And Markham? How do I convince Markham?

Chapter 12

The two men sat close together, hunched over the kitchen table, looking at a yellow writing tablet trying to decipher the scribbled writing of what was clearly a draft. One's age was evident by sprinkles of gray in his hair and softness around the belly. On closer look, the younger one had the same shape head, the same wavy hair, albeit a rich brown, and broader shoulders. Any observer would have easily guessed that they were father and son.

George had been apprehensive about showing his draft to Werner, whose standards for writing were high: clarity, strong verbs, honesty. "Leave the propaganda to the politicians," his father would say.

The glow and thrill of coming in third in the Henley race still lingered. The bronze medal with its white and blue ribbon now hung over the knob of a closet door as a reminder of what had been and what might yet be possible. George thought the embedded sculler on the bronze medallion looked like someone from an Eakins painting. When George brought it home, he laid the prize alongside a copy of an Eakins sculler painting in his art history book. While admiring the art, he would often conjecture what it would be like to row in the distant places depicted in the artist's paintings. Novels brought other worlds to readers but art, even more so. The depictions were already there to ponder and expand one's imagination.

"Needs some rewriting, but we'll print it," said his father. "It might bring some happiness to people here to know that two German Jews helped to bring a bronze to Germany. That could be the focus—the theme, you know. We need something in this country to lift the spirits." He decided to wait before telling him what had happened to his grandfather.

"No," George said, pushing the writing tablet aside. "There's nothing there about Arthur and me being Jewish, and it's not going to bring any glory to Germany if that information is included. Instead, we print a description of the race, how close it was . . . and the setting. I'm sure the readers here would like a bit of description of the English . . . how they behave at a race and how they dress. Women spectators wore fancy hats with big brims often adorned with flowers, and some of the men even had top hats." He paused. "Dare I say that I think some of the dresses were made of chiffon?" He smiled. "And some of the men wore morning coats along with their top hats?" He touched his father's arm. "I want this article to bring some light into people's lives."

Werner Grossinger walked to the kitchen sink, turned on the tap, filled a glass with water, and took a few sips before returning to the table. This is not the time for wine, he thought. I need a clear head unadulterated by diminishing clarity brought by a glass of merlot. He sipped the water, contemplating his son, shoulders hunched, eyes staring at his writing draft.

"They took your grandfather away to jail last week on the suspicion that he was a Communist because he was teaching about Karl Marx," Werner said softly, trying to quell the dilemma in his head. Honesty. Clarity. Support my son. Make him stronger. Don't frighten him. But make him aware.

George looked up. "Is he all right? Grandmother must have been frightened."

"Back home, a little shaken and thinking of leaving for Palestine. They both are."

"Palestine? When did they become Zionists?"

"How do you even know what a Zionist is?" Werner was sure that this subject had not been discussed in the twenty years since George was born, and now suddenly, Zionism was on both their lips.

George proceeded to tell his father he had not written the kidnapping story in his notebook. He had felt it would be too dangerous should anyone come across it, but he had every detail of the incident embedded in his memory. It kept repeating itself as an hour-long movie in black and white with very few shades of gray, mostly at nighttime as he was trying to get to sleep. But it never overshadowed the winning of bronze for Germany.

He ended his description of the kidnapping saga with, "But that's not what's most important," said George. "Germany won a bronze. We won bronze for Germany. That's important." His father had not said a word during the entire recitation of what had to be a frightening event.

"You think so?"

These last words came from his mother, who had entered the kitchen at the tail end of the conversation.

She repeated, "You think so? That's what's most important?" She sat down and took George's hand in hers—a gesture she had not done in many years. "You are lucky, my son, that you are here to tell the story. Unfortunately, some are not so lucky. Tonight, Abraham Grosser did not show up for rehearsal, and no one knows where he is. Fortunately, we have substitutes who are willing to step in. But not a Jew among them." She paused. "I need a glass of wine."

"George suddenly knows about the Zionists because he met them in London," said Werner, going to the credenza and pouring a glass of wine.

"Yes. It was an unfortunate part of an exciting trip," said George.

"Unfortunate! Unfortunate!" Frieda Grossinger let go of her son's hand and stood over him, wine glass in hand. "For God's sake. Your grandfather was just held hostage in jail. The Jews in the orchestra are disappearing. Your father cannot print the truth, you are kidnapped by Zionists, and all you can come up with is the word 'unfortunate?'"

"But I am still rowing for the club. Nobody asks about our foreskin. Arthur and I were selected for the eight, and we are working our way toward the Olympics. Olympics in 1936, Mother. How exciting would that be?"

"Only if we're still alive," snapped Frieda but decided at that moment not to voice her concerns further, continuing to sip her wine slowly. She realized her words came out of frustration with no clear direction of the right thing to do.

Werner would not let up. "You honestly think that they are going to let Jews row in the Olympics? Just look around you."

"Coach Messinger wouldn't take us out of the boat. We're too good," George said, trying to keep his voice moderate. "And we could be rowing singles. Arthur and I are good enough to compete in singles."

"You think Messinger has all that power?" his father demanded. "That he is not worried if he is going to put Jews in a winning eight? How naïve can you be?"

Frieda sat with her head in her hands. She spoke barely above a whisper. "All this shouting and discussing isn't going to solve anything. Print George's article. Let him return to rowing. Who knows? Something good may come out of it for everyone." She downed the rest of the wine quickly.

~~~

George left the house at 5:00 a.m. in the dark of the next day, books in a backpack, and mounted his bike to ride the five miles to the club. He whistled one of his favorite songs from America, "Makin Whoopee." The little English he knew taught him to love the way the words "June" and "honeymoon" rhymed, and he guessed what "whoopee" was. He was looking forward to the joy of the crew seeing each other again, even Henry, and the recognition of honor from other rowers who would be at their lockers just as the sun was inching over the horizon. He imagined the water to be still and mirror-like at this morning hour.

Loud voices greeted George, with everyone wishing each other congratulations. George noted that three or four of his teammates hugged each other. He decided to greet Arthur with a firm handshake and a smile. I must make a note in my book, he thought, because it is unusual for Germans to be hugging one another. It's just that winning brings out much joy. It does, he thought. It really does. He had read that the rush of adrenaline had been linked to bringing on a state of euphoria. He could not stop smiling.

When Coach Messinger entered the locker room, everyone quieted down, took to the benches to await the congratulatory speech. Part of that speech would be, of course, telling them how they could do better to win the gold at the Olympics. George took out his notebook, thinking he would write an article about Messinger. Of course, he would check with the coach to make sure the quotes were accurate. He had learned that from his father. "Don't misquote. Don't assume you heard it accurately. Verify that you heard it accurately."

Messinger spoke, trying to control the conflicts within. "My voice is a bit hoarse from all the shouting in England, but the club and I are proud of you. You lost by only four seconds to Sweden. Now let's think about how we can take off those seconds, but we have other things to think about as well."

"I'm going to work on strengthening the legs. Propulsion with the legs has got to be stronger," said Arthur, practically jumping out of his seat. "I'm recommending that for everyone."

Messinger took a deep breath. "Yes, that's good for everyone, but not important for you and George."

"That's not necessary for you to say, Coach Messinger." George was emphatic. "We will do whatever anyone else does. Every bit of extra work improves the body, improves the stroke, improves the row."

Messinger looked over the heads of the young men sitting below him. It was as though he was waiting for someone or something to come through the door. Finally, he returned his gaze to the rowers.

"Jews will not be allowed to practice with us to prepare for the Olympics. The order just through from Goebbels," Messinger said quietly and slowly, his voice quavering. "Now that Hitler is fully committed to hosting the Olympics and is convinced that certain people are enemies of the state and can't be trusted, I repeat, Jews will not be allowed to practice with us to prepare for the Olympics." He started to walk away. "I have nothing more to add."

"But . . ." Arthur did not finish his sentence when he saw tears in his coach's eyes. As he got to the door of the locker room, Messinger turned and said, "No practice this morning. You should leave the club and get to your classes on time."

George and Arthur remained seated as all the rowers walked past them, eyes averted. Henry was the last one at the door. "It will be for the good of Germany that you will be treated as the vermin that you are. You were responsible for our defeat in the last war. This is what my father has told me. Now we have leaders who know and believe it."

George exchanged a glance with Arthur that he hoped transmitted the words, "ignore him." He knew that this was a widely believed legend propagated by the defeated Germans.

But the coxswain continued. "In our leader's own words, 'National Socialism affirms the heroic doctrine of the value of blood, race, and character as well as the external laws of selection.' I have memorized those words. I suggest you two do the same."

A bolt shot through Arthur, and he lunged at the coxswain. His one hundred ninety-pound, six-foot height could undoubtedly have taken the five-foot five-inch coxswain down, but George grabbed Arthur around the waist and tackled him to the ground. "This will not get us anywhere."

Henry grinned, standing over them. "Just like two Jews to try to save the world, but they wind up on the ground."

"Don't say anything," said George as Henry walked out the door, "and don't go running after him." They lay on their backs on the cold floor of the locker room.

"We have to do something about this," said Arthur as he pulled himself up to the bench.

"Yes, we have to find a way to continue rowing," said George, brushing himself off sitting alongside his friend.

CHAPTER 13

At 6:30 in the morning light, Martin Wilder stood with a mug of coffee in hand on the balcony of the Hebrew Boat Club, assessing the flow of the Spree River. One of his favorite morning rituals before he went out to row his single was to drink a cup of coffee, which he believed gave him an extra boost of energy. At fifty-two, he was beginning to feel that caffeine was a necessity and not a luxury. Coffee and wine had been hard to get in the worldwide depression, so most Germans had settled for tea as a morning beverage and beer as an evening drink, but Wilder spent the extra money for coffee.

The rains had come suddenly and unpredictably in the night, and this morning's occasional wind blew in blasts of air, creating ripples in the river, which would make rowers more cautious. The air felt good, but Wilder noted some of the outside boats were not tied down and needed to be secured in light of the weather. He would have to speak to the members and remind them. If you were hurrying off to observe the Sabbath, you needed to prepare for extra time to secure the boats. Not even Sabbath prayers to God were going to take care of the boats without human help. Everyone, religiously observant or not, needed to tie down the boats. Otherwise, in the event of a storm that brought a downriver surge, they could be floating down the Spree, never to be seen again.

He ran down the outside steps to tie boats to racks and was surprised to see two bicycles outside the front bay doors—doors wide enough to permit rowers to carry eights and fours down to the dock for practice. Wilder turned to see two young men—he guessed them to be about twenty—roaming around, clearly in search of something. They did not appear to be the SS goons who had lately been reported harassing some of the members who took boats out in the early evening.

"Can I help you?" Wilder asked.

"We couldn't get in your bay doors to see your boats," said Arthur, "so we decided to take a look around."

"Of course, you couldn't get in." Wilder stood, arms akimbo, as though to undergird his authoritative statement. "Not that anyone can easily steal a boat, but this is private property." He added, "People don't usually come around wanting to look at our boats. They come here wanting to row, so the doors are locked until it is time for our members to be out on the water. Strangers rarely show up."

"But it says Hebrew Boat Club above your door. Therefore, we are not strangers," George said, hoping that his light tone would assure this older man that they were not unwanted trespassers, or worse, SS dummkopfs who had come to do damage. "And we do want to row."

"Come upstairs, and we'll talk," Wilder said, thinking of late that he had heard stranger stories, and he was always looking to introduce young men to the sport he was so passionate about. Arthur began with the news of being barred from the rowing program at the Germania Rowing club and how much they wanted to continue to practice rowing. They were going to commit to singles. They were Jewish, so why couldn't they train at the Hebrew Rowing Club and participate in the Olympics?

"Yes, and we just came back from England. Our Germania Club eight came in third," George interjected, thinking that this statement would be further assurance of their desire and determination to row.

Martin Wilder sat back impassively on a worn leather sofa throughout the entire story. The words had come out in a continuous stream alternately between George and Arthur, and if a pause existed in the narrative, Wilder merely had to nod his head, and the two young men read it as a signal to continue.

"And you never thought of coming before today?" Wilder motioned to a six-foot round table topped with an oilcloth of miniature red roses on a pure white glossy background. "After all, this is a Hebrew rowing club, and you are Jewish." While they sat down, Martin rose to retrieve glasses of water and set them before the rowers. "Drink. You need to hydrate after biking here."

"We tried out for the club eight at Germania to row in England. We got selected. We didn't think past that," said Arthur, looking at George for affirmation.

George nodded, hoping that his face didn't reveal the truth. Hebrew Rowing Club was something they had never considered because Judaism wasn't prominent in their lives. Being Jewish, yes, but no religious school and no holiday observances. He and Arthur had heard you were supposed to fast to better reflect on your sins and atone for them, but they both ate on Yom Kippur because they usually rowed that day as well.

As if reading George's mind, Martin asked, "Did you fast on Yom Kippur?"

"We couldn't because we needed energy to row," said Arthur quickly.

"Well, for your information, we don't row on Yom Kippur, and we do have Zionists who are members here—ardent Jews, but they probably didn't fast either," Martin said. Arthur and George put their glasses of water down on the table simultaneously and exchanged a glance.

"Oh, I see," said Martin. "You react to Zionist, but you wouldn't know a piece of matzoh if I placed it in front of you. Am I right?" He could barely contain the sarcasm—something, of late, that he had been trying to control, especially when he heard his fellow rowers at the club express a positive sentiment for the new regime.

At that moment, George knew he needed to be the next one to speak in this awkward conversation. "We only know what a Zionist is because we rowed in England," George said softly.

"Mm," said Martin. George and Arthur simultaneously took a sip of water, set down the glasses again, and eyed the floor. Arthur cleared his throat. "We were competing in London . . ." when Martin interrupted. "Wait, if this is going to be another interesting story, I want to get Amos Schindler here."

Amos Schindler must have been downstairs in the boat bay because after a brief trip down the steps, Martin came back with a man in tow, about ten years older but with no sign of excess fat on his limber six-foot-two frame.

"This is Amos Schindler. He coaches and knows all the quirks of the boats here." Amos smiled. "As well as the members."

"Sit," said Martin. "There's going to be a story here." He waved a directing hand. "Go ahead, Arthur. "

Arthur continued relating the events of their capture and return to dorm rooms in London by men who called themselves Zionists.

"And what did they want from you?" asked Schindler, who, like Wilder, sat attentively in anticipation, ignoring an offered glass of water.

George hesitated. "They wanted us to get boats and rowers to Palestine so that Jews could participate in the Olympics." Silence followed.

"Please repeat," said Schindler.

George repeated that sentence a bit more slowly, word for word, as though he were speaking to someone hard of hearing.

"And this is one way we could encourage Jews to emigrate to Palestine," Arthur added, seeing his hosts' attentiveness to the story.

"And what did you think about that?" Martin asked, his voice barely above a whisper.

"We were surprised," said George. "At first, frightened. We weren't sure if they were a bit deranged." George had decided there was no way to go with this story but bare honesty. No embellishment. Honesty. Clarity. His father's words.

"Were you frightened when the Reichstag fire occurred?" Both George and Arthur were taken aback by Wilder's sudden intensity. He continued; his voice raised. "You didn't think it was a plot the Nazi party devised to turn everyone against the Communists and later the Jews?" George and his father had discussed that possibility as a news story but decided it could bring problems for the paper from the government. He avoided the question.

A silence settled over the room. Eyes lowered in awkwardness. Amos stood up. "Come. Martin takes things seriously. I'm a bit more optimistic. So, down to the bay. We have two singles for you. We will see how well you row and if you want to train here under the Hebrew banner."

"Yes," said Martin. "And we'll see if we . . . if we want you to train here."

"Maybe, we should take out doubles first, with one of you in each bow," Arthur said tentatively. "We don't know this portion of the river."

"No. If you're going to represent us, it's going to be in a single, and I will be in the motorboat," said Schindler. "No time like the present. The embers in Germany are being stoked. According to Martin, we're just about ready to burn. But we must go on with life. So, when do you want to begin?"

"As soon as possible," said George. Arthur repeated, "As soon as possible."

⚊⚊

George and Arthur lowered themselves into the singles more tentatively than their usual approach in the eight. They were accustomed to eight rowers entering together and stabilizing the boat. A narrow single demanded more stability—both inner and outer, mental and physical. George slowly lowered his body into the boat, slid first his left and then right foot into the well-worn foot straps, grabbed the oar handles with his right hand, and pushed hard away from the dock with this left hand, following precise instructions from Schindler. Arthur tried to copy George's movements. No coxswain. Just a new coach in a nearby boat. "A few more directions," shouted Schindler. "Backside centered on the seat. Knees vertical, never moving left or right.

Eyes on the horizon. Sit straight and hands level. Just like the eight. Again, hands level. Okay? Ready?"

Arthur and George started tentatively on the slide at first, barely reaching the complete length of the catch—the moment the blade turns to enter the water. Then, after about ten minutes with Schindler's instructions in mind, they both traveled the entire length of the slide towards the catch with arms extended. They did this awkwardly at first, clearly missing the balance that six other rowers and a coxswain would typically give them in an eight. Finally, the river was wide enough so they could row side by side, with Schindler, observing in the motorboat ahead of them, one hand on the steering wheel, megaphone in the other. He assessed their ability to row, and the extent of their previous training as the only different directions he gave them were to row "port" or "starboard" to help them stay on the proper path.

For the next ten minutes, they continued to row with greater ease, with the distance growing between the puddles and the ripples the oars made at the catch and release. As they feathered, they kept their blades about three inches off the water, burying them at just the proper height, just beneath the surface at the catch. Schindler smiled as he saw their natural ability. He yelled at them. "Different from an eight?"

George and Arthur both nodded. He raised his megaphone. "Let's take it up a notch. There's no one behind you. Align your boats next to each other. Wait till I give the command. Sit ready."

They relaxed shoulders, sat upright at three-quarters slide, blades level with the water at the catch. This was the moment to race and racing against each other it would be. Schindler got close enough to them to call without the megaphone, "Ready! Row!"

He eagerly watched as they both sprinted off blades buried just at the correct height and two short slides before the full slide. They had been well trained. He had heard about the coaching abilities of Messinger, so he wasn't surprised at Arthur and George's level of discipline, but he knew they didn't have much experience as single scullers. Today that didn't seem to matter. It was as though someone had thrown competition dust over them as they rowed, trying to maintain a competitive pace, both breathing hard in short bursts, as Messinger had taught them.

George slowed a bit as he thought, *I won't be able to keep this up much longer. I have to conserve some energy for the finish.*

"Another five hundred meters," shouted Schindler. George responded with his racer's body and mind. For those next five hundred meters, he kept saying to himself, "legs, legs, legs," and poured on the power. He had pulled ahead of Arthur, and when he heard "stop" from the coach, he had beaten Arthur by five seconds.

"Row back to the boathouse, and I'll meet you there," shouted Schindler.

Wilder was there at the boat bay waiting for them. George and Arthur skillfully lifted their starboard oars onto the dock and slowly glided into place, one after the other. They then helped each other return the sculls to the racks. George's observational skills told him that the boats were all in good condition—wooden shells gleamed in the sunlight streaming from the outside, and oars were neatly paired in slots along the wall. Many fours, doubles, and singles. Only one eight.

"So," asked Arthur, "can we train here?"

"The Hebrew Rowing Club welcomes you with open arms. Germania will regret losing you. I can tell already," Schindler said. "I'm sure Wilder will agree."

CHAPTER 14

It was official. George was now working as an intern at the newspaper. Gradually, he had learned to love the production of the newspaper and saw that it went far beyond gathering data and information to get news, or "truth to the populace," as his father would say. Three floors of the building held people who worked with machines and their minds to get the story out to *Der Tagblatt*'s readers. First and second floors housed the editor's offices and typists, usually women, typing the reporter's information to be typeset. The basement housed workers who received the set metal type, then fed it onto enormous rolls of paper that took two men to boost onto a machine so paper would feed continuously.

George had learned how to walk quickly on the first floor and basement through the cigarette smoke that seemed to waft in a permeable forever fog. He wondered when it becomes an imperative that a cigarette accompany thinking, writing, chatting, conferencing. The coach had always cautioned them about the dangers of cigarette smoking. "It will wreck your lungs" was his favorite foreboding comment, and it had stuck with George and most of his teammates. Fortunately, the third floor where the papers were stacked into manageable bundles for delivery was smoke-free.

His father's corner office on the first floor, equipped to receive cables and seeming accessible to anyone during his workday, always felt chaotic. George noted that the secretary would run cables to the newsroom after his father had looked them over quickly and decided if the information was newsworthy. From those cables, Werner designated reporters for specific assignments. In George's eyes, people always seemed to be coming in and out of Werner's office with a pencil behind one ear, a pad of paper in one hand, and a cigarette between finger tips. His father often reminded him that "news" meant something new was happening in the world. Readers liked a fresh story, and it was their obligation to give it to them, but it was up to him as editor to determine if it was "newsworthy." A significant responsibility, he frequently pointed out.

"But we are walking a fine line here," his father had told George. "Other newspapers are being forced to print whatever Hitler's henchmen tell them to print. If there's a street fight between the Communists and the SA, the Communists always start it. So far, we have some leeway, but if we tell too many truths they'd rather not think about, the so-called authorities will shut us down immediately." He paused. "And we can never go so far as to choose our own words. We use the word 'citizens' now instead of 'workers' whenever possible, even when reporting about labor issues. That appeases the government."

The sports editor, Heinrich Grosz, had welcomed George's article about the regatta in England and thanked him for specifically avoiding any mention of participation of Jews in the eights or the removal of Jews from further involvement at his former club. "It's enough for the propaganda minister. He will be happy to know that Germany received a bronze medal. And we will name the coach, of course," he explained and somehow felt the need to add, "Your teammates will be proud even without their names." George nodded but was concerned that the rest of the crew of eight would blame him and Arthur for their lack of recognition. He had decided, though, not to worry too much since he was no longer rowing with them. He also thought their families had already probably told them to "ignore the Jewish rowers. It's safer."

Grosz, who had been in the trenches in The Great War, was acutely aware of how leaders could manipulate citizens or push them to a fervor of idiotic patriotism that costs lives. When he returned from war, he had resolved that even when the subject was Germany's crushing loss, he would be a truth-teller. Unfortunately, Grosz, the reporter, now weighed truth by telling only part of the story. He appeased his conscience by saying he would never write an account with an actual lie.

Grosz and Werner Grossinger had even decided not to report on the Hebrew Rowing Club or other Jewish affiliated sports teams. They hoped their readers read into cues and code words when reading anything positive about Jewish winners. Reporters would disguise the event with words like "historic" or "diverse." Somehow, their very distinct readership had been clever enough to pick up on the real meaning of the language. With it all, the paper was able to maintain a substantial circulation. None of the newspaper vendors denied delivery of *Der Tagblatt*, and the newspaper sold out at the kiosks daily

Today, after reading information from an anonymous source in Berlin,

Werner asked for a meeting with his news editor, Henry Hess. Werner found George in his wanderings through the plant and asked him to be present. At times, George felt lost in the intern process; his father always seemed busy. He was grateful when called in. Perhaps he would be given a specific assignment.

As he sat in his father's office strewn with papers all over the floor and on his massive desk, George shifted his chair, so he could be ready to hear whatever his father and editor Hess had to say. He wasn't sure if he would have anything to contribute—just yet. His father was blunt. "There is news that a list will be published of people who are going to lose their German citizenship. I know they include Henrich Mann, Lion Feuchstwanger, Ernst Toller, and Kurt Tucholsky. All Jewish. What do we do?" George had never heard his father be quite so blunt and direct. Even when George had to be reprimanded, his father had seemed to do it with an intellectual edge rather than being harsh. "Was there a better way you could have handled that situation?" seemed to be his father's favorite question.

"Didn't one of them have an Aryan spouse—you know someone who is Christian?" asked Hess.

"I know what an Aryan spouse means," Werner retorted. "That's not what I'm asking you."

George noted the palpable tension, and he understood. His father wanted to print the truth, and he also wanted the newspaper to continue with as much authenticity as possible. Printing *almost true* stories had never been his style, and as editor-in-chief, he took seriously the need to inform readers. Werner Grossinger had argued with Hess about printing details of the story of a rally covering Hitler. Goebbels had sent them the crowd size. Informants had told them otherwise; it was much smaller. *Der Tagblatt* printed the truth, and it hadn't drawn any government reprisal.

Another story told of SA members rampaging through neighborhoods and knocking over trash containers. The newspaper printed Goebbels' denial, which said the young men were on a cleanup mission.

"We wrote an opinion piece condemning the ruffians that set the Reichstag fire, knowing full well that they probably did it themselves so the Nazis could blame the Jews for something else." It was Hess beginning his litany. He continued. "It was sort of a half-truth story."

"We have run advertisements with swastikas on children's balls. The department store, KaDaWe, promotes them almost daily. We have reported on the election of Franklin Delano Roosevelt in America, but we write nothing about his programs that help people out of the Great Depression. Instead, we only write about how he closed down all the banks. Like a dictator."

Werner interjected. "I know. I know. And our leader can make laws without consulting the Reichstag, and I am forced to express my approval." He took a breath. "But you know, there is power in words. You just hope your readers are smart enough to also be able to decipher what is behind the words."

George knew, at this moment, that his father was dealing with the conflict going on in his soul, between keeping the newspaper alive and printing accurate news. He watched attentively, wanting to say something but unsure when to interject. The Zionism question was burning a hole in his brain now that it seemed to be entering his life capriciously at every turn.

"There is a rumor they are thinking of instituting their secret police—a Gestapo," his father continued. "Just what we need to frighten people into submission. The party having its own police unit."

George blurted out. "Do we have a Zionist organization here?"

"Where? In the office?"

"In Germany. In Berlin."

"There were rumors we had a Zionist office in the building. I never explored it. Why the subject of Zionism in Berlin?" asked his father. He tossed out the question for Hess' enlightenment, and George took the bait. He told the news editor the story of his kidnapping and the bizarre requests from the British Zionists. He then pushed for more information. Were the German Zionists that extreme, and where were they, and were they worth writing about?

Hess noted the enthusiasm in the young man's voice as well as the naiveté in his thinking about the power of the press. "I guess they're worth interviewing," said Hess, "but I'm not sure we want to write about them unless we want to destroy them. Hitler probably identifies them with Communists—anyone who's not a member of the National Socialists, anyone who's not an Aryan could be in danger." He added, "You should keep your story to yourself. Maybe for your memoirs. Not for now."

George persisted. "Let me set up the meeting. I think I have an idea of how to find and appeal to them and what would work with them for the good of the newspaper."

Werner was torn between his desire to encourage his son and his anxiety about a constantly evolving political situation.

"You do this on your own," said Hess. "The newspaper won't have anything to do with what the Zionists want." Hess didn't even look at his boss for approval. They had already staked out the parameters that would keep the newspaper going.

"But there was this huge rally at Madison Square Garden in New York over books the SA burned," said George. "The Zionists promoted it, and why shouldn't they? It was mostly Jewish authors whose books we burned. But they were also upset for Bertold Brecht, Ernest Hemingway, Erich Maria Remarque. Right? Libraries here will no longer carry their books, either. Just because they espoused liberal causes."

"Yes," said Hess testily. "We decided to cover it and write an angry opinion piece against . . . " He paused to allow the silence to filter. "The rally, that is. There was a Jewish flag alongside the American flag. As I said, it was an angry opinion piece. That's why we're still in business." He got up. "Discussion over and by the way we didn't burn the books, the SA did."

George remained quiet. He worried how the daily events would affect his studies and rowing plans. Could he please his father as an intern? Werner looked at him apprehensively. He knew George was thinking about how to get back to rowing, and at the same time, recent events had awakened his assimilated Jewish identity. Werner hoped that whatever George had in mind would also be good for *Der Tagblatt*—it still provided readers a modest semblance of truth.

Chapter 15

Isaac Sherman raised the window shades in his small office, wondering how long the dark clouds would bring rain. He looked down and saw a sea of open black umbrellas offering more darkness on the street before turning his attention to the papers on his desk. Several of his clients were looking for loans from the banks, and they turned to him for help in filling out the applications. Isaac, as an accountant, had worked frequently with Danatbank, with its Jewish senior partner, Jakob Goldstein, but he understood it was now under Nazi surveillance. A textile firm had defaulted on its payments, causing a crisis in the bank.

Isaac pushed the papers aside, understanding there might be little that he could do. He turned his attention to the newspaper headlines of *Der Sturmer*. Was it printing any more lies about ritual murders by Jews? He had written letters in protest. "No, we do not drink the blood of children." He wrote out of frustration since he knew the newspaper would never print his missives. He wondered if his protest letters were shared in the *Sturmer* office, with men making jokes about the letters' foolishness, knowing the words came from an ardent Zionist and a Jewish accountant. He had long ago given up the hope that Hitler would condemn false arguments, especially if the Fuhrer's ego were involved. And he suspected Hitler and his friends approved of anything that stirred animosity against the Jews.

It was no longer the Germany of the Weimar Republic where Jews were looked upon as ordinary citizens and had easy access to all of society's offerings; where they could even conduct experiments that won a Nobel Prize—Fritz Haber for the synthesis of ammonia in its elements. Isaac had it imprinted in his memory because it brought so much pride to his community. "See," his mother had told him. "See what happens when you study."

The sudden opening of the office door interrupted his thoughts. Julius Abrahams, his partner, came flying through, breathless. "They need boats. They need to start a program for some Arabs and Jews. They need boats."

Isaac smiled. This was just like Julius, coming in with wild fantasies while all he wanted was for *Der Sturmer* to print one of his letters. He silently hoped that whatever Julius was going on about would bring in more business. They needed to have clients and expand beyond their regular clientele, mainly members of the synagogue—right below his office window.

"Sit down. Have a glass of tea and explain. Start with a first paragraph."

Julius explained that he had a letter from his cousin in a kibbutz near Wadi Ali in Palestine. They had a British soldier who was an outstanding rower and would train Arab and Palestinian youngsters to compete in the Olympics.

"The Olympics? Already?" said Isaac, putting two glasses of hot tea and cubes of sugar on the desk. He had long ago given up trying to curb his sarcasm. It had been handed down from generation to generation. He just had to be careful when working with clients or potential clients. Some understood that his sarcasm came from angst; others had no clue from what brought about angst in the first place.

"Maybe, I got a little carried away," said Julius sheepishly, dunking his tea bag several times before placing it on a napkin. "Apparently on the Kishon River . . . near Haifa." He wrapped a paper napkin around the glass and added three cubes of sugar, stirring slowly with a spoon before lifting the glass to his lips. "You're right. We need to start from the beginning. He said they needed boats. Do you know what kind of boats and where are we going to get those boats that we know nothing about?" He paused. "I know how to convince people why they should go to Palestine. I know how to help people keep track of their money if they have a business. But boats. That's another story."

"Werner Grossinger," said Isaac. "You know him? You know his son? I think he knows about the kind of boats they need." He went to a dented, green metal, three-drawer filing cabinet, reached for the bottom drawer, and pulled out three manila folders. "Here," he sighed, laying them on the table. "Here is information all about boats. Companies in England, Switzerland, Canada." He looked out the window and stared at the dark sky. "If we live long enough, maybe we'll do business with a boat company in England."

Julius began rifling through the folders. "Germany, too?" He asked the question easily, knowing Isaac was simply a collector of all kinds of information connected to Judaism and potential clients. Even ones that might be considered far-fetched. But, once Jews began rowing in Germany and establishing their rowing clubs, Sherman would have created a file about people in the clubs and its possibility as a source of clients.

"So they'll come from here. The boats, I mean. Right from Germany. Right? That's the easiest thing to do," Isaac said and continued to sip from the glass, trying to hide his enthusiasm. He had often been accused of reacting first and thinking later, but he had a mind that refused to take a rest from his agitated thoughts. The dedicated Zionist knew enough about rowing to imagine boats and oars arriving at a dock in Haifa, and young Israelis coming in their trucks and jeeps already having figured out how to load 8.2-meter wooden boats, protecting them on the top of old cars with blankets below and pillows on top. In reality, he was looking to make enough money to have these impossible dreams come true. Therefore, more clients.

Julius resumed looking through the photographs in the file from races on the Thames in England. Some of the photos showed people in boats with eight men and a smaller person sitting in front. Others had four men. Isaac had learned about boats through his rowing on Lake Plötzensee where he and his father would spend part of a Saturday instead of going to a synagogue. "It's good to be quiet on the water," his father had said. "And watch the birds and plants that God has given us." He would then take a few strokes with his oar, pause, and say, "Just look. Just look and wonder." Those were the days when Jews, like his father, who taught high school history, took comfort in the Weimar Republic.

"We'll never be able to do this," Isaac suddenly muttered.

"What do you mean? We haven't even started," said Julius. "We raise money. We make contacts. We find a big boat. We ship." He took a sip of tea. "We could even ship arms in the boats. No one will know."

"Look," said Isaac pointing to the photographs. "Some boats are 18.9 meters. Some are 13.4 meters. We don't have a ship that can take those." He looked up. "And do we want to risk this project by shipping arms? Too dangerous. We have other ways to send guns."

"So," said Julius. "We'll start with the small boats. What did you say? 8.2 meters? And they're wood. Won't weigh as much as aluminum."

"And maybe we can get some money from our clients," said Isaac. "We just have to convince them it's for a good cause." He looked away. He did not want Julius to see the tears welling up.

~~~

During the next few days, Julius contacted all the Jewish rowing clubs in Berlin as well as Zollenger, a Swiss manufacturer of boats, because one member had a contact there.

"Who knew?" said Isaac. "Who knew we would ever have rowing clubs? Did we row across the Red Sea? No, it opened, and we walked. Did we row in Noah's Ark?" He turned his palms up—the questioning gesture. "It just floated, didn't it? Even then, they knew how to make boats that just floated. "

Julius understood a response wasn't necessary. He knew Isaac was prone to Old Testament passages when mulling over hard decisions.

Ultimately, from the Jewish rowing clubs, they could get a commitment of five old wooden singles and oars. Isaac and Julius recruited George Grossinger and Arthur Schwartz to check the boats to see if they were still rowable. Martin Wilder and Amos Schindler had recommended the boys. Not only had they earned a reputation in the Zionist community from the London contacts, but George and Arthur were now showing up regularly for practice at the Hebrew Rowing Club—five days a week. If Julius and Isaac had taken the time to talk to George, they would have heard that he was beginning to think about the Hebrew Rowing Club as a path to the Olympics. George and Arthur had been impressed by Schindler's coaching.

From George and Arthur, the two accountants learned some boats had seats and foot straps missing, but they were all replaceable parts. Even bent riggers were replaceable. Just as long as the hulls were intact. Zollenger, the Swiss company, wasn't responding to any calls and telegrams, but George and Arthur confirmed that they were a great manufacturer of boats. Isaac Sherman and Julius Abrahams were exceedingly grateful for the young men's skills and intensity.

⁓

"And just exactly how are you and the Zionists planning to transport these boats?" Werner Grossinger asked George while taking a chicken drumstick from the plate that Frieda was passing. Before taking the first bite, he said, "Ahh, I know, you are planning to row it with your friend, Arthur, directly to the port of Haifa." He took a bite. "But they don't have a double." He looked up, waiting for a reaction.

"This is no time to be sarcastic," Frieda said, putting down the plate in the center of the table. "Your son is trying to do something extraordinary in these terrible times. We have just lost our best cellist because he was Jewish."

"Don't forget, I run a newspaper. I know what it's like to be treading water—trying to keep one's head above and at the same time not taken away to prison, never to be seen again. Besides, would our son even know the route?"

"What's the difference?" Frieda said. "He's not going to be rowing there." At times sarcasm could be energizing for conversation. Tonight, it was beginning to feel tiresome to George.

"I would know enough to start on the Elbe River to the North Sea. I would consult a navigation map to get to the Mediterranean," George said, trying to bring down the tenor of the argument. "Of course, I'm not going to be rowing there. It's a tentative route for a ship." He stood up from the table. "Good dinner, mother, but I need to be excused to work on a plan. I just have to show it to some Zionists."

Frieda and Werner watched their son go upstairs, undoubtedly, to dream about a spot in the Olympics.

"So, what do you think?" said Werner. "Suddenly Zionism and Zionists are on his lips?"

"It's the rowing. It's the passion for rowing. I understand it about music. You thrive on the stories for your newspaper," said Frieda.

"Are you worried?" asked Werner. "Isn't he overzealous?"

"It runs in the family," Frieda responded. "Didn't we rescue my father from jail?"

~~~

Isaac Sherman and Julius Abrahams grew increasingly grateful for George and Arthur's skills and commitment. They had rowable boats which had been checked out by these two young rowers. Through a client who worked down at the docks checking ships in and out of the port, Isaac determined one ship was available to transport boats to Haifa.

"It's called the USS California," said Isaac. "They'll let us put the boats in containers. $2,000.00." He saw Julius blanch at the sum. "They are shipping cars—Mercedes-Benzes."

"Who's they?" said Julius, ever wary, knowing that papers needed to be in proper order to get in and out of ports. And now, the German government was making it even harder.

"The ship is leaving from the Port of Hamburg to arrive in the Mediterranean and specifically to the port of Haifa," Isaac said. "That's all the information we need." He began tapping a pencil rapidly on the desk. "Forget about 'they' for the moment. We'll raise the money. We'll offer

$10,000. Maybe Lionel Hartmann would give us a loan."

Isaac tried to avoid the scathing look from Julius at the mention of Lionel Hartmann. He couldn't understand how any Jew would be part of the Nazi party, let alone cast a vote for it.

"Think of him as our spy," said Isaac brusquely. "Now for logistics. Getting the boats on the boat." He smiled at his wordplay, but Julius remained stone-faced.

"The guns. We need to think of the guns," said Julius. "Guns and papers. If we're going to do this, we're going to do it right."

Isaac sighed. Julius would not give up about the guns. "All right. I can see it now—guns hidden in the boats. Boats and oars in the containers and papers in hand to give to the dockmaster, who is probably a Nazi. We are doing battle our way." He went over to the steaming kettle and poured the hot water in Julius' glass, which held a teabag.

"Here, have another glass of tea."

Chapter *16*

"Guns and boats, guns and boats, guns and boats." In Palestine, Moses Goodman walked the perimeter of his plot of land—enough for a small white stucco house with a red roof, a minuscule garden, and a chicken coop—muttering these words over and over again. He paused, admiring the growth of the eucalyptus trees he had planted ten years ago. They were the smaller variety, but they had done their work and absorbed the unhealthy swamp water that had dominated this crowded acre of land. Fertile soil now replaced the fetid underbelly.

He resumed his walk, interposing a different chant. In his youth in Poland, he had learned a Hebrew prayer as a child in synagogue, repeating it in a sing-song voice—the Shema. "Hear o Israel, Our Lord the God is One." Yes, he had learned it through repetition, and found it soothing and helped him get through an awkward adolescence, a growth spurt at eighteen, and the harsh early years in Palestine. He never thought, though, that "guns and boats" would be coming out of his mouth, alternating with sacred prayers.

Isaac Sherman from the Zionist office in Berlin had sent a telegram saying that boats for rowing would be arriving and guns for . . . ? Well, it was not specified what the guns were for. *I guess the gun runners assumed we would know what the instruments of terror and destruction were for,* Goodman thought. Who could he tell? Who could he call on for help? Certainly not Safid Khalidi because he would immediately alert his community that Jews were being supplied with guns, putting Safid in an awkward position. He was supposed to be working as a conciliator with the newly arrived Jewish immigrants.

Khalidi was trying to convince his fellow Arab villagers that Jews should be welcome. The Jews that started arriving in the 1920s demonstrated that they cared for their families and the land. They were improving it. What could be better than that? They were also able to buy out Arabs who no longer wanted to farm or hadn't been able to make their land productive. What could be wrong with that?

The British would have to be involved, Goodman thought as he continued the routine of surveying his property. Somehow, they would know how to get the rowing boats safely off the USS California and transport them to that God-forsaken warehouse along the river because God knows, boats and I have no history. Planting orange trees and raising goats, yes. Boats for rowing, no.

Would Captain Ben Leicester be helpful? Would he be able to continue teaching rowing as part of his duties? Would his superiors be supportive? Goodman knew the British could be prickly at times. He always preferred dealing with Arabs; they had equal distrust of the British.

"Enough worry," he said aloud to himself and pulled the telegram out of his pocket and checked the date. "Arriving September 16th." He took quick, deep breaths. "That's two days from now." He ran inside his home, two rooms furnished with a scattering of tables, chairs, and beds. A gas cylinder fueled the cooking stove, and an icebox held one large block of ice. His British-installed telephone had a prominent place on the one table. As village leader, Goodman had been awarded a phone by the British government. He knew the British were testing the proposition that gaining loyalty from a population could be won with treats rather than threats—although sometimes the latter was necessary. He grabbed the handset.

Who was he going to call? Leicester? What about the guns? His Zionist connection here in Palestine? That was it. He could help. He was delighted he remembered Gordon Glick. At his desk, Goodman searched through a sheaf of scattered papers that held a shortlist of telephone numbers somewhere. It was one of the few numbers he had written down since not that many people had telephones. Human contact, delivering messages by drivers from run-down cars and trucks, and even donkeys had been the mainstays of communication. He slowly dialed the number.

"Gordon Glick?" said Goodman to the voice that picked up the receiver.

"Moses Goodman?" said the voice on the other end.

"How did you know?" said Goodman.

"They told me to expect a call from a Goodman, a man who would sound anxious and excited at the same time because—we, the Zionists—were doing something fantastic and dangerous—all at the same time. I heard that in your voice."

"You're not serious," said Goodman, wondering at the lightness in the man's voice.

"Only partially. I received a telegram yesterday from Zionist headquarters in London about the boats and guns and just was waiting for a call and made a deduction." Glick paused. "We're also lucky we don't have a party line so we can make plans." The playfulness was now gone from his voice.

"What about the guns?" said Goodman. "I can get the British to help with the boats. I'm not so sure about the guns."

"The guns will be taken off the boat at night, before the Brits get involved, by some very intrepid Jews who know how to fight—those who have stopped studying the Torah, you know, and instead are studying the Chinese book, *The Art of War*, where one has to depend on an educated understanding of the enemy. We Jews are good at that, aren't we? Good at educating ourselves."

This is no time, thought Goodman, to get into a discussion of Jews who fight and Jews who study. In his mind, a necessity for fighting and study existed side by side, and he was sure whenever the Jews had an official army, that the generals would be guided by both and would prepare for battle with books as well as weapons.

"I hear silence," said Glick. "Good. No arguments. Just follow the directions. Get your British friend, Leicester, to help with the boats. We will do the guns."

"And you will get them past the inspectors? "

"We will."

Goodman hung up and wondered if he would ever get that feeling of calm he heard in Glick's voice, the confidence that enabled him to sound so decisive and sure.

———

The director of the port, Ahib ben Salaman, held a clipboard in his hand while British officer Teddy Simon stood, shifting from one foot to another, indicating his impatience. Lieutenant Colonel Markham had given him the assignment to see that the boats were properly removed from the ship and delivered. Markham had also told him to be on the lookout for guns. He had been alerted that the Haganah made it their business to know departures and arrivals of large ships. Haganah had functioned as a paramilitary organization since 1920 to deal with Arab Palestinian revolts against Jewish settlements. That was the impetus for guns making their way to this small strip of land. Simon eagerly complied with the orders. He had been a rower and followed his family's tradition of British soldiering.

"Please, sir. The English, it is slowing me down, but I will get there," sighed ben Salaman.

"They are in order," said the British officer. He saluted unnecessarily. "Besides, we run the port. We inspect the boats. We check what's on board. Kapish?" said Simon, using the phrase that had become the vernacular and seemed to be understood by everyone—Arabs, Jews, and even members of the Baha'i faith. He held himself back from adding that ben Salaman was here just because of the good graces of the British trying to find jobs for natives. Work kept rebellion at bay and might develop some loyal followers for the British. Maybe some whom they could trust to divulge brewing plots. History revealed that no population learned to love the people they saw as conquerors.

Ben Salaman continued to peer at the papers before him, slowly turning to the second sheet. "Ah, I see. Five boats." He looked up. "How do you put boats in a ship?"

"Small boats," said Simon impatiently. "Something you've never seen." He grinned. "But you will like seeing them."

"Yes, yes," said ben Salaman. "Okay. We unload. You bring your jeeps down closer to the boat."

Simon gave him a jaunty military salute. "Yes, sir. At your service, sir."

Ben Salaman shrugged him off. As he and Simon walked out the office door, Salman waved his hand in the direction of the five jeeps that had been discreetly waiting at the perimeter of the dock.

Simon wrapped a cotton bandana around his nose and mouth. "The smell from these oil tankers is getting to me. Something I can't get used to though clearly, you have." That statement elicited a proud smile from ben Salaman. "Yes, Sahib. We are happy to have the oil here. It makes us part of a new history. Oil production is important to the world."

Ben Salaman turned to the crowd of stevedores that had been waiting at the office door for their directions of the day. No day at the port was the same as the day before. Unloading could involve furniture, animals, Persian rugs, automobiles, bags of grain, used clothing. This was a first for small boats—long, sleek boats, he had been told. He held up his two hands to the stevedores, showing ten fingers. The leader pointed to ten men in the crowd, and they slowly made their way toward ben Salaman.

"Here," said Simon, taking out a photo from his briefcase and passing it in front of the men. All peered intently. Some nodded, indicating they understood, but Simon knew they had never seen what they were going to unload either in person or in pictures. It wasn't in their culture or their education, or their history. A history that was in the process of change.

"Two to a boat," he said. Simon was grateful for his rowing experience before he joined the British army. "You will put each end on a shoulder." He looked over to ben Salaman for a translation and hoped it was accurate. He knew one person could carry a boat over his head if he knew how to distribute the weight, but he didn't trust "first-timers" to do it correctly. Besides, it might be tight in the hold, and two people might need to extricate the boat from its storage.

The stevedores, all less than five feet, seven inches and lean in build, came out of the hold of the ship with the forty-pound boats held high over their heads, trying to appear confident while at the same time, stooping to pick up an oar left on the floor. Teddy Simon walked over to the first two and demonstrated how to distribute the weight on one shoulder that freed up the other hand for the oar. Over the head may look more manly but was not necessary. Then, each boat with its set of oars was lifted onto the back of an open jeep and tied down with rope by its British drivers, who openly cheered as each boat arrived for placement.

"Think you'll be rowing?" Simon asked one of the fellow British soldiers driving the jeep.

"No, not me, but I'd like to see what these medieval morons can do," he answered while hoisting the boat on top of the pillows of the jeep and covering it with a torn blanket.

Teddy Simon glowered at him. "Keep that talk to yourself. You never know who's picked up English. They're not as dumb as you think."

He radioed Markham. "Boats are on the jeeps," he said.

"Guns?" Markham asked.

Glick was silent for a moment. "Don't see any. Do you want me to do a search?"

"No," said Markham. "We need to figure out a way to get the boats to the warehouse. Maybe that'll satisfy Leicester for the time being."

He put the phone down, thinking that he would have them search the boat tomorrow for guns. He had yet to understand that the Haganah had resources to unload guns during the small hours of the morning when hardly anyone was up and about. Baksheesh had not been lost upon them when the Jews came here.

Markham worried. Arabs and Jews rowing boats together might bring about a modicum of peace, but additional weapons in the area just meant more chaos and paths to turmoil. Nevertheless, he would tell Simon he had done a good job unloading the rowing boats and let Leicester know the boats were here to help fulfill a dream. He would let Teddy Simon pursue the search for guns.

CHAPTER 17

Leicester awoke slowly on the narrow bed set against a wall of his one-room stucco house. His looked like every other home built quickly to house newly arrived immigrants. The only thing that distinguished it was a British Austin army jeep to the right of the Lebanese cedar wooden front door with steel-gated windows on either side.

The two-burner stove supplied by a gas cylinder served him well—even though he wasn't much of a cook. And army life had accustomed him to an outhouse. A reader of Middle East adventure stories, he eagerly embraced the climate. Desert-dry air suited him.

He pictured himself as a sort of Lawrence of Arabia, able to connect with the populace, whoever it might be at the moment, so he was not surprised at a knock at his door with shouts of "Captain Leicester, Captain Leicester" in clipped Arabic between the pounding. He had learned to recognize the difference almost immediately between an Arab and a Jew when they spoke his mother tongue. A Jew's English speech was always more languid, almost musical, with the voice rising at the end—an Arab usually spoke with clipped diction. Voice gave it away more than appearance because Leicester had discovered that, yes, dark-skinned Jews lived in Palestine—they were not all pale from Germany and Poland. They could be as light-skinned as Disraeli, the only prominent English Jew he had learned about in history. In that same history class, he had also learned that there were Ethiopian Jews; they would undoubtedly be dark-skinned and fast runners.

He peered through the window to see Ahmad standing outside the door, sweat pouring down his brow. He had probably been wearing the same clothes for the last three days, Leicester thought.

"They're coming," Ahmad shouted as soon as Leicester opened the door. Leicester smiled, thinking that those words were close to the supposed words of Paul Revere at the time of the American colonies, trying to remove the shackles of Great Britain. And I suspect, he thought, they will want to do that here. Who likes strangers in their land? Meantime, I've moved into their neighborhood to promote peace. We'll see.

"Who's coming?" said Leicester.

"The boats," said Ahmad excitedly. "The boats that you will use to teach us how to row. Remember, you promised." His brown eyes pleaded.

Why hadn't anyone told me, Leicester wondered? Wasn't he in charge of keeping relations friendly between the two potentially ready-for-blood enemies?

"They're at the dock, tied on to jeeps. Now, what do we do?"

"Ask the drivers to take them to the boathouse. Run, and I'll meet you there after my shower." The shower, also outdoors, consisted of a corrugated tin wraparound for some privacy and pipes configured to allow water to flow down onto his head and body.

"Go," he said, but Ahmad just stood there.

"We have no drivers there. So, someone has to find people who know how to drive a jeep," said Ahmad.

"Well, how did the jeeps get there?" said Leicester, moving to pick up a bar of soap and a towel.

"Something like the Ha-ga-nah." Ahmad eked out the word that Leicester recognized as a Jewish movement that had been driving his commander Markham crazy. No amount of discussion with the Jewish community leaders could keep these so-called terrorists at bay.

"Well, Ahmad," said Leicester. "The trick is to get your terrorists to become your best friends." He put his arm around the young boy's shoulder. "My shower, and then we go to Moses Goodman and see what he knows. And we'll go in my jeep—the car that works the best around these unpredictable roads." He grinned at the boy. "That's why you should never give up your donkey."

Leicester and Ahmad both knew that these roads, carved out of swamps, once held papyrus over eight feet tall and scorpions and snakes that roamed in and out of that vegetation. It was not that long ago that drinking water and washing water became available to the residents daily. The town had a small clinic, and while medicine was available to cure malaria, fewer people contracted it since scientists had recently developed procedures to keep the mosquito population down based on Israel Jacob Kligler's work. In 1927 he founded the "Malaria Research Station" of the Hebrew University in Rosh Pina, where pioneering fieldwork was carried out relating to eradicating malaria.

Now, in 1933, a doctor, who visited three times a week, had convinced the population that washing hands would cut down on dysentery. The nurse, Hana, from the Palestinian community, was eager to implement British hygiene methods.

Arriving at Goodman's house, Leicester was surprised to see six young men already there. What didn't surprise him was their attire in khaki pants and shirts. Of late, many dressed in this uniform. He assumed they were worn to make them appear army-like, or perhaps behave as military. The contrast was a dark-haired young woman who sat among them with a bowl of grapes in her lap, scissors in hand, snipping off bunches to give each of the young men. "Eat," she said. "You get energy when you eat."

When one of the young men said, "Thanks, Naomi," Leicester realized she must be Moses Goodman's wife. She sat among the young men, trying to position herself as an equal and helpful soldier. I hope they know they are not the military, Leicester thought, because this so-called land—not even an official country—never had any government-authorized armed forces. Leicester, having grown up in a military family and having studied military history, appreciated and worried about guerrilla forces; some militia grew out of a sense of conviction to build the good; others were bent on evil.

He sighed silently. My god. They all have rifles slung over their shoulders. What's worse, they look natural wearing them. Why don't they understand that the British army is here to defend and protect them?

The arrival of approximately 80,000 Jews in 1929, fleeing the pogroms of Poland, had prompted the Arabs to take up arms, destroying property and killing 133 of the recently arrived, unarmed Jews. The British were here to prevent the violence.

"You look prepared for a skirmish," said Leicester. "Aren't we all just getting ready to learn how to row?" He turned to Naomi. "Surely, Mrs. Goodman, you can assure them they don't need their rifles."

Her husband, who had come in, quietly spoke. "Welcome," said Goodman. "The rifles are part of the need to protect ourselves. We have no intention of harming others. But what's most important is that you now have five drivers for your jeeps and your boats."

Ben was startled when one of the young men stood and whispered, "And where do we find the guns?" Naomi quickly pulled him down to the closest chair and stood up to go to the kitchen area, her back turned toward the group. She began turning the water faucet off and on. She, too, had been attired in khaki that clung to her sturdy frame. Her long, black hair was tied up in a practical bun held together with only the skinniest of clips. Leicester watched Moses Goodman's eyes follow her with joy. Her husband knew that this woman never put a drop of makeup on her face and was proud of it.

Goodman glared at the hapless soldier whose blush from his neck to his forehead appeared as suddenly as the unwanted comment had been uttered. Goodman understood that if Leicester knew the guns were on that ship along with the boats, he would be required to order the confiscation of guns. Possibly the boats as well. The British were in charge. They were the court, the judge, and the jury.

Naomi came back to the group with a plate of biscuits and passed them casually to the soldier who had spoken. "You need more food, Ari," she said. "The hunger has gone to your head. There are no guns. We wouldn't be doing something so foolish."

"The boats, they're what's important," Goodman said quickly, giving an approving glance to his wife and eyeing Leicester, who seemed to be watching the group with a detached air.

These British, thought Goodman, always try to be calm and collected, but I know they are calculating. That man who seemingly can row a boat and shoot a rifle simultaneously, I know he's plotting something.

"Yes, the boats. They're what's important." Leicester sensed a need for affirmation on his part. "Shall we drive in my jeep down to the dock? Then, we can drive to the warehouse where we will keep the boats. I can check them over, and we can begin learning to row. That's why we're here. Right?"

Leicester's blood pressure had risen, so he hoped his words had come out in a cool, comprehensible way. Yes, he had heard the statement about the guns, but right now, he was to remain in command and not give away to emotion or threat. This provocation will be looked into, he thought, but not now. He knew the history. British timidity had made the Mufti grow bolder. We can't let these Jewish pioneers with their unbound sense of righteousness think that they can dominate the situation. We've got Amin al-Husseini under control now that he is Grand Mufti of Jerusalem—appointed by Herbert Samuel, a Jew and a Zionist, would you believe. We've made Husseini an ally. Now, we've got to do the same with these newcomers to the land. We've got to create love between them instead of hate. Or, if not love, at least, peace.

Naomi Goodman stood with the empty plate in her hand. "Right," she said. "These young men will help to drive the jeeps with the boats. Right, Moshe?" With that, the five young men climbed into the back of the jeep with Naomi sliding into the seat next to Leicester. "They need a guiding hand," she said when the young captain raised his eyebrows at her joining them. He refrained from saying anything, knowing that women were thought of as important to Jewish settlement in Palestine.

~~~

The army jeep loaded with its six passengers and driver stopped just short of the dock with the USS California in sight. Alongside, appearing quite diminutive, stood five jeeps, each with a boat tied to its roof with ropes. Leicester suspected the jeeps were leftovers from The Great War, and the boats could have been of a similar vintage.

Naomi leaned over before exiting the jeep. "You know we have been able to smuggle in arms under our skirts and market baskets," she said almost in a whisper. "We wouldn't be so foolish as to do it here, especially with your help with the boats." Leicester could sense the tenseness of the five. Usually, the Israelis were talkative among themselves. Nonstop talking and commenting seemed to be a cultural trait.

Leicester wanted to believe her; he needed to get boats to the warehouse to teach rowing, to build community. He didn't want to be leading a charge on discovering unauthorized weapons.

"We're here to drive the boats to the warehouse," said Leicester to an official standing with a clipboard. He waved his hand, directing the others out of the jeep onto the dock. He stood for a moment, in back of the last jeep in line, contemplating the wood that still managed to gleam even though the boats were visibly old. The foot straps, in particular, looked dirty and unkempt, and gunk covered the boat tracks. Two boats had no sliding seats. *Maybe I can find someone to make them out of wood.* He looked around and realized the young men and Naomi were staring at him, waiting for him to give an order—and some direction to make sure the jeeps laden with boats be driven correctly.

"Okay," Leicester said. "All you have to do is drive slowly and avoid any potholes along the way and follow me to the warehouse." No one moved. "Just take any jeep you want," he barked.

"When a British officer is in charge, they expect precise directions, but otherwise, they are perfectly capable of making decisions on their own," explained Naomi, seeing his exasperation.

Leicester wondered if this was a subtle message that meant they had already taken charge of the guns. Always on the alert, he had not forsaken his military duty; he had prepared the commandant of his boat retrieval mission, so he was not surprised when Harry Markham pulled up in his jeep on the dock next to the USS California. Leicester knew the young people were waiting for the signal to leave, but he could not avoid his allegiance to the British Crown. Markham was checking up on his junior officer.

Markham's face was taut and composed. "We heard about the possibility of guns being shipped along with boats. And you are here helping these people with their boats?" He stepped close to Leicester, his face just five inches away. The captain stood still and snapped his right hand to a military salute. "Yes, sir. They need to row. Boats will serve the peace better than guns."

Naomi stepped in. "You will find no guns. It was just about the boats," she said. "We want our young people to row just like you English do." Leicester had never seen a young civilian woman approach an English officer with so little trepidation, but he had seen this unabashed behavior on the part of many Jews. He wondered if this form of direct confrontation bode well for the country's future.

CHAPTER *18*

In his German schoolrooms, Werner Grossinger had been schooled on the American Revolution. He could recite from memory the First Amendment to the United States Constitution: freedom of speech, press, religion, assembly, and protest. In his university journalism classes, prior to The Great War, the amendments were repeated with reverence. It was a time professors sought to broaden student knowledge, a time before Germany became focused on petty grievances.

Werner stood at the window of his office, looking down at the street to see people walking by with umbrellas to protect them from the wind-driven rain. He thought that umbrellas also prevented them from looking up and seeing flags with a swastika on a field of white surrounded with red. He was standing eye level with the array of flags that hung from second-story windows. How quickly the swastika flag had replaced the black, red, and yellow flag of the Weimar Republic, Werner thought. It's as though the Weimar Republic had never existed, although it had removed the Kaiser and replaced an Emperor with a republic. The generals who signed the Treaty of Versailles would be turning purple with anxiety and frustration. Who could have ever anticipated such a change? Normally quiet citizens seeing Communists everywhere and reporting on them; Germans beating each other up for perceived slights against the new government. Certainly not Christopher Isherwood, who was coming for an interview to ask the newspaper to promote his book. Or maybe he wanted a job. One never knows which way the world was turning, Werner thought.

—ww—

"So, Mr. Isherwood, what's an Englishman doing here in Berlin?" asked Werner of the lean, elegantly clad man who sat with legs carefully crossed so as not to disturb the crease in his pant leg. George sat nearby with a notepad. It was part of his training to observe how interview stories were done. Werner would give him a shot at taking notes and writing an article. But no guarantee that the newspaper would print it, Werner had told him. You have to explain that right away to anyone sitting for an interview. Certainly, they were coming to talk to publicize their work, but the writer's work had to be interesting for the newspaper readers and well written.

"I needed to get out of England, and I heard that Berlin was sympathetic to people like me," Isherwood said with a slight smile. George noted Isherwood spoke with assurance—a trait that he would like to develop. The author continued. "I like men."

Werner looked down, his hands clasped together under his chin. He looked up slowly, pausing slightly. "This is a different Berlin. Did you not see all the flags before you came in? People like you, the Communists, the Jews—they're starting to have a hard time. I don't know if you've noticed it's not the same Berlin, Mr. Isherwood."

"Call me Christopher," he said and leaned forward. "There are still pockets of places where I feel welcome here. Berlin has cabarets like no other place in the world."

George, scribbling rapidly, was grateful he had read Isherwood's book, *The Memorial.* He had come with questions relating to this man as an author but wondered, being an Englishman, if he had ever been to a regatta. Rowing and regattas still were at the front of George's mind, and he always associated the English with rowing. After all, that's where the sport started and had a formidable tradition.

"George, do you want to ask Mr. Isherwood a question?" Werner said.

"Yes," said George, looking down at his notes quickly decided to ask a book-related question. "Your book, *The Memorial,* what was the inspiration? Did your father serve in the war? "

"Yes—and let me tell you ahead of time that the part of the book that talks of the young man wanting to be part of the homosexual life in Berlin is me. There's nothing better to use than your own material. Just the names are different. But did you like the book? Were you engaged in the story?" Isherwood sat back, smiling, waiting for a response.

George hadn't liked the book. Maybe he hadn't given it sufficient attention. His heart was in his studies and rowing. Even his friendship with Arthur had taken a back seat, and right now, he was in the midst of trying to help his family withstand the onslaught of Hitler's ever-limiting strategies on freedom of the press and expression. But he had an assignment to write an article about this interview. He plunged ahead, deciding it was his interview. He didn't need to answer Isherwood's questions.

"Are you comfortable if we write about your . . . your . . ."

"Sexuality?" Isherwood offered.

George turned a shade of pink. "Yes. Your . . . sexuality."

Before Isherwood could answer, Werner interjected. "Our news editor will make a decision. You understand, Mr. Isherwood, we are caught between truth-telling and a particularly harsh minister of propaganda?"

George impulsively diverted the discussion before Isherwood could respond to his father's rhetorical question.

"Did you ever attend any regattas in England? I mean while you lived there? I'm interested in Cambridge-Oxford races that took place on the Thames."

George didn't look up, knowing his father would be annoyed at his impetuous interruption.

"I'm not sure that's at all relevant to my book," said Isherwood, frowning.

"You'd be surprised what lengths we go to in order to make a story interesting, nowadays, especially when we have to limit truth-telling," said Werner, surprising George. He was annoyed with George's interjection of rowing, but at the same time, his fatherly protectiveness came to the fore.

George thought Isherwood sniffed before responding. "I don't know much, except they have been competing since the mid-1800s. That's a long time, isn't it? And there are tactics to winning the race on a course that's rather shaped like an S. It all has something to do with the current and the bends on the river." Did he sniff again before adding, "It's not my field of interest." George continued to scribble away on his notepad. He paused, looking up briefly at the writer. "Did you know the Cambridge-Oxford race rowed upstream and timed to start with the incoming flood tide?"

Isherwood stood up, wrapping a long silk scarf around his neck. "I think you've gotten enough information for your article."

~~~

The book review of *The Memorial* that George wrote extolled a father/son relationship with a homosexual friend, living after The Great War. He had managed to include a sentence about the author's interest and knowledge about the rowing history of England. His article never ran. George never knew if it was the reference to homosexuality or The Great War. Werner and the book review editor had decided that it would receive opposition from the Minister of Propaganda's office and was not in the newspaper's best interest.

Werner turned his attention to the advertising department. He leafed through yesterday's newspaper to see that Hertie's department store was now running ads in *Der Tagblatt* for its linens, promoted as "white sales." Werner had a moment of consciousness when the ad department wanted to solicit them for advertising dollars now that the new regime had forced Hertie's Jewish owner, Tietz, to give up the exclusive stores he founded. Now that they were Aryanized, should the paper accept their dollars?

The conflict was momentary. *Der Tagblatt* needed the money to keep going, and Goebbels might be interested in why their newspaper didn't have Hertie's ads while, in other newspapers, Hertie furniture ads leapt off the page. He couldn't risk it. This, Werner thought, is how I make decisions now—on the scale of how many people it will affect. Too many would lose their jobs, he rationalized. So, we will take the ads for Hertie. And for the International Auto and Motorcycle Show. Not that many people had the money to afford a car or motorcycle, but life was better with fantasies. The newspaper editor knew that people who couldn't afford a car or motorcycle were now making sure they had a radio.

Radios seemed to be blaring from everywhere. If Werner opened his office window on a warm day, they could be heard booming from open windows. It was as though the new toy became an addiction through its possibility of "newness" every hour—a recent briefing from the Minister of Propaganda, from the Fuhrer himself. The Volksempfanger was a subsidized radio with limited stations that allowed the population to hear Wagner's music and evening broadcasts from the BBC. Still, the rabble-rousing rhetoric of the Third Reich dominated the broadcasts. Werner could tell when people were listening to Third Reich propaganda even when he couldn't hear it; through the windows he could see listeners with contented smiles. They liked to hear that Germany was on its way up. The dominant message was that the German people just had to listen to the Fuhrer and defeat Communists—that's all it would take.

How long can I keep this up, Werner wondered? Trying to shape truth to suit both me and Hitler? He looked up to see photographer Franz Godel standing outside his office door with photos in hand.

"How am I supposed to cover this?" Franz asked, walking in and placing the photos on the editor's desk.

He recognized the photos of Hans Maikowski and Josef Zauritz and knew the radios would be blaring with the news of their state funeral.

"Just cover it the way you would for anyone semi-important," said the editor.

"Did you have too much beer last night?" Godel responded. "These are not just locals. One is an SA officer, and the other is a cop."

"So?" said Werner, sorting through papers on his desk and holding onto a cigarette with the edge of his lips.

"They killed Communists. There will be an army battalion at the funeral marching in goose step to some military music. . . just like the horns that come in for Sigfried's "Funeral March." You know, from *Gotterdamerung*."

"I know. Of course, I know it's from *Gotterdammerung*. I live with Frieda."

"The funeral will be blasted over the radio," Godel continued, apparently ignoring his boss's last comment. "The entire country will hear about it as though they were the best men that were ever born in Germany. And you want to cover it as though they were just semi-important?"

Werner ground his cigarette into the ashtray in anger. "We cover it as a news story . . . and . . . and someone writes an editorial."

"Get your son to do it," smiled Godel. "It will be a good experience for him in gilding the lies. He needs more experience after the Isherwood try. And it will keep *Der Tagblatt* alive."

He gave the assignment to George, knowing he'd be disappointed that he could not connect rowing with these men. Werner was happy George had a positive passion, but he worried that his love for rowing gave him tunnel vision, and a good reporter had to have an expansive view of the world.

> *Germany honors its dead with a State Funeral at the Berliner Dom Cathedral. Honors were given to Hans Eberhard Mailowski, Leader of a Storm Trooper Unit (SA Sturm 33), and Police Sergeant Josef Zauritz, who were both shot during a valiant fight with Communists. The martyrs were honored with the presence of Hitler, Goebbels, and Goering. A hearse pulled by special horses was followed by a squadron of Stormtroopers carrying wreaths. Pallbearers in top hats carried the coffins.*

The story ran with no problems. George had come through.

CHAPTER 19

Frieda sat with hands clasped under her chin, eyes shut, listening to Clara Fuchs play Joseph Achron's *Violin Concerto No. 1*. In the five years that Clara, now twenty, had been studying with her, she had become a serious violinist, hoping to apply for a spot at the Berlin Conservatory. Her pale shoulder-length blonde hair parted on the side and slight frame gave her movie-star looks. But music was her passion—not capturing admiring glances. Clara played with the intensity, accuracy, and fierceness that the music deserved—she had memorized the concerto to focus on technique to produce the brilliant sound of the composer's intentions. Clara ended the last measure with a delicate flourish and smile, but her beloved teacher was frowning. With her violin in her lap and bow on the stand, hands folded, the violin student waited expectantly for a critique. She knew Frieda to be unsparing both in her praise and her criticism.

"They will never accept you now with a piece by Achron," Frieda said quietly.

"What? What are you saying? I have been practicing this piece for months." Clara tried to quiet her anxiety. She revered her teacher. Her music-loving parents had taught respect for talented musicians. Her mother also had had aspirations to be a professional violinist but had turned her energies into being a homemaker and encouraging Clara to fulfill her passion.

"I'm truly sorry, but if you want a Conservatory spot, we will have to start you on another piece," Frieda said. She touched Clara's hands that now clasped the violin neck tightly and offered her a tissue as tears welled up in her blue eyes.

"Look, you started this piece before the Nazis came to power. You're a smart young lady, right? You know what's been happening. You've got to understand you will be making choices if you want to pursue a musical career. There is news that Hitler likes music—especially Wagner. But it is too risky right now to pick a piece by Achron." She paused. "He's Jewish."

"But he's not even so Jewish, is he?" Clara stammered. "He lives now and works in the United States, performing all kinds of music. It doesn't make sense here. What is the obstacle?" Clara had regained her composure. "I'm not playing his Hebrew melodies." Frieda was not at all surprised that this remarkable student knew about his other works.

"Yes, what exactly is the obstacle?" George said. He had entered the music room and overheard the end of the conversation. Usually, he would avoid interacting with his mother's students, but he liked Clara. He noticed her blue eyes lit up with intensity while she played, and he admired the way she pinned her hair on the top of her head, removed from her shoulders so it wouldn't interfere with her playing. George saw that small gesture as evidence of her fervor and commitment to her music and less of a concern about her vanity. He had little patience for young women who spent time thinking about how they looked.

Clara blushed when she saw her teacher's son. Frieda turned quickly. "You know this is my private time," she said sharply.

"It's all right," said Clara. "My lesson is over but I, too, would like clarity on the obstacle."

"Yes, mother. What is the obstacle?"

"He has a close relationship with Arnold Schoenberg, an even more prominent Jewish composer. Schoenberg has told the world that Achron is one of the most underrated modern composers. Unfortunately, the German government has labeled both their music as degenerate." Frieda sighed. "We will have to choose another piece for you. Something by Mozart, Beethoven, or Bach. Something from the old masters. Achron and Schoenberg are too modern and too Jewish. That's it."

Clara smiled, hoping it would belie the sadness she felt. "I will look for something by Bach. I like his sonata solos for violin," said Clara.

"I'm glad to see you are determined," said George. "Come, I will walk you to the door."

Frieda sat silent and looked at her son with a bit of wonder. Where had he picked up this maturity? This ability to give a young woman, clearly struggling, a compliment and a polite offer of an accompanied walk to the door, albeit brief. Clara had always been able to find her way herself from the music room to the front door, and George knew this. Frieda kept her eyes from expressing astonishment when George picked up her student's violin case and helped her with her light jacket.

At the door, Clara let down her hair and thanked George. She also decided at that moment to plant a kiss on George's cheek. George responded by pulling her close to him and kissing her fully on her lips. For a brief second, he thought, thank goodness, no lipstick. In that momentary flash of thankfulness, she surprised him, kissed him back, opened the door, and closed it quickly behind her.

"Everything, all right, George?" called his mother.

George stood for a moment, looking out the window of the door, observing Clara walking home quickly. He smiled broadly when she turned and gave him a happy wave as though she knew he would be watching. He waved back a bit sheepishly.

He went upstairs to deal with a tricky statistics problem from today's class before his father came home for dinner. As George sat at his desk to pore over the assignment, he realized he could not focus even though he usually enjoyed the challenge of working through problems. They gave him a sense of orderliness. He returned to staring out his second-floor window, encountering only a large maple tree, beginning to sprout winged samaras, and wondered how long it would take for them to fall. He had a fleeting thought that he needed to research their role in the tree's growth. Shaking his head, he returned to his statistics book and the notepad next to it. He picked up a pencil to work through an equation but started doodling and realized he had drawn an outline of Clara, darkened her lengthy hair, and made her eyes nearly black with gray pencil.

He raced downstairs.

"What's Clara's telephone number?"

His mother smiled. "Usually, when you come flying down the stairs, you want to know what's for dinner." She went to search for the number in her diary. "Remember, she probably has a party line. You need to be careful. So as a mother, may I ask what you are planning to do? Discuss the appointment of Richard Strauss as the head of the Reich Music Chamber? Already a Nazi supporter."

George knew his mother's sarcastic remarks came from her frustration in dealing with the uncertainties that many musicians were facing. Last week, the orchestra was forbidden to play Mendelssohn's *Midsummer's Night Dream*, although it had been a musicians' and audience favorite. Mendelssohn seemed to appeal to music lovers of all ranks. George knew that his mother particularly loved that piece with its onslaught of many violins playing right at the beginning to produce a gigantic, inspiring sound.

Frieda handed George a piece of paper with Clara's scribbled number.

"And Mendelssohn didn't even remain Jewish. No more of his music just because he was born into a famous Jewish family." She took a deep breath. "Enough. Dinner will be ready soon." She had been fuming about Strauss ever since his appointment.

George had to make the call from the phone in the foyer, but he didn't care if his mother overheard. He knew he should make the call before he lost his nerve.

"Clara," he said when she answered, "do you want to go with me to see *The Threepenny Opera* before the government says it cannot be performed anymore?"

It seemed to him that the silence on the other end lasted five hours.

"It this George Grossinger?" she asked.

"Yes, it is. Sorry, I didn't introduce myself." *Should I tell her I'm nervous? Too late.*

"Can you just wait a minute? I need to ask my parents something."

This time the wait only seemed to last a few minutes because Clara returned saying, "If you get tickets for a Saturday night so that it won't interfere with my classes, I can go with you. My parents say that it is all right."

The Threepenny Opera was in its final weeks at the Schiffbauerdamm theater. His mother had informed him that Goebbels had ordered the play shut down because of its satirical tone and its emphasis on the plight of the poor. Germans didn't need this—they needed something uplifting. Besides, Kurt Weill, who wrote the music, was Jewish and a cantor's son. That alone would have been enough to shut it down.

"Good. We will ride our bikes together to the theater. I will pick you up at your house."

—⁓—

That Saturday night, bicycles, Opels, Mercedes-Benzes, and trolleys filled the wide German streets in the Mitte district. Most noticeable were the flags hanging from windows—flags with the swastika embedded on a white circle bordered by red. Clara was waiting outside her apartment building, standing next to her bike, and George waved to her to join him alongside. He was pleased when he saw her comfortably attired in slacks, the kind he knew were worn by famous movie stars like Marlene Dietrich and Katharine Hepburn in America. George was just beginning to figure out what he liked in women, and for an unfathomable reason, this image of Clara pleased him.

She easily hoisted herself onto the seat of her bike and, without missing a beat, began to ride next to him. She yelled over. "Think of a piece of music and ride to it. We will get there faster."

George knew that some of his teammates rowed to whatever music was in their heads to maintain the necessary steady rhythm. But he usually had nothing in his mind during his training sessions on the water but the words of his coach. "Easy on the slide. Catch. More on the slide. Knees vertical. Oars level with the water. Pressure from the feet." At this moment, he could not begin to think of a piece of music, although he had heard a good deal from his mother. Clara shouted, "Bach's *Brandenburg Concerto No. 1 in F major*." Thank goodness. He knew it. And it seemed to work. They pedaled along almost at the same speed, avoiding the few cars and trolleys. By keeping their eyes on the road, they could ignore the sights of the Nazi flags adorning buildings.

George waved his left arm, signaling to pull over in front of the theater next to a bike lock stand. As they dismounted, they failed to notice three young men who started to encircle them. They were dressed in paramilitary uniforms, knee-high brown boots, medals, and knives sheathed in leather pouches belted across their shoulders. George thought he recognized one or two of them from university, but he wasn't sure. It was time to deflect.

"Where did you get the war uniforms? My father served, but you look too young," George said. He thought he needed to be the one to step up. One of the young men came in closer. George reached for Clara's hand and pulled her in behind him. He felt the cold shiver in her fingers.

"What do you want? We are just here to see the show," George said, hoping the fear in his voice didn't show.

"You want to see a show with music by a Jew?" said one of the men.

"You want to see a show about poor people who are beggars?" said the other.

Clara stepped out from behind George. "Jews write very good music. Have you ever heard of Mendelssohn, Meyerbeer? I think Kurt Weill wrote interesting music. George and I would like to hear it."

Her forcefulness surprised George and seemed to encourage him.

"Yes, and there's Mahler, too." At that moment, George was grateful for a mother who not only played music but lived it as well. George was also aware a small crowd had gathered and silently watched the interaction. Some seemed ready to step forward to defend them.

That may have prompted the three to begin a retreat. The tallest one spoke. "You will see. This music, this show, will not be here that long. It is degenerate. We need to uphold the German race like Wagner does. Richard Strauss says so."

"So does Goebbels," said another, backing away, and the small crowd began to disperse.

George had a parting comment to the young men as he led Clara to the entrance and into the theater. "This is no way for civilized people to act," he said and quickly walked with Clara to their seats. George waited for the theater to darken, the curtain to go up, and the orchestra to begin the overture with its "Ballad of Mack the Knife." He took Clara's hand, and they sat with hands clasped throughout the entire performance until the curtain came down. It was a night to remember for many reasons.

CHAPTER 20

George and Clara bicycled back in silence through the dark streets, grateful for clear skies and lighted street lamps to help avoid pedestrians and the few cars still traveling. Trolleys had abandoned nightly runs an hour ago. When the young couple left the theater, they quickly mounted their bikes, silently thankful their means of transport was still there and had not been damaged. This time, they rode back with no music in their heads, just stoic stillness. George had thought of exchanging a few words about the music and songs he liked—particularly the one about McHeath, but he read Clara's worried face as saying, "not now."

During the show, George had forced himself to bring his attention back to the performance because his mind wandered to a worrisome scenario. What if those hoodlums came back and destroyed the bikes? How would they get home? He was sure Clara had similar thoughts.

When they arrived at her building, she slowed her bike and gracefully dismounted. She didn't hesitate. It was as though manners were perpetually at the forefront. "I had a wonderful time, George." George was grateful for the kindness of the comment. He thought her voice even had a musical quality.

"I'm glad you did," George said hurriedly, standing astride his bike and then quickly pushing the pedal to get into gear. He rode off without even a backward glance. Clara stood for just a moment, her face set in a quizzical smile, and turned to go inside to write a brief note in her diary: "Saw The Threepenny Opera with violin teacher's son. Wonderful, exciting music, and I liked George, but he is either terrified of me or preoccupied about this upsetting incident of hoodlums confronting us. Or maybe both." She would discuss this complicated evening with her mother tomorrow—an evening of unusual music, thuggery, and possible stirring of love. She mused, *muddled thoughts are so much more challenging to sort through than the measures of a Mozart sonata.*

George arrived home, grateful that no one was up to question him. The music, the impending danger from the brown-shirt kids. They were just kids. How did they learn to be so tough? How did they learn to think that way about Jews? The thoughts swirling through his mind didn't cease. I just need to uncomplicate life. Take some moments and quiet this whirling in my head.

Instead of going to bed, he sat at his desk and began writing quickly on a piece of paper. Olympics, rowing, practice, Hebrew Rowing Club, Zionists. He paused. And Clara. How does one sort through these and stop the unrelenting buzzing in the brain? He stared out the window and saw the reflection of his pale self. He grabbed a pen and quickly scribbled, "The only thing necessary for the triumph of evil is for good men to do nothing." His history professor had told him that it was a famous quote of Edmund Burke, and he was an Irishman who had served in the British parliament and earned the respect of many as a philosopher. But the professor had stressed that Burke was not as great as Immanuel Kant, their German philosopher. The professor had written on the blackboard in large handwriting, "Live your life as though every act were to become a universal law." It was right here that the vision of Clara appeared strongly with his first impulsive kiss. Where did that impulsivity and passion come from? Could that act become a universal law? When you are overcome with emotion, do you just act on it? His German and family background of orderliness and self-control questioned it. With the repetition of that quote in his brain and Clara, George could think about sleep.

～～

"I'll be home late today," said George to his mother as he was gathering his books to leave for university.

"What's on your schedule?" said Frieda as she stood at the sink washing the breakfast dishes. "Maybe you can recruit some violin students for me," she said with a half-laugh. "Mine seem to be diminishing by the minute." She paused. "They also seem to be finding substitutes for me for the concerts, claiming that in the spirit of the Third Reich, they need to be giving more people a chance." She scoffed. "More unqualified people. Can't even play in tune."

"Mother, what would you think if there was a way for me to enter a regatta that was close to Palestine?" He paused and waited for a verbal reaction. He had always known her to be a quiet reflector whatever provocative comment came her way. This time was no different. Frieda also knew her son was far from impulsive, so he had given careful thought to this question.

"What are you thinking?" she said, drying a large plate slowly with a dishtowel.

He stopped gathering his books and papers. "I'm thinking that we need to imagine leaving Germany and more than 'imagine,' we need to find a way to do it." He paused. "What do you know about Spain?"

Frieda continued taking the plates, drying them carefully, and placing them back in the cupboard. It was as though this mundane act gave her permission to think carefully before responding.

"They'll never let us leave without taking everything away from us. They'll make us turn over our bank account. This apartment. We own this apartment. And grandmother and grandfather. What about them? You've seen what the authorities have done to grandpa. Just leave? I doubt it." Frieda answered as though she had also been thinking of the need to do something.

George knew how important it was for his parents to be able to financially take care of him, themselves, and his grandparents. "That's just what I'm thinking of—a way to leave and outwit the government. I think rowing may play a part. I just need to figure it out."

"You father? What does he say about this?"

"I haven't discussed this with him. It just came to me last night that this is a possibility for us." He paused and returned to sit at the kitchen table. "No. It didn't just come to me. Ever since I've been to the Hebrew Rowing Club and I found out they are shipping boats to Palestine, a little nudge of a dream has come up. You know how ideas grow. A smidgen of thought appears, and then it grows into a paragraph and then an essay." He smiled. "I'm now at the paragraph stage. I think I need to talk to Arthur about this as well."

"Try talking to your father first," she said. "We have to take this paragraph of an idea and discuss it as a family." She put the last breakfast dish in the cabinet.

"And now I have to practice, even if I don't have a seat in the orchestra. Practicing helps me think I'm preparing for a future seat in an orchestra." She closed the cabinet door. "Also, if you don't keep practicing, you can just start going backward. Never a good idea."

She had heard her son's suggestion was based on reality, but she couldn't begin to think about what it would mean to leave her home country. Even thinking those words "home country" brought tears to her eyes.

~~~

The next day, George biked to the Hebrew Rowing Club, glad to see that he was the only one there to row this late Saturday afternoon. He knew that most of the members were not observant, but maybe it was somebody's bar mitzvah—an event for a thirteen-year-old Jewish boy's life that he was just becoming accustomed to hearing about now that he was an official member of this club.

He parked his bike in the club's outdoor space and opened the bay doors, pleased to see his favorite single, Mozart, there. He thought his mother would be pleased that the club had named some boats after famous composers. It said something about the intellectual level of members, and reasoned intellectual achievement was important to the family. His second favorite boat was Nietzsche, given by one club member who found Nietzsche's words honorable. He would have to discuss with Clara how anyone could find anything right about this particular philosopher.

After a quick change to shorts and a long-sleeved wool shirt to absorb the cold, George moved the wooden boat from the rack just at shoulder height and lifted it above his head, steadying it with one hand while grabbing the oars that now had his name on them. He had made an agreement with the club that if he were allowed to place masking tape with his name on the oar handle, he would come once a month to check that the oars were aligned correctly in their spaces. He sensed it was a reluctant agreement that the club took pride in its accessibility of equipment, but he had pointed out that, since oars are shared—he just wanted the pair he liked easier to find.

At the dock's edge, he rolled the boat gently, so the skeg cleared the dock and placed the hull in the water. As he knelt on the dock to set oars in oarlocks, he expressed silent gratitude for having a setting to take him away from the unpleasant thoughts of his night out with Clara and the threat of the brown shirts. He appreciated that the foot stretchers were in the same place. No one else has probably rowed it, he thought. He held the two oar handles in his right hand, stepped in with his right foot, lowered himself onto the seat, and deftly put his left foot and then right foot into the stretchers. With one push, he was off the dock, turned his head slightly, out of habit. The gesture was unnecessary since no one else was on the river, but that routine was ingrained. An hour of practice would allow him to return before dark.

The river's glass-like surface brought about a special connection for him. He could just concentrate on perfecting his rowing stroke and not think about battling winds that could roil the water. In addition, the rains had held off for a few days, which meant that the rate of water flow was nearly equal going both up and downstream.

He would start with a slow slide, work his way up to thirty-three strokes per minute and maintain each progression for a minute. He had been reading more articles about techniques that improve the rower's strength, and interval training was beginning to trickle into the reports. From there, while shifting from a stroke rate of twenty-seven to twenty-nine, Thomas Eakins came to mind and an artistic depiction of rowers along with the menacing brown-shirts who had been so threatening just the night before. How does the world reconcile that the human spirit is capable of such beauty and ugliness?

He conjured up an image of Clara with her at his side, and when she had turned to kiss him. He shook that image off quickly. Not now. He did ten strokes at full pressure, ten more at lesser pressure, and began to enter a pause as he saw another rower approaching. Well, I guess I don't have the river to myself. He picked up the pace when he recognized Arthur's back, slowed down, and waited for Arthur to catch up.

"You didn't call me," yelled Arthur. "We usually help each other with the boats."

"Too preoccupied." George stopped, rested over the oar handles held together with his right hand.

"With what?"

"Nazi Germany. A girl."

"We need to talk."

"Are you willing to talk about leaving Germany?" Just uttering these words to his friends while sitting in the middle of a river where no one else could hear them except the occasional egret that landed on a branch of a low tree gave him a surge of courage.

"Yes. My family and I have been discussing it." Arthur took a few strokes because the river's natural flow had begun to shift his boat away from George's.

"Okay, we'll have a deeper conversation tomorrow, but not without a race back to the dock." Arthur smiled because he knew that no matter the turmoil in the world, George's competitive spirit still thrived. The two raced back to the dock as fading daylight began to cast shadows on the river.

CHAPTER 21

The quiet was unnerving. George was used to waking up in the morning, hearing his mother practicing musical phrases. He marveled at her ability to play the same measure repeatedly on her precious violin. To him, each measure sounded faultless, but he knew his mother's combined talent and perfectionism would insist on practice making the music virtually flawless. She would tell her students that "practice may not always make it perfect, but it will always make the music reach new heights."

He had decided he would wait until she gave some indication she was ready for a serious discussion. He was beginning to understand that not every anxious thought needed to be brought to the fore immediately. Some moments were more appropriate than others to bring up worries. The critical topic, again, would have to be about leaving Germany with his parents. The encounter with the SA kid gangsters at the theater had unnerved him. George headed downstairs with his rowing clothing tossed into his briefcase since practice required that he be at the boat club every day after school; workouts were critical in taking seconds off his 2,000-meter sprint. He also needed to see if enlisting the aid of the club to get to Palestine was possible—boats, yes, but people—actual human beings, was another story. Germany would undoubtedly be imposing restrictions on products and human emigration.

His mother sat at the kitchen table with a music score on the table, absent-mindedly eating a piece of toast.

"Preparing for tonight's rehearsal?" George popped two slices of bread into the toaster, taking out a jar of gooseberry jam from the cupboard. His grandparents had helped him cultivate a taste for this extraordinary fruit. They frequently reminded him it had traveled well from England to Germany to suggest that one's horizons could always expand.

She didn't look up until she had turned the page. George knew she was looking at a piece of music, trying to hear the precise notes in her head. It was a regular part of her practicing schedule—to listen carefully. She did it to maintain this particular skill of being able to read and hear exact notes in the music simultaneously. Frieda had explained to him that most musicians could hear the music but not always with perfect pitch. She had wondered if she should pursue the study of perfect pitch as a genetic or learned trait as an academic line of inquiry.

"No, I'm not rehearsing tonight. Ludwig told me not to show up for the next two concerts. He said they want to give training time to possible substitutes." She retrieved additional coffee from the drip aluminum percolator that remained on the stove over a tiny burner light. Coffee was always hot and ready for anyone entering the kitchen for breakfast—a family tradition.

"That's a bunch of nonsense." Werner Grossinger walked over and poured himself a cup of coffee, then bent over to kiss his wife on her forehead. Before he set the cup down on the table, he added two cubes of sugar and cream. "Your mother is just being stoic, maybe optimistic, but definitely not a truth-teller."

"But . . ." Frieda interjected.

"No 'buts,' Werner insisted. "You're probably never going back to play as long as Hitler is in power."

"You told me he might not get away with everything—Franz Richter took him to court," said George. He was now absorbing every bit of news that might be needed for his budding plan for leaving the country.

Werner paused, taking an affectionate look at his son. He had long ago given up tousling his hair or giving him an encouraging pat on the back. Hugs were never a family practice. As a father, he could not refrain from thinking that this only child who had been so focused on rowing—and at times, his studies—was now beginning to understand the wider world and think beyond his own needs. His son was still green as a newspaper reporter, but he was growing.

"And look what happened. Richter is now in Dachau prison—amazingly, we have secured a telephone line to talk to him. I've gotten permission on the basis that it's going to let people think twice before anyone dares to challenge any of Hitler's policies. Richter had the Fuhrer on the stand for three hours in court and look where it got Richter—prison." George watched his father's face grow even more stern. "And you are going to forgo your classes at university and your rowing practice, if necessary, and interview this man for the newspaper."

George stared at his father and shot a glance of appeal at his mother. "Shouldn't you give this to a more experienced reporter?" George's somber expression belied his anxiety, to which his father was not oblivious.

Werner's hand went to his son's shoulder.

"No one wants to do it. They are afraid for themselves and their families. You, on the other hand, you are young, and youthfulness could be used as an excuse if necessary. Besides, Goebbels sees this as an opportunity to tell the government's story but we can shape the information to get at the truth and also please him. Our readers have become very sophisticated." He paused. "We can also leave your name off the story."

George knew the SS had also become more sophisticated. They had a way of finding out or even converting lies into truth. Still, he was not ready to challenge his father.

George turned to his mother, who had sat watchful and silent throughout the exchange.

"What do you think, Mother?"

Her voice was so low that George strained to hear her. "I've given up thinking and predicting. I have you, my parents, my violin, and music that I love to play. That is all I'm certain about."

"But you might get called back to the orchestra." At that moment, boosting his mother's spirits was a priority for him. He hoped there was some truth in the words.

"We'll see." She sighed. "But I guess my motherly advice would be that you should do the interview. School and rowing can wait. We might inspire other people to do the right thing. That's about all we have now—doing whatever it takes in subduing this regime without getting imprisoned or killed."

"Then it's settled," Werner said. "After your last class at university, be at the newspaper office."

"But rowing practice," George insisted.

"Not today," said his father. "It's more important to interview a hero so our readers understand that the current regime cannot extinguish justice. Franz Richter's story needs to be told."

—ᵐᵐᵐ—

At the newspaper, George sat at the desk with the telephone and special line. He ran his hands through his hair several times and rubbed them together as though preparing for a fight, but Rudolph Lizst, who was at his side, knew this was just nervousness. Lizst, an expert in telecommunications, understood this was an extraordinary venture—to speak to a prisoner—a prisoner who was an esteemed lawyer, who had dared to question Hitler for three hours on the stand successfully but still managed to wind up at Dachau.

"Are you ready?" Lizst asked. "I've received a go-ahead that they are waiting for the call. The commandant has offered up his office—undoubtedly to be able to listen in."

George nodded. Lizst dialed the number he read from a small slip of paper.

Remarkably, no static existed on the call, and Dachau had ensured there would be no party line. It didn't matter, thought George. His father promised that the truth would be published. His father also had entrusted him a great deal, leaving him to interview a man who had confronted Hitler in a trial, had won, and was now imprisoned.

"Franz Richter, here." It was an assertive voice on the other end of the line.

George swallowed and looked at his pad for his prepared questions. He had worked with Lizst to ask those that would obtain the most information. They might change as the interview went on, but he needed to think about the words that would make Richter feel comfortable and elicit the truth. Avoid unnecessary pleasantries. He posed the first question, making sure to speak precisely and clearly. Telephone lines were sometimes less than perfect.

"Do you think you're guilty of the offenses with which you are charged?"

Richter didn't hesitate. "I am guilty of cross-examining a man for three hours and proving that Hitler had pushed the SA to take out his enemies one by one. The law was entirely disregarded, and if I am anything, I am a man of the law."

George set aside the pad and decided to push in a different direction. "Do you think that the public understands that the SA are lawless, loyal only to Hitler, and not the people of Germany?"

"That's a bold statement coming from someone who is such a young reporter. I can tell by your voice—you are still quite young." Richter hadn't lost his skills as a challenger and questioner.

"That does not answer the question," asserted George, surprising himself at his challenge. "Do you think the public understood that the SA was doing Hitler's bidding when they stabbed innocent workers because the thugs thought they were Communists?"

For a moment, just for a moment, George thought he would bring in his encounter outside the theater with the SA and how much it had impacted him, but then he remembered he was a reporter and was supposed to be as objective as possible. He, being intimidated by recent violence, shouldn't be a part of the narrative.

Richter answered slowly. "It is my job to discover the truth, and if the public chooses to deny it, there's nothing I can do about it." He paused. "I suppose we cannot wipe away ignorance as much as we would want. Just think. German academics once influenced the entire world. Our leaders had integrity."

"So, you discover, he lied," George said. "You had enough evidence to convict him of perjury. But the conviction of perjury did not stand. We have an obligation to explain that to our readers."

"That is up to your editors, I suppose. I will tell you—corrupt judges. Judges who are intimidated by Hitler and forget that they are there to uphold the law. This is a dangerous place for any country since every country is a step away from easily falling into fascism. Just look at Mussolini in Italy."

~~~

George turned to Lizst, who had sat stiffly by his side—far enough to indicate that he knew this was George's interview, but close enough in case of any technical problems. He had heard George's questions and thought them worthy of a good newspaper interview. He would know more when he saw Richter's responses which George was writing rapidly on his notepad as the prisoner spoke.

Lizst's face finally relaxed when he heard George ask the question, "But Mussolini took power long before you were sent to prison. Do you see a connection?" This was important to clarify for readers, and it would require careful writing that reflected truth but didn't bring Goebbels' wrath upon the newspaper.

Complete silence reigned in response to the last question. George looked to Lizst, wondering if the line had gone dead. Then a tired voice spoke, "I only have a few minutes left, and all I can tell you is the Third Reich conjured evidence that connected me to the Reichstag fire, and therefore, I was sent to prison for their propaganda and lies." Richter's voice gained strength. "I defend truth, and I don't care if they're Communists or Nazis, but Germany has forgotten the rule of law. It has forgotten trial by jury." The prisoner's tone was a blend of animus and despair.

George heard a voice on the other end, telling Richter that his time was up; he needed to return to his cell. The young reporter searched for the right words to end the conversation. "You have a reputation for pursuing justice. I hope this article can help in your pursuit."

"I have no hope," Richter responded. "When the rule of law is gone, hope is not possible. When people assign godlike qualities to one man, all hope is gone. Let some of us remain brave enough to tell the truth."

With those final words, Richter hung up the phone. George wrote Richter's last words, slowly trying to remember them precisely as he spoke them. George wasn't sure how he was going to write the story; his father would undoubtedly have input, but more than ever, Richter's words about the absence of the rule of law made him more aware that he was going to pursue the best way for him and his family to leave Germany.

Chapter 22

Isaac Sherman had been reading the day's newspaper at his desk, wondering if he could believe the positive news that factory orders for goods were picking up when he was startled by the sharp knock on the office door. He and his partner, Julius, had taken to locking their office door now that SA members were becoming more emboldened and audacious—and unpredictable in their violence in the streets. The partners could hardly believe that the SA loyalists were some of the same soldiers they had served with in The Great War.

Awareness of relevant history to their political inclinations was prominent on the office walls. A newspaper clipping with a November 1923 date held a framed place: "Six Hundred SA Members Attempt to Overthrow the Weimar Republic" with the word "disgrace" that Sherman had written over it to serve as a reminder that the republic was fragile.

The letters on their office door read "Sherman & Abrahams, Accountants." Many in the building knew they were committed Zionists, and up to this point, they had not been the object of an attack. Still, Isaac and Julius had decided to take precautions and only open their office door to people they recognized.

"Yes, who is it?" Isaac called out. The rapping on the door continued. The second time he uttered the same words, he shouted, hoping the increased volume would frighten off an unwanted visitor.

"It's George Grossinger. Open the door, please."

Isaac quickly opened the door. What did the kid want now? The German Zionists had already helped fulfill a request for boats. Sherman knew they were in Palestine. Maybe the Arabs and the Jews were already rowing in them and, for all he knew, were vowing to become best friends. What more could he want?

"My partner, Abrahams, isn't here yet," said Sherman. Without waiting for a response, he turned on the switch of an electric tea kettle that had already been filled with water. "Whatever you want, you can always have a glass of tea." Sherman returned to his desk and waved to George to take a seat on the opposite side. George didn't particularly want tea, but he understood this was part of the getting to know one another ritual—to ascertain if you were a trustworthy person and a "mensch." A word he was beginning to understand had a particular resonance in encounters with certain Jews. Not precisely biblical, but important.

"So, you are here for a reason," Sherman said, setting two glasses on the desk with a jar of sugar cubes. "If you want more boats, we need to have Julius here. But I can tell you it's going to be hard to convince him to send more boats to Palestine." Sherman leaned forward on his elbows. "Because they don't need more boats. They need money. They need trees. They need people. Maybe a few guns here and there." He lifted the glass to his lips, blew on the rim, and took a sip.

"Exactly," said George, practically pouncing at the moment of silent reprieve. "I want to find a way to get to Palestine with my friend, Arthur Schwartz, to explore the possibility of living there and leaving Germany."

"And?" said Sherman, putting the glass down slowly.

"And I want to see if your Zionists will help my friend take an exploratory trip to Palestine—to see where our families can live—to see where we can row."

Just at that moment, Julius Abrahams entered the office, throwing his briefcase on a desk and hanging his coat and hat on a coat rack pole.

"He's back," said Sherman, motioning at George.

"I can see he's back. I don't need an announcement for that," said Abrahams, sitting at the other desk so close to his partner's that they would have had an easy reach for a hug, but to any close observer of German customs, it would have been an unlikely scenario.

George stood as his parents had taught him. "When an older person enters a room, and you are already seated, you stand." Werner and Frieda had imprinted politeness on George's psyche. Julius Abrahams glanced at some papers on his desk, waved dismissively, and George sat down with the gesture of bare acknowledgment, taking a sip of his tea which somehow had managed to remain warm in the glass.

"Do we have enough money to help send two young men to Palestine for a few days–or a week—to see if they can find a place to live with their families?" Sherman asked and watched as Julius stirred three sugar cubes in his tea, apparently determined to have them dissolve before he said another word.

Still silent, Julius looked over at George, who nodded because Isaac Sherman had perfectly explained his concern directly without embellishment. George had come to admire the directness and no-nonsense attitude of the Zionists he met along with the endless glasses of tea and sugar cubes. He was beginning to think all this tea-drinking was a way of slowing the conversation, either to give time for more reflection or simply to assess the people in the room.

"And row," George added after a moment. He thought about explaining his idea that rowing could change the world. George had been delighted to see athletes from foreign lands unable to communicate because of language barriers but somehow connecting and even bonding because they understood the language of rowing. Rowers earned respect and admiration for their prowess regardless of country, race, or religion. But this was not the time for such an explanation. Give these gentlemen their chance to say what is on their minds.

"Just because the British are in Palestine, it doesn't mean that rowing would be anything like rowing in England. You realize that don't you?" Julius Abrahams knew that he had to dispel any romantic notions anyone might have about living in Palestine. He had been there enough times to know that swamps, mosquitoes, poor irrigation, and unhappy Arabs could dampen anyone's dreams. A place where Jews could be free to set up their government and laws would mean never having to worry about pogroms and discrimination, but it didn't guarantee an easy life or happiness. He had lived long enough to understand that some joy had to come from within the individual. He was worried about unhappy people who saw moving to a new land vanquishing their problems. No, he knew, whoever wants to emigrate to Palestine must come from sturdy and resilient stock. As he was pondering, he thought Freud would probably say the same thing, especially now that his books were being burned.

George was quick to reply. "I understand that living conditions might be difficult, and honestly, if I think they are too difficult for my family, especially my grandparents, I will consider other options, but right now, I feel compelled to explore a potential escape with a friend."

"Ah, so you have a good friend, who is willing to go?"

"Yes, at least to visit. I'm not sure about his commitment to settle there." George took a breath. "I want you to understand that I understand struggle; rowing to win a race, to test your endurance is incredibly difficult. You need to learn to push on with the minimum oxygen you have in your body."

Abrahams smiled, peering over his glasses perched on the bridge of his nose. "Not as hard as dealing with a group of people who are threatened by your very existence and don't want you there. You do know there's resistance from the Arabs?"

"And you think we are wanted here?" George startled himself with the ferocity of his counterattack.

Abrahams sighed. "You're right. And I think it's going to become increasingly hard."

"So?" queried George. "What do you think? You'll find the money to send us?"

Abrahams leaned back in his chair, spreading his arms up in a gesture of defeat or acknowledgment. George wasn't sure which. "So, my friend Isaac is going to open the books and see if we have any money to help with this crazy idea."

George watched as Isaac Sherman pulled a large black and maroon book from one massive pile on his desk and began perusing it slowly, going up and down a page with a finger, turning to the next page and doing the same, adjusting his spectacles from moment to moment.

George thought he might help and started to speak but refrained when Julius Abrahams quietly shook his head. George interpreted that as "let him do his work."

"Yes, we can do it," Sherman sighed. "We have enough money to send you and a friend." He turned to Abrahams. "We will have to do some juggling, but this young man has made a convincing case."

George jumped up and leaned over to shake Sherman's hand.

"Yes, you want to shake my hand now, and I hope you will want to do the same when you return." Sherman slowly closed the account book. "You will have six days there, and you will be staying on a kibbutz near Mount Carmel. I know they will take you in. You may also run into members of the Royal Fusiliers—a fighting unit that we have helped to organize based on their victories in the 1920s."

"But we are not about fighting," said George. "Besides, that is far from rowing in Haifa, isn't it?" he protested, trying to maintain his profound gratitude in his voice.

"Look, Palestine is not all about rowing. You'll go to a kibbutz to see how people get together to make something out of nothing. It's the land for them. For you, it may be the river, the boat, but for them, it's making something out of nothing. Maybe you'll learn a little bit more about life," said Sherman.

"Get your passports and papers in order. We will arrange for the flights on Deutsche Lufthansa. Right now, it's relatively easy to get you out of Germany and back. However, the future may be more problematic," said Abrahams, clearly the one in charge of extraordinary arrangements.

George was already at the door when Isaac Sherman said, "And study some English when you're on the plane. You'll need it there. The British are in charge. It helps to speak their language."

—···—

That evening, George waited until dinner was over and watched his mother and father retire to the living room. A console radio took up space that had previously held a large plant—a philodendron—that seemed to thrive, now near the kitchen window, despite the sullen Berlin sky. As much as they disliked the news that came forth from the speaker, proclaiming victories in neighborhoods where Communists had been defeated, praising SA members for singing the "Horst Wessel Song" when they finished cleaning up a street, the family felt compelled to listen. What came across the airwaves was an absolute barometer of the moment. George watched his father grind down a cigarette in disgust at the reporting of a Munich attorney, Dr. Michael Siegel, being marched through the streets barefoot with a sign around his neck: "I will never again complain to the police." The reporter seemed to express glee. Siegel had filed a complaint against the unwarranted and unauthorized arrest of his client, Mr. Uhlfelder, owner of a department store, which led to this disgusting act of police brutality.

George wasn't sure what to do when he saw his father cover his face with his hands and his mother sit impassively staring at the floor. He counted to ten.

"I would like to go to Palestine with Arthur to see what the land offers us in the way of . . . freedom." He waited. He wasn't sure if these were the right words, but they came out of his mouth spontaneously.

His father, dropping his hands in his lap, stared at his son and looked at Frieda, who quietly nodded. "Go," he said. "Go as soon as possible. I am thinking that Germany is no longer our country."

—···—

The landing at the small Haifa airport was smooth, and George and Arthur were grateful that it was daytime so they could see the shoreline of the city. They were keenly aware of the lush green that overwhelmed the few buildings, many of which seemed to have a flag of Great Britain attached to a window, gleaming in the bright sunshine. The brightness of the March sun in contrast to the bleak gray of Berlin startled them.

The two young men entered the one hangar that stood at the edge of the runway. What appeared to them to be a young boy stood with a rifle slung over his shoulder, a cigarette dangling from his lips, and a sign with their names in his hands. George handed him a slip of paper with the words Ein Or and Mount Carmel. The boy nodded and proceeded without comment to a jeep pockmarked with dents and rust, an open-air cab with rugged tires.

George and Arthur had looked at a map prior to leaving and saw their destination was southeast of Haifa. They anticipated a short half-hour ride by jeep. They eagerly climbed into the back and threw their suitcases into the small open trunk, not even trying to contain their excitement. Anticipation had kept them going through all the days of preparation—passports, luggage, appropriate clothing, and writing pads because surely there would be fascinating stories. This first adventure began in wondrous silence with a journey over rough roads, which sometimes narrowed down to lanes where only one car or donkey could pass at a time. Even the bumpy ride delighted the newly arrived travelers. "This is like the excitement at the end of a race when you've won," said George.

"More like the beginning," said Arthur, "with its sense of anticipation. This is all about the excitement of the unexpected, isn't it?"

"Look," said George, pointing to the passing landscape. "Saplings. It looks like trees growing next to a swamp."

The driver uttered his first words in halting English. "A Jew went to Baghdad and stole date palm saplings. Smuggled them here."

"I guess there's no holding newcomers back," said George.

"I only understand the word newcomers," said the driver. "We are not newcomers. This is our land. It says so in the Bible."

George looked at Arthur and shook his head. We won't win this conversation. They both had read enough history that they knew two people claimed the land, but they were determined to see if Palestine could become a safe haven for Jews who wanted to survive and row.

CHAPTER 23

The young driver stopped the jeep in front of a twenty-foot-high narrow stone tower with a difficult-to-find entrance and barracks surrounded by barbed wire. George and Arthur were delighted to see what appeared to be a teenage boy, rifle slung over one shoulder, waving to them from the other side. Someone knew of their arrival.

His high-pitched voice came through clearly. "The tower light shines at night to pick up our enemies. We do this to be safe in our land." He continued waving. "Come in beyond the tower, and you will find yourself in the midst of a fort. Gadi Aloni will be out to greet you. You will know him because he will give you each a giant hug." With that very terse introduction, George and Arthur followed the boy, grateful for the warmth of the sun and enough blue sky to limit the sight and sting of barbed wire.

Isaac Sherman had provided a short tutorial to the young men before they left Germany and had informed them of the efforts of British engineers who saw the need for protective surveillance. "Communities need special protection," Isaac Sherman had said. "We built schools and hospitals. Finally, we realized we'd have to raise money not just for water supplies but for protection as well. We also needed to be aware of the need for defense and safekeeping of our community."

Gadi Aloni's most distinct feature was graying curly hair, cropped short, above a tan face wrinkled prematurely by the sun. He, too, had what appeared to be the ubiquitous rifle slung over one shoulder. He strode to meet them. The gun did not interfere with his ability to envelop Arthur first and then George in a wraparound bear hug. He nearly lifted lightweight Arthur off his feet.

"Come into the dining room. Supper first, and then I will take you to your rooms. You are thinking of making aliyah?" Aloni continued as they followed. "I bet you didn't know we had our first arrival of Jews in the 1880s. We need more."

Arthur and George decided Aloni was not waiting for a conversational response. They entered the most prominent building amidst ten smaller buildings that George knew must serve as homes because in front of each was a small garden and a mezuzah affixed to a door frame. George couldn't believe it. Were there oranges growing in front of their homes? Three outhouses in the back appeared to be shared among homeowners. He and Arthur had been told they would not have their customary facilities. So what? he thought. He had rowed until he felt his heart would fall out of his chest. He had rowed hour-long practices, containing his bodily needs until he could reach a bathroom. Outhouses did not faze him.

Setting their suitcases at the entrance, they entered a large dining room. Pots of potatoes, string beans, and chicken thighs sat on each burner of the gas-powered cylinders. Salads of chopped-up tomatoes, cucumbers, and an unidentified green herb sat in large bowls on each of the ten rectangular tables that filled up the rest of the space in the room. Stoves, sinks, tables, and chairs. George wondered if people ate every meal here.

"We use this same room when we need to gather to discuss not only our salvation but how to get rid of mosquitoes, plant trees, and get people like you to settle here. We need you," Gadi said, removing a flask from his jacket pocket, taking a swig, and offering it to George and Arthur, who both shook their heads. "Especially the young and the strong. We are building a country."

"We're in training," said George. "No alcohol and no cigarettes. Nothing bad for the body."

"Speaking of bodies," said Arthur, "where is your closest body of water?"

"You are near the Na'Aman River, and we're working on creating a fish farm nearby," Aloni said with a twinkle in his eye. He waited because usually, when he mentioned the word "fish farm" to foreigners or strangers, they had questions, but since no questions were forthcoming, Aloni forged on. "It is not fit for your rowing."

George started to speak, but Gadi lifted a hand to silence. "I know because somehow this British colonel, Leicester, I think his name is, has come by every day to ask about your arrival." Aloni shrugged his shoulders. "So, we talked. So, now I'm a little bit informed about your rowing. But before you set foot out of here, you will have rifle training so that you can defend yourselves in case of danger as you explore this area. You know . . . be in control."

"But we did not come for rifle training," protested George.

"Let's hear what he has to say," said Arthur. "We are their guests. This is their country." He lightly touched his friend's shoulder. George shrugged.

Arthur continued. "We came to see if we could live here and if rifle training is a small part of this life, so be it. Let's remember that street violence has taken over Germany. Maybe we should have the ability to do something about it."

"I see your friend has his head on his shoulders," said Aloni. "Breakfast tomorrow at 7:00 a.m. and rifle training practice immediately after that." Aloni took George's hand in his in a rough clasp. "You will get to rowing, my young man, I promise you. You have a British officer to help you. That's an answer to a lot around here. Some people are not happy about their presence, but, right now, they serve a purpose."

—ᴡᴡ—

At breakfast the following day, the dining room was full of a sea of light blue. Individuals in blue shirts, shorts, long pants dominated the room, as did chatter. Everyone seemed to be talking to someone. Cigarette smoke filled the air, and cigarettes rested on ashtrays right alongside the steaming cups of coffee and tea.

A young man with dark, curly hair waved them over with their trays of oatmeal, eggs, and toast. George wondered if all the young people had dark, curly hair. "Jonathan," he said. "I will be your rifle instructor today. But first, sit and eat. You should know the eggs come right from the chickens on the farm, and we bake our bread." He smiled. "Right now, we get boxes of Quaker Oats from someone who has a rich relative in the United States, so we eat oatmeal. And the refrigerator. That came from someone's uncle, again in America. We depend on you Zionists."

"Well, I'm not sure I'm a Zionist," said George, taking a few bites of toast along with sips of coffee. Arthur did the same, eating quickly, sensing that they would not have that much time to eat.

"Of course, you are. You're coming to see if you want to live in Palestine. That's enough. And when you finish your rifle training, you'll be a full-fledged Zionist—able to take care of yourself and your family. No more ghetto Jews who are afraid of their own shadow, let alone a stupid edict from the government." He stood, adjusting the rifle over his shoulder with one hand and putting on a brimmed cotton hat—a smaller floppier version of the British white pith helmet with the other hand.

"Do we go by jeep?" Arthur asked.

Jonathan grinned. "No, we will walk 1000 meters. Voila! There we have enough land to practice on. Land we cleared."

Arthur and George smiled back to acknowledge his pride. They had been with enough Zionists now to know that part of many conversations would be about swampland that had been cleared and was now overflowing with forests and orchards of fruit. Next, they would probably hear about fish farms.

The range consisted of a sparse meadow surrounded by cedar trees, which had probably been there for hundreds of years. Some of them had trunks two feet wide.

Jonathan laid two rifles on the bare earth with a few seedlings of grass struggling to grow. "Maybe these came on the same ship as your boats. That should give you motivation," Jonathan said. "But first, safety. You do not touch these things until you understand their power. Never stand in front of a gun." He pulled two plastic toy pistols from his pocket and handed them to Arthur and George. "Again, from America," he said. "Just practice pulling the trigger. Get the feel of it in your finger." He demonstrated with deftness that indicated competence rather than swagger. Then, he handed each young man a pair of winter earmuffs.

"But it is not winter here," said Arthur, laughing.

"These could have come from Germany, so don't say America again. I know they weren't made here," said George.

"They are the best we have to protect your hearing," said Jonathan. "And there will also be a recoil from the gun. Watch." Placing the earmuffs on, he then demonstrated, aiming the rifle at one of the trees, slowly pulling the trigger.

"So, you have been using what I think is a German-designed rifle." George pulled out a notebook. "Wait, just one minute. Before I shoot, since I might not be alive afterward, I want information."

Jonathan grinned. "We can have a debriefing later for your notebook. You will be alive. It's a 7.65 mm M1903 Mauser. It has a range of 600 meters, and I would say a leftover from the Ottoman Empire. That's why we need all the military hardware we can get. Even if they come buried in hulls of boats."

George was not surprised that Jonathan knew about guns being shipped by boat. He was beginning to get the idea that access to information was not only keeping individuals alive but encouraging the possibility of a homeland as well. Having security and information were the modus operandi of the day here in Palestine. It had been beginning to feel that way in Germany, too. Daily conversations had revolved around news of the day and what one needed to do to stay safe.

"Let me try," said Arthur. "I've learned how to follow directions from my rowing coaches and coxswains." Arthur deftly took the rifle and aimed. "Make sure you rest it on your shoulder," Jonathan said. Arthur readjusted the gun, took aim, and pulled the trigger. Startled by the recoil, nevertheless, he gave a satisfied smile and said, "Enough. It's George's turn. I hit the tree."

No one had noticed Ben Leicester standing off to the side, observing. He understood it was important not to startle anyone with a rifle in his hand. He watched as the other young man reluctantly took the weapon, put on earmuffs, and aimed at the same tree. "Try to match me," said Arthur. "Try to aim at the same spot."

Leicester watched as this young man followed his friend's direction and managed a shot that made its mark nearly next to his friend's bullet hole. "Teammates," he thought. The scene reminded him of the times he and his rowing friends spent joyous times together away from the boat. He recognized the camaraderie instantly.

Ben stepped forward and shouted, "Bravo! But that's not why you're here, and I doubt that you'll need any of that where we're going." The British army officer decided this was not the time to tell them Arabs, of late, had been ambushing cars and even donkey carriers on some roads.

He moved toward them, extending his hand to Jonathan. "Captain Ben Leicester, determined to have these men help me with rowing now that we have boats."

"Of course," murmured Jonathan, avoiding his offer of a handshake. He had yet to make his peace with any of the British, even those with good intentions. "We were told you would be arriving. Otherwise, you would not have easy access to find us here on the shooting range."

George and Arthur eagerly extended their hands to Leicester, nearly simultaneously, and Leicester laughed, shaking George's hand first, then Arthur's. "Happy to feel the strength in your hands," he said. "Now, let's get you to the warehouse and the river. That's why you're here. Right? To help promote rowing and teach it?"

"Yes," said George. "Of course," said Arthur, following him to the jeep, grateful to be off the range and onto the road to take them to the river. Just looking at the reed-like vegetation along the wayside as they drove, with the anticipation of a body of water to be rowed upon, created a level of internal excitement that they both understood—no words needed to be exchanged.

No scenery needed to be remarked upon.

At the warehouse, Leicester turned the combination lock and easily pushed open the wide doors. "Need to have a lock now that we have more boats, although I don't know how anyone would get them out of here. Hard for a donkey to carry them. But they would be useful for firewood."

George and Arthur stared at the boats, with each end resting on one-foot wooden boxes with colorful labels. Labels with Blue Lagoon, College Heights, Meander were plastered on the sides. Oranges from the United States? It must have been a while ago; for now, fruit was thriving in orchards here.

"Gentlemen. Here are your boats. There is your river," the army captain said, pointing to the flow of water that was not more than six feet away. "Shall we have a trial row?"

No more words were exchanged. Sandals were quickly removed and left by the door. Each of the three men found a set of oars to place by the side of the river. They helped move three singles to the water's edge. Two lined up, one at the front, the other at the bow of a boat to carry it, place it in water, shallow enough so they could easily seat themselves and put their feet into foot holders. One by one, they pushed off from the shore with a starboard oar and slowly started the rowing stroke, focusing on getting bodies in sync with the boat and the water. Leicester noted their level of comfort and control and gradually raised the stroke rate to see how far they could be pushed. They good-naturedly matched the captain's pace, and he happily watched as they skillfully rowed 8,000 meters of Kishon River for the first time. On the return, Leicester gladly let them outrace him.

"So, gentlemen," asked Leicester after they carefully returned the boats to the warehouse. "You will be staying to give lessons for young people of the village?"

"Yes," Arthur and George said in near unison. Their joy was palpable, and the row had reenergized them. That was the delight in rowing. Afterward, despite an extraordinary output of energy, the body responds with an uplifted spirit and a sense of accomplishment.

Chapter 24

Fortunately, in the early dawn, with the sun barely peeking over the horizon, Ein Or was lit intermittently by a circling tower light. George and Arthur stood outside the barbed wire fencing of the kibbutz, thumbs out, hitchhiking. Aloni had told them that this is what everyone did there—try to hitch a ride with one of the passing cars or even on the back of a motorcycle at any hour of the day. George thought back to the streets of Berlin, his encounter after the movies with Clara, and the near brawl with street thugs. He had been grateful the SA thugs had not touched their bikes because the last thing he would have tried was to hitch a ride with a stranger to get home.

"I think someone is stopping for us," said Arthur, and he stepped out into the road as a car slowed down. When the driver rolled down the window, Arthur showed him a piece of paper on which Leicester had drawn directions to the warehouse near the Kishon River.

George and Arthur knew that Leicester could have picked them up but understood that he wanted to test their initiative. Living in this land without the infrastructure that usually supported a civilized society, one's ability to fend for oneself and make things happen appeared to be a litmus test to acceptance—and maybe survival. For George and Arthur, it was not too different from racing at strange venues and finding ways of setting a pace to push themselves beyond everyday personal endurance. "Exceeding" and "overcoming" were two words imprinted on their cell structure.

The rowers were determined to find a way to get to the boathouse by themselves. They would not bother the people of the kibbutz, who all seemed busy with chores. George also had heard that Leicester admired people who thrived in this milieu. George wondered about Leicester's background since he noted the captain seemed so happy here.

"Ah, the warehouse," said the driver in English with an inflection they did not recognize, "Gabriel Rossi," he said. "With relatives in Italy, just in case, you wondered about my accent." George took him to be about his age and attributed his somewhat wrinkled skin to sun.

"Have you been here long?" asked George, taking out his notepad. He had not forgotten his father's directions to be aware that everyday life can be turned into a story. "We're visiting here from Germany," he added.

"Since before the fourth century and Constantine and Christian migration," said the driver, smiling slightly.

"No, you," said George, understanding the moment of subtle humor. He had had an excellent Middle East professor who not only taught the area's complicated history but posed the question: did conquerors ever think that taking over another land that wasn't theirs would bring about complications in the daily lives of its future citizens? Land for land's sake often brought about war and ongoing conflict. He and Arthur were a part of that history today, with Arabs and Jews disputing about selling, owning, and taking land.

"Well, really, since Mussolini," said Rossi. "My mother and father saw that he would not be good for the Jews—Jews who had lived in Italy peacefully since the sixteenth century—because, at heart, Mussolini is a dictator. Dictators have no moral compass. If it suits them, it's the right thing to do. They get corrupted by the power. You're from Germany? You have your brown shirts. We have our black shirts." During the monologue, Rossi waved at each passing car coming in the other direction, and a horn toot came in acknowledgment. "Here, there are still possibilities of a righteous place on earth. Here, an Abraham Lincoln would be welcome."

George wondered if everyone he met would be a philosopher and a historian and discuss existential reasons on how to live. And did everyone know everyone else?

Rossi stopped the car at the entrance road to the warehouse.

"You're here to row?" asked Rossi.

"Yes, how did you know?" Arthur asked.

"It's still a small country, so we know everything important. Word of mouth works phenomenally well here. It's what keeps us going." As Arthur and George exited the car and said their thanks, Rossi pulled away, saying," Watch out for Arab kids. Never know when one is going to turn on you."

"Not if you teach them how to row," George retaliated, hoping his words reached Rossi as he sped away. Arthur gave him an approving pat on the back for encouragement, but each knew this was potential conflict territory despite incredible sunshine and friendly dispositions.

Walking down the narrow road with bulrushes growing on each side, Arthur spotted Leicester with four teenagers, dressed in shorts, T-shirts, and sandals. One girl had a flowered kerchief wrapped around her hair, and

George could see curls springing out from the edges. The young men all had dark hair, and George and Arthur could not distinguish Arab from Jew.

George tried to think back to his first coaching days with Messinger. What was the tone Messinger took? How authoritative was his coaching style? How much did he physically demonstrate? George decided he would have to adopt his own coaching style—he and Arthur were strangers in a new land, where rowing had not been a tradition and where land ownership issues prompted daily arguments, sometimes turning dangerous. Some had heard "effendis were selling to the Jews," and were uncertain of the implications. Well, things were not going that well in Germany either; that should be no reason to give up on rowing where the possibility of camaraderie and teamwork went a long way to nurture friendship.

Leicester, dressed in his British summer uniform, greeted them each with a handshake. "You only have six singles," Leicester said, sensing that George was trying to figure out a way to start.

"Thank you," said George. "And do they already know how to get their oars first and how to carry the boat to the water?" Arthur asked.

"Yes, we do." It was Ethan who ran over to shake their hands. "Nurit, too," he said. "She and I will carry two boats to the water together, and Omar and Ahmad will carry the other two."

"As you can see, that will leave two boats for coaching," said Leicester, "and I'm assuming you will want to take on that task."

"What about you?" asked Arthur

The captain grinned. "Young man. I have other ways of trying to keep the peace. Meetings over land, ditches, roads, malaria. Confiscating guns. They take up my time, but I'll drop by after your first session—in a couple of hours, shall we say?" He saluted sharply and laughed. "I know, not necessary, but if you succeed, you are doing soldierly work and maybe God's work."

George and Arthur returned the salute with a smile and turned to their young charges. "Let's see you get the oars and boats into the river, take your seats, and hold the boat stable with your oars until Arthur and I get in our boats to coach you."

The youngsters stared back at George.

"Coach means we are trying to help you. Make you better. Maybe get to the Olympics." They continued to stare.

Finally, Arthur said, "Just get the oars and boats as you've been taught and get in. We'll explain more later." They were the words for which would-be rowers were waiting.

George and Arthur watched as each took a set of oars leaning against the corrugated metal wall and brought it down to the river's edge. The youngsters returned, and two of them together, carefully yet with a certain grace, picked up the boats poised on wooden orange crates, raised them to shoulders, paused at the shoreline, and brought boats over their heads to gently place at the water's edge, hull side down with the skeg clearing the river's bottom. All four were in shallow water with bare feet and an oar hugging the shore.

"Good," said George.

"You don't have to compliment us," said Omar. "We know what's good. You just have to make us better."

"Make us compete, better," added Ethan.

George frowned and looked at Arthur. How difficult was coaching these kids going to be? Was everyone here this outspoken? Challenging authority? He thought back. Coach Messinger had been sparing in compliments but unsparing in corrections. So be it.

"Now, my boat," directed Arthur. "Just watch." After placing oars near the water's edge, Arthur put one hand on either side of the boat, raised it over his head, and walked it slowly from the door to the water, locked the oars in place, stepped in the boat, and pushed off against the sandy bank, taking a few strokes to remain close to the students. "I will wait till you get into your boats."

"Eventually," George said, joining him, "you'll be able to do what Arthur just did. You'll be stronger and more secure in your ability to carry a single on your own."

Nurit was the only one who nodded, indicating an acceptance, or understanding of George's words. He was beginning to sense he would have to win Omar, Ethan, and Ahmad over.

George and Arthur had agreed that the river was not wide enough for six abreast. They also decided to spend the first ten minutes assessing their rowers. George remembered that Messinger had spent a fair amount of time observing them before making any corrections. George would take Nurit and Ethan. Arthur would take Omar and Ahmad with a 500-meter start. "Let's go," Arthur said. "The plovers and the gulls are here to encourage you," he said just as a flock of birds settled in the bulrushes near the shore. *I am here rowing amid nature instead of the concrete of Berlin*, thought Arthur as he watched Omar and Ahmad take their first supervised strokes with him as a coach.

"I'm going to ask you to row and relax. Say those words to your shoulders, legs, and body. They all have to connect with your mind—the mind reminds you of focus," said George. He watched as Nurit and Ethan took their first strokes, with Ethan having his oars buried too deep in the water and Nurit having moments of anxiety by rushing on the slide.

And so, they rowed the 1,500-meter stretch of river with the two of them reminding the young rowers of oar height, a good ratio of the drive to the recovery. He was grateful that Leicester had taught them the vocabulary of rowing; they understood when they heard, "the legs, then the back, and then the arms. Recovery just the opposite—arms, back, and legs."

George asked them to feel the boat "run out" under them after applying energy from the legs.

Arthur reminded them of a hand's height just beneath the breastbone. He asked them to watch while he demonstrated.

George reminded them of straight backs.

Arthur called out flat legs at the finish.

"Now row, the 1,500 meters back on your own," said George.

With George and Arthur rowing back leisurely, Ethan and Omar seemed to have discovered their natural competitiveness and began racing each other. Their coaches could see that Ethan would burn out because he was not pacing himself to win. His oxygen supply would be depleted, and the lactic acid would start to burn. Omar's deliberate pace won, and he let out a giant yell as he neared the warehouse and raised his arms, letting go of the oars. The next moment he tumbled into the Kishon River and stood in water up to his ankles. He lifted his arms again as the victorious one and did what could only be interpreted as a happy dance, stomping up and down, so the shallow water sent out ripples.

George and Arthur smiled—they knew that feeling of winning, but they also wanted to instill the value of training itself. It built both mind and body. Today they had made a start. They hoped they could harness the enthusiasm to build champions. But first, back to Germany.

CHAPTER 25

Where to go first? George and Arthur had returned to Germany from a place beset with problems—not only malaria and poor roads but also people struggling to live alongside each other, people ambivalent about throwing off the yoke of British domination. At times, interactions had taken on an atmosphere of community warfare because individuals had declared allegiance to tribes rather than a state or a country.

But in this desert land, there were rivers to row and people in which the sport could be nurtured, and that in turn, could give strangers who had previously distrusted one another the opportunity to grow together, to find common purpose. George and Arthur, who had absorbed rowing as their passion, saw all these possibilities but how to translate them to strangers in an alien, primitive land was the challenge. Then again, it was more than a strange land. It was a place that held out the promise of being a homeland—a place to escape the jack-booted SA gangsters who had taken over the streets with violence and intimidation and a government that had adopted discriminatory laws.

George and Arthur's daily conversations included whispers of hope. "Maybe, my mother can find an orchestra where she can play her violin," said George. "And maybe my father will be able to produce a newspaper," he continued. "And my grandparents, they would feel safer there," remembering his grandfather's prison episode.

"I think my family has been lucky so far because customers still come for my father's tailoring. He charges so little," Arthur mused. "Having pants legs at just the right length and just touching the tip of the shoe still seems to be a German preoccupation. But I can see that my mother is worried—that she is at home more, that she does not use the telephone, that she worries there will be a decline in my father's business. She broods a lot."

The friends went to their Hebrew Rowing Club after classes and rowed a double with renewed energy and commitment, with thoughts of possibilities commingled with each stroke. Wilder had been observing their impassioned rowing together, so he wasn't surprised when they requested some time to talk—upstairs and with glasses of tea, of course.

"We would like to coach here," said George to Martin Wilder, deciding to open the conversation directly. Seeing the unresponsive expression on Wilder's face, George added. "Of course, with the permission of Schindler."

"We have not needed more coaches," said Wilder. "Schindler seems to be able to handle all those who want to learn or improve." Each was sitting on the edge of his chair, leaning forward as though preparing for verbal warfare.

"What if we can recruit more members—more novices?" said Arthur. "We would be good with novices."

Wilder motioned them to lean back and relax with an impatient wave of his hand. "You got boats from us to ship to Palestine, and now you want recruits. Why don't you think of working with those who are already here?"

George answered quickly. "Those members already belong to Schindler."

"Yes, they are already Schindler's rowers. They revere him. They revere him for every second he helps them take off their time," said Arthur.

"And you will bring here only Jewish members, right?" said Wilder, uncertain about the proposition and nervous about the direction. More young members? Would the club have enough boats? With wear and tear on vessels, repair and buying new boats was a near-constant management problem. And now, they were living in uncertain times of the Reichstag passing the Enabling Law and making Hitler a virtual dictator. Long-standing club policies and practices would need to be reviewed. Institutions, businesses, clubs must think of ways to deal with and mitigate frightening political winds. Wilder thought the law forbidding the forming of new political parties was most dangerous because Jews had thrived in Germany. When circumstances were not to their liking, they either fled to a new country or, if possible, formed an organization to unite themselves and work against what they conceived of as a looming danger.

"Just nine more young members," said George. He avoided answering the question about their Jewish heritage because he was not sure that he and Arthur could recruit only young Jewish men. They would deal with that issue after recruiting enough for an eight—eight rowers and a coxswain. Arthur smiled back at him. They had taken on the most challenging boat to get eight novices to synchronize their strokes so that they could row in unison and to get all eight fit enough that they could draw on an extra burst of oxygen when needed. And it would be the most satisfying when the team progressed to the point where they realized that their combined effort could get their boat first over the finish line. George and Arthur had been part of that elation after coming in first in a race, raising one arm in the air with joy while maintaining a grip on the oar handle with the other hand. They both knew that triumph of winning a race only furthered their passion. Each victory served as an incentive to go on.

Wilder walked over to the window that overlooked the river where rowers from other clubs rowed in fours, doubles, or singles. He took pleasure in seeing the puddles that created ripples in the water. He smiled when he saw that the distance between ripples was equal. Good rowing, he would think.

He turned back to the question of new rowers. "Yes, it's worth a try. But only as an experiment." Just a glint of excitement grew in his eyes.

"Agreed," said George. "As an experiment." He bit his lip and turned to Arthur. Arthur nodded. It was time to share information.

"We learned to shoot guns when we were in Palestine," George blurted to Wilder. "The people there thought we would need them to protect ourselves," George added.

"So, what are you saying with this earth-shattering piece of information?" Wilder asked, not even trying to hide the sarcasm in his voice. He was not unaware of the rising threat of hooliganism. Boathouses so far had been spared, but this may have been due to their location—far from the city's center.

"Just letting you know that you can call on us for help should you ever feel the boathouse and its rowers need protection," said Arthur. "Sometimes, if SA goons know that there are members who know how to use guns, they will avoid harassment."

"Go, recruit your members," said Wilder. "We'll see about the guns."

———••———

Back at university, George and Arthur quickly got to work. The first order of business was flyers. George used the newspaper's printing press with the permission of his father and the business operations manager. There was still enough paper for *Der Tagblatt* to spare 100 sheets. Their flyers would compete with propaganda posters showing Germany rising from the ashes with Hitler's fist rising in the air. George had thought of Eakins' *Max Schmitt in a Single Scull*, but they ultimately selected a photo of a white-shirted crew rowing an eight, their upright bodies poised with blades just above the water to show the physicality of the sport. The lengthwise perspective of the eight, with the coxswain at the bottom, dominated the page. George and Arthur included only the words, "Come Join Us," their telephone numbers and posted the flyers in dining halls, classrooms, science labs, locker rooms where students prepared for physical education classes. They didn't want anyone calling the Hebrew Rowing Club—that information would come later. They set a date for rowing machine demonstration and trials—the physical education department had purchased five when Hitler came to power. Building strong German men had become a near-constant propaganda theme to wash away the pain of losing The Great War. Although books were burned, the university somehow received monies to purchase athletic equipment for the gymnasium.

Fifteen men showed up, all in their senior year. At first, George found this unusual. Then he decided that they probably either hadn't had the opportunity to row before or realized this was their last chance. To his surprise, Clara's brother, Walter, showed up, as well as Hans.

"We know your ability," George said to Hans. "You didn't have to show up for this."

"I'm just here because I thought it important to know what you were doing since you left our team," he said. "Jews are always up to something to upset the Fuhrer."

"It's not illegal to row, and when Germany enters the Olympics, we want the best, don't we?" said Arthur. He saw Hans's face go dark. "I know, you don't think Jews should take someone else's place, but the Fuhrer does want the best."

"We're just going to show these young men how to use the rowing machine," said George. "Maybe that will give us the best eight possible."

"Not better than the Munich Rowing Club," said Hans.

"Enough," said George, and with that, he got on the rowing machine, placing his insoles in the foot straps as he seated himself, and grabbed the metal handle. Arthur gave intermittent directions directed at the newcomers who observed intently.

"The power comes from the legs."

"Sitting up allows you to breathe."

"The elbows must pass over the knees as you move toward the front."

"Think of fluidity."

With that, five men got on the rowing machines and practiced for ten minutes while either George or Arthur instructed and observed. They tried to see how well the recruits could follow directions and how much stamina they had after an intensive final 30 strokes, usually lasting about a minute. Then another five men and finally the last five. Despite their fatigue, each group stayed to observe and learn from each other. Hans remained throughout the entire session, leaning against a wall, arms folded.

Walter, Clara's brother, was in the last group. "This was an interesting experience," he said. "Clara has often spoken of your interest, or should I say your passion. This is what motivated me to come out."

George had seen Walter execute every command with ease. His six-foot frame easily adapted to the machine, and he seemed able to relax his body to reflect flexibility and grace, trying to emulate the motion on water. George and Arthur knew that rowing on a machine promoted an entirely different feel from being in a boat, especially a single one.

George and Arthur understood they would have to carefully conduct the selection process based on ability, promise, capacity for work, and the likelihood of being an enthusiastic member of the Hebrew Rowing Club. They had not thought much about the filtering process, but as George watched Hans walk around and chat with some of the fifteen young men, he turned to Arthur with a nod, indicating that he should observe. The coxswain had given them a clue without even trying. They would automatically exclude anyone who showed they might have a close association with Hans.

To avoid suspicion, Arthur wrote the names, addresses, and phone numbers of all who had participated. The young recruits' elated expressions showed they had been inspired by the trial practice. No one left without leaving personal information on the notepad that George maintained for his news articles. After all, these young men could be making news someday.

"When do we tell them?" asked Arthur.

"As soon as we talk to Wilder and Schindler to figure out the logistics of our practice time, then we tell them they're going to be rowing under the auspices of the Hebrew Rowing Club," said George. "Remind them they need to show up on time. We'll see how many will show up."

Chapter 26

Werner Grossinger walked carefully from his paper-strewn desk and fumbled as he turned on the wall light switch. He realized that he had been sitting in the dark for at least half an hour, wondering how he would deal with the ever-growing earnestness and passion of his son. George had continued to make a formidable case for the entire family to leave Germany. He assured his parents that a path to entry and creating a life existed through a river in Palestine.

Werner and Frieda had been patient with him, not insisting on a lengthy debriefing about Palestine. If he needed to go to rowing practice at the Hebrew Rowing Club, so be it. They understood that Palestine had been more than a trip. George and Arthur's travels there could be compared to an Odyssean voyage that could remake individuals and help secure a foundation for a new country. As a family, they had been far from religious practices and observances, yet they had enough sense of history to know that when Jews perceived a threat, they were usually ready to think about emigrating. Once leave-taking took place, the emigrants didn't think about returning. As immigrants, they usually made a path for themselves in the new land. Werner wrestled with accommodating George's pleas. The family had vested so much in Germany: Frieda playing with the Berlin Symphony, her father at university, his stake in *Der Tagblatt*, and George's commitment to rowing for Germany. Yes, his son had wanted to bring honor to Germany as well as himself. George had understood that countries earned prestige through the hard work of their athletes, and that idea had motivated him.

In the quiet, Werner heard someone taking two steps at a time on the staircase, and he immediately knew it was George. Footsteps echoed when the building was nearly empty, and no machines were running. He also knew George was planning to come to his office after rowing practice to see if the newspaper could print a story about his experiences in Palestine in the human-interest section. Maybe in that particular department, the article wouldn't be considered political and would pass the censors.

"Sorry, I'm late," George said, dropping his book bag on the floor.

Werner marveled that his son still had enough remaining energy to run up the steps after an afternoon of rowing practice. He and Frieda had heard enough from their son to appreciate the rigors of the sport—the intensity of workouts, the weeks, and months of daily practice just to take a few seconds off a race. Werner understood how to work under pressure to get a newspaper out on time, with accurate information and compelling stories. Still, newspaper pressure was usually a matter of hours, not the seconds George went on about.

Werner nodded, indicating that George should take a seat. "I know your mother wants to hear every detail of your exploits, but you might as well start with me here, so I can figure out if there's a story that the newspaper can realistically print." He paused. "Then you can tell her everything you have not told—what you ate, for example. She's always interested in whether there was enough food for you."

"Food can be part of the story," George protested. "You know, how the settlers get their food, how they drain the swamps for land to be able to produce."

Werner purposely remained silent; he sensed that his son wanted to say more. He could almost feel the pent-up energy just waiting to be released.

"Palestine is going to be our salvation," said George quickly, carefully observing his father's expression. "We are going to have to leave. You know it better than anyone else."

The color rose in Werner's face. Torn between his roles as a father and as an editor, he muttered, "I've not given up on words. Do not underestimate the power of the press."

George waited, expecting his father to throw Benjamin Franklin's words at him, the ones his father had quoted endlessly during dire situations ever since George was a child: "Whoever would overthrow the liberty of a nation must begin by subduing the freedom of the press." Instead, he heard his father say quietly, as though trying to suppress his anger, "At the same time, I'm going to run your story on the glories of rowing in Palestine. Yes, that's what it's going to be all about—nothing about the necessity of Jews going back to their ancestor's homeland or even that Jews row. I omit these subjects because I'm not sure if the Fuhrer just wants us gone from Germany or eliminated from the face of the earth." A vein in his temple throbbed. "I understand that it's hard to know what to do."

George got up, starting for the door. No more needed to be said. "I'm going home to start writing."

"Wait, I want you to join me on another assignment. I liked the way you handled Christopher Isherwood, and we're going to continue to follow him. I think there's another homosexual who's going to make a name for himself in the world—a German."

"Who?"

"Ernest Rohm."

"What about him?"

"He's the one you must watch. Despite flagrant behavior, he appears not to be intimidated by Hitler. I think he wants to exert himself a bit and will sit for an interview. I'll arrange it. You know the *Munchener Post* attacked him because of his homosexuality. Helmut Klotz did the reporting—a former friend of mine and an editor of *Antifaschitische Korrespondenz.*"

"So?" said George.

"Prepare for an interview with him, but don't neglect your studies." He looked up. "And, yes, write the story of rowing in Palestine just the way I told you. No emphasis on Jews and aliyah."

—ᴡᴡ—

Ernest Rohm eagerly agreed to the interview and came dressed to *Der Tagblatt* offices in his German uniform of the SA. It was distinctly different from the usual regalia of those who served under the Reichswehr. Rohm comfortably wore the black uniform, the high boots and held a protective hand on a long sword. Werner Grossinger knew that the days were long gone when German soldiers wore long swords. When Rohm entered, those working at desks sneaked furtive glances as he walked by. Werner had moved some piles of paper around his office to give some illusion of order; he knew Rohm expected to be accorded special status. He even prepared a bottle of schnapps to offer him a drink, a gesture that would not have been considered for any other interview. George sat slightly behind his father, notepad in hand. His father nodded, and George realized that was his signal to pour shots for the commander of the SA—the Oberster SA-Fuhrer and his father. George tried to keep his hand from shaking. *I have just returned from Palestine—a land of swamps, malaria, Arabs, and moments of terrorism. I can do this.*

"So, we begin," said Rohm, stretching out his legs perhaps to accentuate his highly shined black boots and his large body.

George watched his father raise his glass and take a slow, deliberate sip and thought it was like watching a chess game. It was his father's interview to lead, to take control, to dominate. He would not be intimidated by this man's reputation as a swashbuckler with a predilection for running directly into danger. His father was a newspaper editor out to get a story and would know precisely how to move the pieces to get what he wanted.

George, though, was surprised at his father's opening question. "Do you know Christopher Isherwood?"

"That is your first question? I'm the Commandant of the SA. It is not for me to know about writers coming to Berlin."

George made a quick note. Of course, the Commandant knew Isherwood. Why would he have said anything about writers in Berlin? The homosexual community was small, and although Rohm may have been reluctant to talk about it in this interview, George knew the soldier had been quite open about going to Berlin's gay clubs. Hitler had hinted that he wanted to close them down, that they were marring his perfect Aryan vision. Maybe it was Rohm's influence that kept them open.

"I only mentioned him because we just interviewed Isherwood recently over his latest book," said Werner casually, hoping that the conversational tone and schnapps would keep the interview relaxed. He looked down at his notes and moved on. "Many of your SA members come from working-class backgrounds, and I think they were hoping for more pro-union support from you."

Werner had done his homework. Some newspapers still dared to print news against the new regime, and he knew that one of the conflicts worthy of investigation was between the three million SA men led by Rohm and the regular German army. The authorized German military only had 100,000 men. The Treaty of Versailles had limited the legal army. Three million "informal" SA members were Germany's way of breaking free and defying the hated treaty. And Ernest Rohm eagerly led them.

Rohm leaned forward, ready with a reply.

"They will understand that the new chancellor needs my men and me to keep order right now. The pro-union support will come. Look how many Nazi flags are flying. People want structure."

George waited to see how his father was going to pursue the interview. Werner knew that the business community was unhappy with roving gangs seeking dominance. Businesses wanted orderliness in the streets but were not sure that control through threats of violence should be the order of the day.

Werner let Rohm press on. "Look, I will tell you something that your readers will like. We need a revolution against the capitalists. My people will help make that happen. They will follow me to make that happen." He paused, reaching for a cigarette, lighting it, and taking a drag with an air of insolent insouciance. "You're Jewish, right?" he said, and George couldn't figure out if this were a statement or a question. "How come you and your family are not in the banking business? That's where all the Jews are." He flicked an ash into the ashtray.

Werner took a sip from his glass, ignoring the question. It would be foolish to explain why Berlin had so many Jewish bankers when Jews were only one percent of the population. Instead, he asked a question about Rohm's childhood. It brought a smile to the commandant's face, and he seemed content to prattle on about an idyllic family life.

"I think we have enough to impress our readers, and I don't want to take up any more of your valuable time," Werner finally said, rising from his chair to indicate the interview was over. He knew he wasn't going to get any more from him other than propaganda and the need to elevate his SA thugs and eliminate or combine the old guard with them.

Rohm stood, lifted his right arm, and raised his voice almost to a shout. "Heil Hitler!" and he strode out of the office. Father and son watched, horrified as half of the office staff stood with right arms held high and repeated the salute as the officer proudly passed by their desks. Fortunately, Rohm did not turn around to see those who remained seated but kept his eyes focused ahead and walked out with military bearing. George did notice that those who saluted seemed keenly aware of comrades who had not similarly responded. Their eyes said that they had observed.

Werner took a drink that emptied the shot glass. "I have enough for a story. I'll slant it to read that he is the leader of a group of strong supporters of the new regime. It should pass Goebbels' propaganda machine, no doubt." He sighed. "And that, my son, is why Germany is in such trouble. We only get to write half-truths."

~~~

Der Tagblatt never printed the Ernest Rohm article. Almost immediately after the interview, the German government found reason to imprison the soldier. He had come under the ever-watchful eye of Himmler, who felt that the military leader was gaining too much power and conceived of a plot to convict him of attempting to overthrow the government. In an uncharacteristic moment of compassion, Hitler agreed that Rohm should not be executed but should have the choice of suicide. Rohm refused to take the pistol handed to him, and one of his guards shot him.

That was the story the *Der Tagblatt* ran, and the writer said nothing about Rohm's visit to the newspaper. George submitted an article about rowing in Palestine, but it never passed editorial scrutiny, and his father never argued with them. The ability to do his assessment of Rohm during the interview and the subsequent events further convinced George of the need to leave Germany. He thought his father was beginning to think so as well.

CHAPTER 27

More often than not, for the past month or so, George would return home from school or rowing practice to hear music from the living room and find his mother with three other musicians practicing a classical quartet. He was happy to see that the other violinist was Clara, his mother's most promising student. He recognized the violist and cellist as Carl Furstenberg and Ernst Salmonsohn—long-time orchestra members. He sometimes wondered if they were Jewish and had also lost their positions.

He smiled to see books and sheets of music strewn on the floor. As disciplined as his mother was in time and attention to the violin, she was equally lax in her placement of music, especially when she was playing and coaching. The musicianship was critical; putting the music away in its proper place on the bookshelf would come later.

Today it was Fanny Mendelssohn's *String Quartet in Eb Major*—George was almost sure, but he would check with his mother later. She had told him that she was interested in promoting Fanny's music. To him, it sounded like harmonious perfection, just like that feeling one gets when everyone is in sync in a boat—when the oars feather together, and the ripples react as though everyone put his blade in the water at the same mini-second. That wasn't true for his mother because she called a halt in the middle of the andante section of the sonata. "There's no need to rush," he heard her say. He also noted she was trying to contain the tension in her voice. "Let's take it from measure fifteen. Remember, it's andante, not allegro."

He knew of her sense of precision in music. Yet, she would often question the need to start from the beginning when the beginning was already perfect. Frieda had repeatedly expressed her dissatisfaction with conductors who insisted the orchestra commence from the first measure when a mistake was made. The music from the beginning already played in her head so she could pick up wherever she thought necessary. She encouraged her students to do the same.

George recognized his mother's anxiety. Recently, waiting expectantly to be called back to play in her old chair, she expressed some desire to see the conductor, Boris Solomon. What had given her hope? She had told George that she was encouraged by the fact that even though the government had declared a National Day of Mourning for the fallen of the National Democratic Socialist Party as a result of SA gangs leading streets riots, only half the number of people on the street were flying the flag with its Nazi symbol. Maybe, just maybe, the country could be saved.

George puttered around in the kitchen, toasting a piece of pumpernickel on a radiant toaster that got its heat from the gas burner because his father just didn't believe that electric toasters were necessary. It was sort of the same way with his attitude towards a car. "You've got two legs and a bicycle. Two hands on the handles, and it's good for a beating heart," his father would say if someone broached the subject. George smeared apricot jam on the toast he had managed to pull off the metal toaster at just the right moment of brownness and was going to sit down to eat when he heard the scraping of chairs. Was this a good time to talk to this group about the dangers to this country? Did they think, as he did, Germany was headed toward fascism? He had not discussed it with his mother; he knew she would be reluctant.

When Frieda saw her son with a piece of toast about to enter the living room, she raised her hand and waved him back. "You don't come to this room with food. You know that."

George flushed as he made up his mind. "I'll put it back but could everyone wait a minute." He quickly returned the toast to the kitchen and immediately returned as students were getting their jackets. "Wait, please," he said, trying to quell his agitation. "They're going to need musicians. I know Toscanini is thinking of going. Look, there are 60,000 Germans already on their way. You know, mother, you've always talked about the importance of music to have a rich and full life."

Frieda feigned a smile at her son's impulsivity. "George, you haven't started at the first paragraph, which I'm not sure my musicians even want to hear."

George watched the solemn expressions on the faces of his mother's musician friends. He hesitated and then continued. "I'm sorry I started in the middle. I'm talking about going to Palestine. That's where the future is going to be . . . for us. Not here." He waited a few seconds before adding, "And what about Toscanini? He's not coming for the Bayreuth Festival." Frieda was surprised at his knowledge of Toscanini. Did her unmusical son know Furtwangler and Klemperer, she wondered? Did he know of Klemperer's

Jewish background? It didn't matter in music, though. Inspiration and talent counted.

Frieda had heard this plea many times since George had first been approached by the Zionists in London and even more so since his return from Palestine. However, it was the first time he had ever taken it upon himself to confront her music ensemble students. She looked over at Clara. She appeared to be besotted with George and, at the same time, trying to decipher the meaning of his words. Frieda was aware that Clara worshipped at a Catholic church that had expressed opposition to the SA tactics and Goebbels' propaganda.

Suddenly, Frieda became bold. "You all attend a Catholic church. Yes?" With that question, George realized they were not Jewish.

They nodded cautiously, uncertain as to where they stood in the cycle of the conversation.

"What has your priest said?" Frieda almost demanded.

Carl Furstenberg took a small step forward. "Hitler has expressed anti-Christian sentiments as well. He will use religion to divide where it suits him. Uncertainty is just as relevant a political tactic as is bullying or threatening."

"But Hitler is supposed to like music. Richard Strauss is thrilled that we finally have a chancellor that values opera," said Ernest Salmonsohn.

Frieda thought this was a time to relate that Strauss also said Wagner would be played non-stop because he proclaimed that Jews suffer from *Untergang* and *Selbstvernichtung*—destruction and self-annihilation. She looked at George and hoped he saw her expression. Would he please move this discussion along since he had started the conversation?

"The Toscanini letter in *The New York Times*. What's that supposed to mean?" said George, continuing with his theme of citing the beloved conductor.

"You saw that, too," said Carl, waving the bow of his violin excitedly in the air. "I saw that and thought that man has something special in his soul, and maybe our music-loving Fuhrer will take heed, and orchestra leaders will stop boycotting Jewish musicians."

"Well, clearly, Arturo doesn't believe it because he's not coming for the Bayreuth festival. Maybe he would, but he knows of Wagner's anti-Semitic reputation," said Frieda. Frieda had long been following Toscanini's career and lovingly referred to him as Arturo since he started conducting the New York Philharmonic. She had always valued the role of conductor—the person necessary to make musicality and timing come together.

"There," said George. "You have Arturo's brilliant mind understanding it." He turned to Clara who had remained silent. "And how do you feel, Clara?"

"Don't push her," said Frieda. "She came here for playing music—not for a political discussion." Clara gave her a quiet nod of gratitude.

"Who can deny the fear of "Blood and Soil?" said Carl. George smiled. He had an ally in Carl. "After all, we are not all born to be farmers."

"And no one was born to be defined by race," added George. He looked directly at his mother. "I'm sure . . . despite Hitler's propaganda that we will become a master race and we will all work off the land to be good Germans."

Frieda knew of Hitler's love of *Parsifal* and tried to discern what it could mean that he loved this libretto—the pure fool who comes to understand the world, the Holy Spear, the Holy Grail, Kundry, the female version of the Wandering Jew killed by Parsifal as he holds the spear aloft. Was he sentimental? Did simple stories appeal to him? Did he reject Christianity or love it? She often tried to broach the subject with Werner, who said there were more important things to worry about.

"And there is Richard Strauss," Frieda said. All those standing amidst the awkward conversation in the hallway knew of Richard Strauss's apparent ambivalence as head of the Reich Music Chamber. Strauss's doubts were evident in the conflict between the words of the governmental decree that offered reasons for getting rid of Jewish composers and his continued performances of Mendelssohn, Meyerbeer, and Mahler. He didn't think that composers needed to promote the Aryan ideal. Excellent music was excellent music and spoke for itself. Frieda continued, "What was Strauss going to do with Jewish Stefan Zweig as his librettist for *Die schweigsame frau* [*The Silent Woman*] when it was brilliant music?"

"What would you think of going to a place that desperately needs music, music teachers? Kurt Weill has already left." He noticed that Clara paid particular attention to this last comment. Seeing Weill's *The Threepenny Opera* together and expressing their love of it had marked the beginning of their romance. He hoped so anyway; he knew it had been a special day for them despite the intrusion by a gang of SA teenagers.

"But he has gone to America," said Ernst. "I know of others leaving, and Hollywood seems to have a particular attraction." He grimaced. "Not for me, though."

"Not everyone can be a Marlene Dietrich," said Carl. "I also noticed that she's not coming back to Germany, and if she has the opportunity to say something negative about Hitler, she takes it. But we can't all be that courageous," he mused. "And we can't go to America without jobs. She was a famous actress here before she left, remember?"

George was not ready to give up. Although the musicians had been poised to leave, they all remained standing in the hallway. "So, at the end of every concert, could you stand, raise your right arm and shout Sieg Heil? You would join a political party because you were required to do so to have a job even though you opposed everything it stood for?" George surprised himself at the fierceness of his argument and avoided looking over at his mother because he knew she would be disapproving of his tone of voice.

He continued. "And where is Thomas Mann who saw the handwriting on the wall when his books were burned? Is he still in Germany?" The author had gone into exile, and some had mentioned Switzerland as his current place of residence.

Clara took the question as rhetorical. "It is time to go, George. Thank you, Frieda, for such excellent coaching. Same time, next week?" Frieda sighed as the other musicians rushed out the door, seemingly relieved at the cue to leave.

Maybe, they will, at least, start to think about the dangers of staying here, George told himself.

Frieda drew in a long breath, and George heard relief in her sigh as she exhaled. He followed her into the kitchen, where she had gone to dice onions to prepare for dinner. She used onions as the basis for nearly all her dishes, frying them in butter or oil, depending on what was available, to add flavor to whatever dish she was making. The tears were flowing. She looked up from the task. "It's the onions. It's just the onions. Why don't you find some music on the radio to distract me?"

George turned up the radio in the living room so she could hear it in the kitchen. An American woman, Ethel Waters, was singing "Stormy Weather."

Should he tell his mother that this is what democracy brings—a Negro woman singing music written by two Jews? He watched as his mother prepared for dinner and listened to the song. He noticed she still had tears in her eyes, although she had long ago finished dicing onions.

CHAPTER 28

George stood outside Professor Ziegler's classroom door and glanced at the notes for the assigned reading, Remarque's *All Quiet on the Western Front*. He was late, but the lecture hall was only one-quarter full. He thought— maybe only twelve students. Yes, he remembered, some students had decided they would boycott the class when the professor had assigned the book. After all, Remarque's book had been part of the book burning by the German Student Union students. Still, until this point, the university had allowed professors freedom to teach their curriculum. At the same time, George knew that classes depended on student enrollment. He wondered what Professor Ziegler's decision would be about assigning a grade for those who didn't attend. Another anti-intellectual student protest, George thought.

Werner had told him *All Quiet on the Western Fron*t was an important book and "would probably be read in school rooms for the next fifty years," his father had said unequivocally. "Even though some think the German soldiers weren't depicted as heroes. But war is hell. Isn't it? Isn't that what Remarque was trying to say?" George had sensed at that moment his father wasn't looking for a response from him. He remembered how proud his father had been when his newspaper had printed Remarque's book in serial form.

As a family, they had gone to see the movie adaptation in Berlin's Mozart Hall. They were upset when the next night, 150 Nazi SA members decided to enter the theater shouting "Judenfilm."

"I mean, did those thugs know that Lewis Milestone and Carl Laemmle were Jewish, or partly Jewish?" sputtered his father. "Is that why? Something is wrong here. I know because, at the newspaper, the movie editor wrote a positive review while Goebbels tried to prevent it from being shown. But word got out about how good the movie is. You can't stop word of mouth, can you? Besides, movies are the palaces of wonderful escapism. You deny people places to forget their ordinary lives and partake in drama; you might as well give up on life." George knew his father was speaking from his heart and head—he felt about free speech the way his mother felt about music. Both his parents had shown him that strong passion for anything worthwhile could promote a life of courage, which meant attempting to overcome the most daunting obstacles.

"Need I say the words, 'handwriting on the wall again?'" Frieda had asked. "And what is Jewish about a film that paints the horrors of war? Isn't Remarque being nominated for a Nobel Peace Prize a good thing?" Frieda, who had been schooled and raised in music competitions, was always keenly aware of announcements of international prizes.

George had reminded them that he had to read the book as an assignment from Professor Ziegler, so maybe Fredrich Wilhelm university was still in the good graces of the government. Or maybe there weren't enough SA thugs to go around. George imagined that the commandant strategically deployed them to have substantial impact and create terror. He also suspected that fewer people would now see the movie: random attacks instilled fear. But copies of the book were still available—maybe not in public libraries, but at underground bookstores, at the right time of evening. Again, word of mouth was critical since the government had decreed that all private copies were to be turned over to the Gestapo.

George took his seat behind the row of fifteen students. He continued to strive to be a reporter; he hoped to observe students' reactions to the professor and, thus, the book. Also, he wanted to know what made these fifteen students so different from the rest of the eighty others who did not show up. Jewish? Courageous? Defiant? Backbone of steel? Unaware?

George saw that Ziegler had written on the board, "Why is this an anti-war book? Why is the government opposed to the book and the movie?"

The answers to the first question came rapidly from students who had been taught to stand when they answered. After each student spoke, and Professor Ziegler had nodded to acknowledge the answer, he would turn to the next student with a hand raised. George wondered if this nearly military decorum was expected at other universities. He tried to make notes of their comments.

"Soldiers are shown with shattered limbs. Also, horses are destroyed." Somehow this student felt compelled to add, "I imagine that animal lovers would find this part very hard."

"The men are starving. The government doesn't do a decent job feeding them. So, they look through garbage for food."

"The commanding officers are shown almost as depraved. It is the young recruits who do all the dirty work."

George tried to note the students' names who spoke, hoping to talk to them after class. Did the book influence them to embrace the anti-war theory, or was there something in their home life that made them think this way?

His thinking was interrupted. "And you, Mr. Grossinger?" George stood up sharply when the professor called on him directly. He thought Ziegler looked more worried than usual.

"It's death and destruction. The troops do not stand up well to the onslaught, although there are a few who could be called heroes." George sat down quickly.

"So, what do you think of Paul Baumer? Hero or not?"

George wondered if Ziegler directed this query solely to him. He knew this question pierced the heart and soul of the novel. Could one consider Baumer a hero because the soldier suffered from, yet returned to, fighting? He didn't think he could frame his response coherently.

Fortunately, the ordinarily passive Gregor Reich stood up. "No, he felt too much pain and remorse when he stabbed the French soldier. That is not what one needs to do to be considered a hero. You cannot worry about the enemy. Baumer was not a hero."

The professor waved his hand, indicating that Reich should sit.

Fredrick Furstenberg stood. "I think our leaders would like a fairy tale depiction of the German soldier—always in the right, always winning, always strong. Never thinking twice about killing the human right next to them who could be a brother, a son, a husband, and important to someone's family."

George looked up from his notes, trying to see Furstenberg's facial expression because he couldn't quite get the tone of voice. Was it bordering on sarcasm or matter of fact?

He didn't have the opportunity to finish his observation because Gustav Hagen stood immediately. George was startled to see him wearing a Nazi armband. He should not have been surprised at the words that came out of his mouth.

"The Treaty of Versailles still is like a cloud over our heads. It is the Jews and Marxists who contributed to our defeat. This book makes it seem as though our German soldiers are weak." George held his breath as Gustav raised his right hand and shouted, "Heil Hitler." Gregor Reich jumped up and imitated Hagen and then turned to the students who had remained sitting in stunned silence. "Do we honor Germany of today, or do we not? This book must be banned forever."

George watched Professor Ziegler sit down at his desk, shoulders slumped, closing Remarque's book gently. He knew that Hagen and Reich were waiting for the rest of the students to give the salute. In that instance, George thought, I want to be alive and not in prison so I can leave. Trying to control his trembling, he stood and shouted, "Heil Hitler." All the other students followed and, without waiting to be formally dismissed, left the classroom.

George, the last to leave, scribbled a note to Professor Ziegler and left it quietly on the desk. "You need to think of leaving." George didn't know what the professor had decided to do because when he went to class the next day, the sign on the door said, "Class is canceled." George decided that he would hide his copy of *All Quiet on the Western Front* in a safe place where it would be difficult for a stranger to find.

CHAPTER 29

Colonel Robert Moss sat behind his desk at 70 Whitehall Street, shifting reports from one spot to another, reading a paragraph from one piece of paper and then from another with the fleeting thought that he would soon need reading glasses. He worried that any habit of concentration had been entirely lost or forgotten. It was as though the bureaucrats at Number 10 Downing Street thought the Palestine fiasco could be solved with reams of paper and words that only added to the dilemma. And conferences. He could not begin to count the number of times the Ministry had invited Zionists and Arabs to sit around a conference table—usually huge—to help them see that two peoples could live on this one piece of land. They could each acknowledge the history of Jesus' birthplace; they just had to learn to accept each other as having rightful access to this malaria-possessed, water-deprived area.

The 1920 San Remo Conference decided England was to prepare Palestine for self-rule, but how does that happen with a squabbling family questioning who had sired the children? It was one of the biblical tales that even God found hard to resolve. Moreover, it was one thing to fight the organized army of a country—quite something else to fight its terrorists' groups that did not follow the rules of international warfare. The 175,000 Palestinian Jews no longer believed all they needed to do was dodge and escape when they were threatened; they included a new breed now committed to fighting back and protecting their land.

Every day it seemed more strife occurred that needed to be sorted. Receiving illegal ships with desperate Jews from Poland and Lithuania was nearly manageable. Just deny entry and force them to turn away. But resolving the fighting between the Husseinis and the Nashasibis families was another story. Clan warfare was like terrorist warfare—impossible to control or decipher with its unpredictable but threatening behavior. Colonel Robert Moss was beginning to tire of it all; it wasn't what the British had signed up for after Balfour.

The intercom buzzed. Moss took a swig from the silver flask kept in his drawer for such moments of tension. He had been waiting for Captain Ben

Leicester to arrive from Palestine and give his assessment directly, for that was the only way Moss could come close to the truth and perhaps arrive at some reconciliation of the problem. Moss knew that most of the British military favored the Arabs; a few understood the history of the Jews. But he knew Ben Leicester had a visionary's hope. The young captain had spoken of his dream to get these two people to live peacefully alongside each other on a narrow, slight stretch of land. Ben didn't share the British concern about the Arabs' ability and inclination to limit the British government's access to its oil fields. On the other hand, he didn't think issues should all be about oil—and possible access to the Suez Canal.

Leicester entered, saluted sharply, and surveyed the office. It had been a while since he had been back in England, let alone in direct contact with his supervising Colonel. Prime Minister Ramsey McDonald's photo hung on a wall behind Moss alongside King George V in military regalia. After returning the customary salute, Moss asked Leicester to take a seat.

"He won't be here long," Moss said, turning to look at McDonald's photo. "Getting old. It's Stanley Baldwin and Neville Chamberlain who are running the country." He reached for a paper on his desk. "Just received a release that Churchill is warning us about the rise of Nazi power under Hitler. He's unhappy about German rearmament." He reshuffled the paper. "But that's not why you're here." He looked up—eyes focused. "Is it?"

Leicester drew a breath and shook his head. "In a way, that's why I'm here. The Arabs want their independence. There's no doubt about that. And in nearly every household I enter, they see the Jews who are arriving as interlopers taking up their land—despite many Jews being there for years. They want us to throw the Jews out or find some way to destroy them. But the Jews are desperate to leave Germany. And Palestine is their most welcoming destination."

Moss made his customary gesture of interlocking his fingers and placing them under his chin. "Even though the Arabs are getting money for that land and turning it over to the Jews, deeds and all." Moss had taken time to study some of the land transactions—unlike British real estate transactions, after all, these people never had the Magna Carta and were still living under tribal rule—and he thought to himself, never uttering the words aloud, "they don't understand the rule of law—not even Islamic law."

"The Arabs feel they're being taken advantage of, so they're seeking revenge," said Ben. "They started by just vandalizing orchards that are important to the Jews, but there are murmurings that they're going to ramp up their operations to demolish what railroad tracks are in place. People who depended on their land are now landless."

"You've come here to tell me what I already know. Tell me how to solve the problem."

Ben hesitated. "I've already begun. I've started a rowing program between the Jewish and Arab youth, and I did it with six boats—old ones, sir—that arrived from German rowing clubs."

Moss's hands unfolded. He began to drum his fingers on the desk. "I don't mean to sound more cynical than usual, but I can't seem to help myself in this case. You want to solve murders, arson, revenge, lawlessness through rowing? I mean, these people are still celebrating Saladin's capture of Jerusalem in the twelfth century." Moss reached for his flask, poured some whiskey into a glass, and offered it to Ben. "I just can't seem to get through a day without some of this recently."

Ben decided to ignore the irrelevant bigotry of his commanding officer. "I have a way—a possibility," said Ben, taking a sip rather than a swig of the whiskey. He wanted to remain clear headed throughout his narrative. He proceeded to explain how these two young German rowers, George Grossinger and Arthur Schwartz, had come to Palestine through Zionist connections, managed to smuggle in sculls, and had given young people in the village—both Arab and Jews—rowing lessons, which seemed to relieve some of the tension. It could even begin to build trust.

"Go on," said Moss. "Although I've outgrown my belief in fairy tales, I'm always up for a good story. And I also know that the Arabs will never beat us or conquer the newly arrived Jews. As I've said, they're leaving places they never want to go back to."

"These rowers want to come to Palestine to live. Their families see the danger in Germany and want to settle there. They need our help." He said these words quietly but with a forceful simplicity, almost as a preparation for the Colonel's angry response.

"There are all these damn Jewish Agencies to help them. It's as though they've flooded the universe with organizations trying to help Jews."

"These 'damn Jewish Agencies,' as you call them, do not know the worldwide rowing community—hate to stereotype, but they were not traditionally rowers. Their backgrounds were more like tailors and scholars," said Ben, realizing he was skating on thin ice with his history. He understood

Moss knew no more than he did, and Moss was also dealing in hyperbole. They were not "flooding the universe." Instead, they were hoping to help people escape persecution and find freedom.

Leicester moved his swivel chair closer to the desk and took another small sip as he watched Moss continue to drink from the flask. "I want to use the resources of the British Mandate to help two families get there. They have two young men who will help the rowing program grow," he said somberly. "Look, it may not bring peace between Arabs and Jews, but it's not going to hurt either. We don't want governing to be turned back over to the League of Nations. They gave the Mandate to the British because they thought we could do it. The words are imprinted in my heart: 'to provide administrative advice and assistance by a Mandatory until such time as they can stand alone.' Isn't that what everyone wants? Stand alone and stand alongside each other peacefully. That's what the Balfour Declaration intended."

Colonel Robert Moss took in the earnestness of Ben Leicester, who reminded him of himself when he was younger and more idealistic—much more idealistic, in fact. *I guess I should be thanking God that there are still people who just think we need to do good deeds, and everything will be all right. Peace on earth and all that stuff.*

"I don't need a history lesson," Moss said testily. "I need you to tell me just exactly how you think this should be done. Building a rowing program in a country caught up in draining swamps, absorbing refugees, and fighting riots?"

Ben hesitated. "We're going to have to turn to the London Zionists for help." He tried to ignore Moss's startled expression that turned into a stare. "Of course, we'll verify that they are not caught up with Haganah, let alone Irgun gangsters."

Ben, fortunately, already had that assurance from George Grossinger. Ben had found out that George had maintained contact with the men who had kidnapped him to get the boats to Palestine. Chaim Halevi, Abraham Felder, Joshua Greenberg, and Ron Schwartzman were names that Ben Leicester never thought would enter his universe but right now, their names were written on a piece of paper that George had given him. They would help. They were the English Zionists, and wasn't Sir Herbert Samuel, High Commissioner of Palestine, a Zionist?

"Shall I set up an invitation, sir?" Ben asked

Ben thought Schwartzman and Felder should be invited to Robert

Moss's office at Whitehall. They were the most English of all the Zionists in manners and affect. But the Colonel would not be serving glasses of tea as a courteous gesture. Ben saw the meeting as a contest of Zionists convincing and winning Moss over because the reputation of the English had somewhat soured from the time of the Mandate. They were not bringing peace to the region, and neither were they pleasing the hearts and minds of the Arabs.

"Go ahead. Just give me some lead time so that I can be prepared for ungodly earnestness," muttered Moss.

"So?" said Schwartzman happily, taking the whiskey offered to him by Colonel Moss. He tossed it back quickly, avoiding the look he knew Abraham Felder was sending him. Felder had warned him to behave as though he were in a room with a man of authority, not schmoozing with friends. Politeness, attentiveness, and strict limits on sarcasm would be appreciated in this round of discussion. As Zionists, Schwartzman and Felder wanted to do whatever they could to help refugees get to Palestine. Still, they knew the Zionists' group was entirely dependent on the British—the ones in command both here and there—for military support.

"Good to have a schnapps with both of you military gentlemen, but I know we are here for a specific reason," said Schwartzman, who received a quiet nod from his friends to take the lead, to be the spokesman.

Leicester looked to Moss, whose body language was basically at rest. Ben interpreted this to mean that he was to take the lead for the British military. Moss would jump in when he thought necessary.

Leicester made his case as forcefully as he knew how. Leicester knew how to make boats move through water with both his mind and body. Now he would have to use his mind and words; he wanted them to be convinced to give these men a reason to fight as passionately as him to bring rowing to Palestine, but he would have to address the appeal with clarity. He drew a breath.

"Gentlemen. I would like you to help specific German families and help them to come to Palestine. Their son and his friend are competitive rowers, and it's what . . . it's what Palestine needs to survive." He took another breath and resumed before anyone could say anything because he knew that was an outlandish statement. "Well, not exactly survive, but it will build strength and character for a flourishing country, and I know that's what you are all about." He had decided ahead of time that he would end his appeal with a compliment.

"So," said Schwartzman, stretching out his legs in front of him. "So, you are asking us for imagination, courage . . . and, of course, money." He wanted to linger on this moment—a moment when Zionists were being called upon to help the British military. He looked at Felder and hoped he understood this point in history was to be savored.

Felder was staring out the window. Their temporary capture of George and Arthur in London had paid off in an unexpected way. Who would have thought that such a daring deed would bring them into the office of Colonel Robert Moss?

"Yes, yes," said Leicester. "But we will also give you our military support when appropriate. We want to help that family leave Germany. Right now, we know there are grandparents involved and parents who have given their professional lives to Germany. You need to convince them to leave, let them know they will receive help." He looked toward Moss, who he could see was not going to say anything. "We will do what we can to help," Leicester added.

Felder held out his glass to Leicester. "One for the road," he said. He quickly drank it and said, "We will get back to you." His quick approach to the door indicated to Schwartzman no more words needed to be exchanged.

Leicester thought that was a good sign before he sank into the chair with exhaustion.

"Not even a thank you," said Moss.

"We don't need a thank you. We need 'yes, we will help,'" said Leicester. "Maybe even time to send up a prayer."

CHAPTER *30*

The atmosphere at the Hebrew Rowing Club simmered with anticipation and anxiety for Martin Wilder and Amos Schindler, active members since the club's founding in 1920. Would George Grossinger and Arthur Schwartz be able to coach new rowers to become confident and competitive? The older long-time members stood at the club's balcony overlooking the Spree, running a bit fast because of last night's rain. The gray Saturday morning sky was not promising. Despite last night's downpour, the river was rowable and Wilder wasn't surprised to see two singles already pushing off from the dock. Wilder understood that many rowers appreciated the river's calm at dawn when there were fewer boats with which to contend. Good rowers always knew they had to be aware of coming close to another boat behind them to avoid collisions. They needed to gather momentum and move to the proper lane to outpace and not interfere with other boats. Schindler noticed some rowers almost had a sixth sense of whether they were close to another boat, while others turned heads every twelve strokes to make sure.

George and Arthur stood on the dock, waiting for the new rowers to arrive. They were to begin coaching recruits, all in their senior year of university, who had never rowed before. They had told the students they wanted to prepare them for the Olympics—that was going to be their level of training, but both Schindler and Wilder knew another motive existed—recruit them for Palestine.

How exactly they were going to do that was still up for question. George and Arthur's trip there had made them dedicated Zionists. Wilder knew that many in the club were Zionists. Still, they were Zionists because they committed themselves to imitate and promote a Jew of strength—wanting to eliminate the stereotypical image of a bearded Jew with Talmud in hand for study. Many German Jews had adopted the "Jew of strength" image since Herzel came to the fore with Zionism in the late 1800s and adapted to German culture. If Zionism promoted the land of Palestine as the place where Jews would thrive, they must be physically fit to build it as their nation. The Hebrew Rowing Club had been established and flourished with the philosophy of the assimilated secular Jew. Could the Third Reich make them give up their respected place in German society? How worried should they be because a flag with a swastika was flying on the balcony of a boathouse down the river?

"You think the rowers will show up?" mused Schindler.

"Are you talking to yourself or me?" said Wilder.

"Both, I think."

"Do you think they understand that this could be a fool's errand, or should I say a fool's rowing practice?"

"You mean because Germany barely earned bronze for bobsled in the Winter Olympics at Lake Placid?" Schindler answered himself. "It was still worldwide depression in 1932. No resources. People were starving. You need food in your belly to compete."

Wilder couldn't resist. "And now, we're swimming in money?"

"No, but it's rowing. You know everything is possible in rowing." Schindler put his arm around his friend's shoulder. "Otherwise, we wouldn't still be here in these Godforsaken times."

"You're right," said Wilder. "And 1936 could be an entirely different year. Germany could be a completely different country with Hitler." Schindler glared at him. "No more talking." They saw three young men out on the dock being greeted by George and Arthur—it was time to observe.

George and Arthur smiled as soon as three young men arrived. Fortunately, the morning was quiet, and the dock was large enough for what they had planned. They politely shook hands.

"We are going to begin, gentlemen, with push-ups," said George. "We do not wait for everyone to arrive before we begin since standing around does nobody any good. Arthur will demonstrate. You follow him." They had completed twenty-five push-ups when six more young men arrived. After a brief handshake and getting a signal from George, the new arrivals joined in. All were dressed in short-sleeved white T-shirts and shorts. They followed the instructions to wear clothing that fit rather tight to the body because loose fabric could get caught in oar handles.

George directed. "Stop when you've reached fifty." He watched to see who did the push-ups in rhythm, who did them accurately copying Arthur's motion, who maintained self-discipline by focusing solely on themselves, and who seemed exhilarated and excited at the end. George had heard that there were countries using rowing machines. One of the English Zionists had told him. But no rowing machines existed in this club and, as far as he knew, or in any of the others. Since depicting the rowing stroke on a machine was not possible, George and Arthur brought out a straight pair to the edge of the dock, having hoisted it overhead from the boathouse, and with precision turned it into the water hull side down. The oars were already ready on the dock. George and Arthur were going to serve as examples of model rowers, demonstrating right from the boat.

"Watch," was all Arthur said, and he knelt and inserted an oar into the oarlock, knowing all eyes were on him. "Much easier on the starboard side," he said. "You'll need to put one foot in the boat to reach port side, or else have a long reach."

Together, they silently appraised the young men, all nearly six feet in height, and whose bodies showed power in their calves and thighs. They also probably didn't realize how lucky they were to have boats that were well maintained and cared for by the club's members.

Just how exactly am I going to do this, George wondered, placing his foot in the rigger to make sure the boat didn't float away. In two strokes, we will be far away from the dock, and these young men will not hear me. They will not be able to connect anything I'm demonstrating with words. They need both. He must have telegraphed his worried look to Arthur. They both looked up at Schindler and Wilder, standing on the balcony, observing. The next thing Arthur and George and nine recruits knew was that two elderly, very fit gentlemen had come down the steps and joined them on the dock.

"We will explain again," said Schindler, "while George and Arthur demonstrate once more." George observed the glint in Schindler's eyes. The long-time coach had happily done this from the capacity of his launch many times, and he had the steps, directions, and movements clearly in his head.

"They're going to place the second set of blades in the metal oarlocks, which will serve as a fulcrum. I'm assuming you all understand what the purpose of a fulcrum is. Good. Only in this case, the oar is not at rest in a fulcrum; it's going to pivot." Schindler saw the blank expression in some. "Just watch."

George knelt to place the second set of wooden oars in the oarlocks. He felt eyes upon him and hoped he demonstrated a certain ease.

"Now, simultaneously, they will grab the handle of the oar, place a right foot on the seat—remember, not in the hull," Wilder said, raising his voice slightly, "lower backsides, extending left foot into the strap, and then the right foot. There, gentlemen, if you have successfully done that without flipping your boat and falling into the water, you are halfway there." The young men watching glanced at each other, some bemused, some worried. Wilder practically danced with joy as he gave his commands. He had enjoyed seeing nervous beginners grow into confident athletes. He also loved reminding accomplished rowers that they had once been tentative beginners.

"Now, notice how they are fidgeting, extending their legs, and pulling the blade handle to their breastbone. They are wiggling to adjust the foot stretcher to the proper size." Schindler noted perplexity on some of the boys' faces. "Don't worry, gentlemen. We will be there to help you as you get into your eight."

George, in the bow, pulled in the starboard oar to his chest bone and angled it so he could push away from the dock.

"Observe," said Schindler. "I know exactly what's in their heads because it's all about timing to balance this extraordinary boat." Wilder smiled because he knew that Schindler had a love affair with the coxless pair, and because it was so challenging, few members at the club cared to take it on and resisted coaching. The port side and starboard side rowers had to achieve perfect balance and synchronicity to keep the boat stable and move quickly. He turned to the young men watching, and with his back to the river, he said, "I'm going to call out what they're doing because I know these words are in their head. Watch how they connect with their bodies." He turned briefly to watch the pair and estimated they had a stroke rate of about twenty-six. He addressed the nine standing almost at attention and said in a rhythm that perfectly matched the rowers—'legs, body, arms, arms, body, legs. That's their mantra, and it will continue stroke after stroke until they decide to change the rate."

George and Arthur rowed with precision for about 500 meters and turned, so they remained within view of the recruits. As they were returning to the dock, they could see Eric Cohen, Walter Fuchs, Robert Mueller, Emil Hagen, Carl Klitzing, Oscar Rathenau, Emil Silberberg, Paul Ditmar, and coxswain Gordon Tornow coming to the edge of the dock to better observe their return and landing. Were these potential recruits for Palestine?

Schindler shouted, "Watch their bodies. Relaxed. Together."

George and Arthur gracefully rowed back to the dock with George lifting the starboard oar and Arthur holding the port oar on the water for stability, both leaning away an inch until the starboard oar settled on the

dock. Sometimes the bow ball at the back of the boat would hit the dock—
but in this case, it was a perfect landing. George and Arthur couldn't be sure,
but Schindler and Wilder seemed pleased. The new students watched with
fierce concentration.

Schindler walked up to George and Arthur as they stepped out of the
boat. "Now, you teach them in the eight. How to carry the boat, right?
You will teach them the discipline, the coordination, right?" George could
recognize Schindler's anxiety. Getting men out in an eight for the first time
with a relatively inexperienced coxswain was daunting. Wilder continued.
"We will put this boat away while you show them how to bring down the
eight."

Arthur motioned to the recruits to gather at the eight. George gave the
sharp command.

"Gentlemen, you will position yourself with four on one side and four
on the other side of the eight. Hoist the boat onto your shoulder. Walk it
carefully down to the dock's edge. Your coxswain will lead the way. Raise it
above your head with two hands. You will carefully swing the boat over in
the water. With the coxswain holding one rigger lest it floats away, get an oar,
place it in a rigger next to a seat, and that will be your seat for today. It will
change in the future."

For a moment, no one moved. Then, "Go, gentlemen," said Arthur.
"Get your boat and place it in the water. Your oars are already there."

George and Arthur looked at each other in amazement as the eight
young men and the coxswain did precisely as they had been instructed. They
carried the boat effortlessly, placed it in the water; placed oars in riggers and
feet in stretchers, gripping the oar handle while fidgeting in their seats. This
was most unusual. They were already thinking and acting like a team. It was
as though they had already rowed together.

George, Arthur, Schindler, and Wilder stood staring at each other while
the young men sat ready in the boat. The critical decision of who would be in
the launch to coach the first row had never been discussed.

Wilder pointed. "There's the launch for the two of you. It has enough
gas for a 10,000-meter row, but that might be a lot for the first time. Blisters
on hands and strained backs. You know about all that, though."

"You have good water," said Schindler. Any hint of wind had died down,
and the position of the sun that now shone through the clouds allowed for the
reflection in the water of the trees that lined the shore.

In the launch, George nodded at the coxswain. He yelled, "Six and eight-seat push off the dock." With pride, George and Arthur watched as the rowers drew in their oars to gain the leverage to push off the dock and, with just the right amount of energy, moved the boat closer to the center of the river. George did the directing while Arthur drove the launch.

"Four of you will set the boat, keeping your oars on the water. Four of you will follow the instructions."

"Don't swing your torso back to an 11 o'clock angle and the finish at 1 o'clock. An exaggeration of the body does not work here." Arthur looked at George giving the commands, and the look reminded George that less is more. Give the briefest, most precise direction, and that would work.

"Make sure your handle passes the knees on the recovery."

"Keep the blade handle coming in below your breastbone."

"Shins—vertical at the catch."

"Toes keep contact with the foot stretcher. Helps with stability. That's where the power comes from. Those feet of yours."

"The most important bit of information ever. Follow the back of the person in front. One to two ratio on drive and recovery."

The two instructors observed those who could not maintain the rhythm, those who could not keep their bodies upright, those who let their oar dip too deep or couldn't grip it correctly. George and Arthur knew that these problems were part of the learning process. Rowers could be trained and these, new to the river, were eager. Their coaches observed moments of coordinated rowing that powered the boat in the right direction. By the end of the two hours, most of the awkwardness and tentativeness had worn off, as shown by their relaxed bodies and the movement of the boat.

Sheer joy and Olympic potential. A powerful combination. They could help in the development of a new Palestine.

For those brief hours on the water, George and Arthur forgot that ninety-five percent of Germans voted in favor of Hitler's foreign policies. For those brief hours of success in the boat, they could ignore the flag with the swastika on the nearby boathouse.

CHAPTER *31*

Leicester arose at 6:30 a.m. from the cot that served as a bed. Still, in his pajamas, he opened the door—it was only ten feet from his bed to the door—and grinned. Sunshine suffused the dry Palestinian air, crept into his bones, and relieved the damp gray he had continuously felt in London. He wondered if scientists ever did any studies on the implications of rain and sunshine on a person's psyche. The euphoria lasted through morning breakfast of sunny-side-up eggs to his finding a delivery of fresh eggs deposited outside his doorway. They had probably been left in the wee hours of the morning from a neighbor. Leicester knew these Arab villagers were grateful they had a reasonably supportive British army officer in their midst because tension certainly brewed.

The Arabs disliked the British for their mandate and for preventing Arab immigration coming from Egypt, Transjordan, and Syria. The British didn't have to worry about the Jews; the Arabs outnumbered them four to one. Leicester knew the British Government was considering limiting the amount of land to Jewish settlers due to Arab political pressure. The Arab population kept growing; they were still having large families. Jews were learning family planning.

Leicester knew if unwanted Jewish refugees kept arriving in ships at the port of Haifa, British plans existed to turn them away from desperately wanted freedom. Maybe if Labor leader Ramsay MacDonald's party held the majority in Parliament, affairs would have been different. But Conservatives now had the power. Palestine had been seen as a thorn in the side of the ruling class—especially when Arab oil was a significant consideration in their dealings and economy. It was as though the British were trying to make up for the Treaty of Versailles by courting the Arabs.

A glance at his watch told Leicester he had time for a short row. He hoped he would see Nurit, Omar, Ahmad, and Ethan. They knew enough to row independently and had enough coaching to begin training for competition. And he knew they would. He had learned to recognize those who would become competitive. They were not afraid to repeat the same drill repeatedly.

They understood what it was that would increase endurance and speed.

When he arrived at the warehouse, he was surprised. Six strange teenage boys and four girls sat on the small portion of cement outside the metal galvanized door, amid weeds struggling to maintain some semblance of growth in the rain-free climate. Nurit, Omar, Ahmad, and Ethan, his four frequent rowers, were not among them.

"Good morning," he said. They answered in English—fortunately not all simultaneously—and he could tell from their accent that they were a mix of Arab and Jewish. He quickly realized that they came with nothing that could be considered a weapon—a large piece of wood, a grenade even. As though reading his mind, they held out their hands and pulled fabric out of their pockets as if to say, "See, nothing here. Just us."

Before he could ask them anything, a girl of about fourteen or fifteen stepped up. "We want to learn what Nurit, Omar, Ahmad, and Ethan are doing."

Leicester was not surprised that they knew what was going on. He had long discovered that in small communities, word of mouth was almost better than the telephone. It was often the only means of communication, and sometimes because of the isolation of distanced lives, gossip fueled the human condition.

He had learned, therefore, that it was critical to maintain contact with people nearby, be a truth teller, and be perceived as a friend—someone they could trust—because rumors could lead to violence. The 1929 riots had started and caused destruction because people believed their land was being stolen. Rumors led Arabs to think that Jews praying at the Western Wall meant taking their right to the Temple Mount—the location of the Dome of the Rock—revered by most Muslims as the place where Muhammed ascended to heaven. A riot that leaves 116 Jews and 110 Arabs dead is not an inconsequential event in a small country. Leicester chased those thoughts out of his head and turned to the immediate situation.

"So, exactly, why are you here?" he asked.

"The same reason you are." He was not sure who responded so quickly.

"And that is?" He knew, but he wanted to hear it spoken. And they did. One by one, without identifying themselves, they iterated a reason.

"We want to row."

"Yes, we know you can teach us."

"It will be good for us."

"I hope it will give me some muscle."

"I want to stop being so bored."

"We know you are a good rower and coach."

The final comment touched him, grateful they didn't all speak at the same time and that he was known for being other than the British oppressor. He would get their names later and quickly opened the door to the makeshift boathouse.

"See, not enough boats here," he said.

"Well, you get in that boat and show us."

He chuckled at the inventive persistence of the last comment. He understood that in a place where no formal instruction existed in any sport, individuals brought their imitating skills into play.

"I hope you don't think that one demonstration will make you rowers." There was no response to his declaration. He realized their body posture implied "we are planting ourselves here until you demonstrate."

"Okay," said Leicester. "Watch and listen. Test afterward, and those who remember every instruction will have a chance to row. That's it." He figured that might eliminate a few because there weren't enough boats to teach all of them. And nobody came with a notebook to take notes. Definitely a test of memory—and desire.

While setting the oars at the shore's edge, Leicester thought to himself, *be brief with the words, defining with the movements. Good. They're watching. Very serious.*

Having removed his sandals, he carried the boat out overhead, turned it hull side down in the water. Fortunately, he was wearing shorts, so he didn't have to worry about any pants legs getting wet.

They all moved closer to the shore edge. Leicester observed that they gave each other enough space to watch carefully.

"Grab the oars. Make sure the oarlocks face forward. This little cuff on the oar needs to press against the rigger. Understand bow and stern." He pointed to the back of the boat first and set the oars in place. He thought it wasn't necessary to teach them about all the parts of the boat. That would come later. Right now, anything related to rowing technique and instruction was all that was important.

"Grab the handles of the two oars together like this in your right hand, step in, feet on the hull, sit on the seat, placing one foot at a time in the straps." He looked up. They were attentive. He had a fleeting thought that they would all be ready for military training. *Should I have one of them repeat what I've done to see if they've got that? No, let me go through more of the process. Let me, at least, get some movement, a couple of strokes in.*

Leicester wiggled in the seat to center his backside in the narrow space and grabbed the oar handles, making sure each thumb was on its edge with fingers loosely wrapped around. Realizing he didn't have enough water and depth to begin the rowing stroke, he pulled in the port oar while keeping the starboard oar flat on the surface and pushed the port oar hard against the river bottom. He could have asked for a push. *Next time*, he thought. *This time it's essential for them to see what they can do for themselves, especially if no one is around. How to start?*

He took a stab at introducing the mental aspects of rowing. "You need to think about what your body is doing with itself, the oars, and your mind," he said. On some faces, he saw blank stares—on others, fierce concentration.

"This is the oar on the square." He demonstrated by turning the blade, so its face was immersed sideways in the water. "You should always be able to see the top of the blade just underneath the surface of the water. When it dips too far below the surface, it loses its efficacy . . . its power . . . its ability to move smoothly through the water." Blank stares. *Too much information in words*, he thought. *They'll get it later when they sit in the boat.*

Leicester sat upright on the small seat of the boat about three-quarters of the way to the stern with his knees bent, almost touching his chest, oars on the square, and simultaneously pulled them through the water as he moved his body back. This time he repeated the stroke to take him midway across the river's width.

"Watch," he practically shouted. "I'm coming back." The distance was so short he could have rowed with the forward motion of the oars, backing the boat in, but the newly minted rowers were not ready. Instead, he placed his port oar flat on the water, and with continuous squaring strokes with the starboard oar, he turned his boat and returned with his back toward them, turning his head only as his oar landed. He smiled at the smattering of applause.

"Wait," he said. "You need to know how to get out of this very narrow, unstable thing. Handles together held with one hand. Stand up. On deck. Left foot out into the water. Then right foot. Grab the boat because its nature is to drift—it's a boat." No one laughed or even smiled. He should have known because humor does not always translate well in other cultures.

"Who's ready to try?" All hands went up. Cheeky kids, thought Leicester. "Okay, third from the left." They looked around. "My left," he said. It was the tallest youngster in the crowd, who looked to be about 5' 8" tall.

"Name?" Leicester asked. He was going to add "rank and serial number," but he thought again, no one would get it.

"Gadi," he said.

"Okay, Gadi, it's all yours," said Leicester, holding on to the boat until Gadi was right next to it, ankle-deep in the water. He joined the others and watched. How much would he need to instruct? To remind? So far, not much as Gadi grabbed the oar handles with one hand, stepped into the boat, and sat down, all in one swift motion. He saw Gadi frown and bite his lip as the boat began to wobble. "Just center yourself on the seat and keep the oars flat on the water. It's the movement of the oars that either stabilizes or not."

"Go, Gadi," said one of the girls. "You can do it. We will learn from you."

The attention of the young men and women had been so focused on Gadi and his first row that no one noticed someone on the other side of the river, creeping along behind the shrubs. Closer observation would have shown that the person wore a black and white keffiyeh, a scarf, and carried a rifle not slung over the shoulder but rather ready for imminent use.

As Gadi took his first tentative strokes, trying to imitate what Leicester had so carefully demonstrated, the entire group began to chant, "Go, Gadi, Go." Then it turned into "Row, Gadi, Row." Their cheering became so loud that no one heard the loud bang—but they all saw Leicester slump. No one needed to say, "he's been shot." They all had experience with terrorism. That terrible swift action of the gunshot deserved a rapid response.

"Someone who can drive the jeep. Go get help," shouted one of the youngsters.

Nicole, who had experience driving, ran to the jeep and quickly backed the vehicle out onto the road. The others gathered around Leicester, assuring him that help was on the way. One young boy knelt, lifted the captain's head, and placed it on his bent knees. No one cried or screamed. That would not help to preserve a life.

Gadi, unnerved, flipped in the river, unable to maintain the boat's stability and having no idea how to get back in. But another eager-to-learn rower, Simon, swam out toward him, and together they propelled the boat back to the shore.

Leicester garnered enough strength to whisper, "Get the boat inside." The ability to get a boat out of the water was a lesson they appeared to have learned well. Gadi and Simon, dripping wet, carried the boat into the warehouse. Naomi picked up the oars.

"We will find him," she said. "Don't worry, British man." She either forgot or couldn't pronounce his name. "And you will continue to teach us to row."

The others stood by, faces somber, unsure of how to help, aware they were players in a tragedy. One by one, they repeated, "Don't worry, British man." And some added. "You will teach us to row."

Leicester heard but didn't respond because just as the jeep arrived carrying the doctor, he passed out.

CHAPTER 32

As Harry Markham sat at his desk observing the brief, unusual morning rain, his momentary thought was, "Thank goodness, maybe it will cool down the rage that has created so much destruction."

Markham, a proud descendant of a military father who had served in India, often told stories about how the British civilized nations, and brought the people not only plumbing but culture—and tea. Markham was beginning to realize he had never heard stories from Indians and how they felt about the British as occupiers. This newly discovered insight undergirded his reporting back to the home office in England that a peaceful solution between Arabs and Jews was impossible, and the Balfour Declaration had done nothing to help. Despite his thinking, the framed copy of a letter from Balfour to Lord Rothschild that gave hope to Zionists hung on a wall facing him. Therefore, it was at the forefront of his thinking every day. He understood that the great politicians didn't know that "national home" had never existed in international law when they promised Jews a homeland. The Balfour Declaration's deliberate vagueness had only further complicated the situation.

The telephone ring startled him. A young man's voice spoke in cryptic sentences. "Leicester's been shot. Stabilized for now. Needs medical care. Where shall we take him?" Somehow, the ragtag group of rowing novices had managed to locate another British soldier.

Well, thought Markham, Rothschild may have screwed up with overpromising in the Balfour Declaration, but he had done good by establishing hospitals in Jerusalem. An American organization, Hadassah, had come along to rehabilitate the hospitals from their neglected state. Because Jerusalem was too far, Hadassah had wisely established the B'nai Zion medical center in Haifa also.

His decision came quickly. "Take him to B'nai Zion in Haifa. It's the closest. I'll alert them. You just do the careful driving and . . . make sure you have someone with a rifle with you. If you're in a British-marked jeep, anything is possible."

The British had concentrated health services mostly in Arab towns since the Jewish community seemed determined to develop its own institutions. Whether their determination came from self-preservation or just passionate interest in science was unclear. Even the political trade union organization, Histadrut, had established a sick fund, a medical insurance program Markham thought remarkable for an underdeveloped country. Well, even Popes had Jewish doctors, so he shouldn't be surprised.

Now he and the British soldiers would have to go about finding the perpetrator. Markham was keenly aware that someone knew who tried to kill Leicester. More than someone, he thought. Probably a whole village knew the perpetrator. Someone wanted to wreak havoc on Leicester's program that had both Arab and Jewish teenagers rowing. Someone wanted the possibility of cooperation to die or just plain wanted to send a message that Arabs and Jews will never live side by side.

The teletype to the home office got him the expected answer. "Do your best. Track down the perpetrator. Warn the village elders that they need to rein in their terrorists. They can do it better than we can."

Markham readied himself with the call to Leicester's family. He knew there was no way to predict how they would react. Some recipients of such a call would express stoicism with the typical English of "Right. I see." Others stifled a sob or two. Whatever the reaction, the British "stiff upper lip" was usually in play.

"It happened while he was teaching some young people to row," Markham explained to Leicester's mother, who responded with momentary silence and then asked quietly, "Where and how?"

Markham explained, and her reaction was, "We must keep the rowing program going. I know my son saw it as really making a change."

Markham also understood that military strength had not and could not make two people love each other and get along.

He pulled into the Arab village of Abu Yesha, where goats roamed alongside chickens and donkeys. He knew the chickens were not for commercial food or egg production because this particular village raised cotton. Markham could tell they were about three months after planting because the dark red petals were beginning to fall, and the green pods of cotton bolls were starting to show. He saw Mahmoud Abadi patiently walking up and down the rows, tenderly pouring vinegar over plants that grew in fields covering about a quarter of an acre, Abadi still wearing the thob—the traditional white garment. However, younger people had given it up for Western dress. It was not uncommon to see young Arabs in khaki pants, jeans, and T-shirts. But Mahmoud, taller than the average Arab, stood out not only for his garment and his height but for his Bedouin background. The young Arab had forsaken the desert background of the Negev and tribal culture when as a teenager, he had managed a trip up North and fell in love with the cooler climate of Haifa and its hills.

That's a lot of vinegar, thought Markham. He also saw the beginnings of saplings—he had known Mahmoud to be intensely interested in agriculture, and the Arabs had observed neighboring Jews planting trees to enrich the soil.

Markham noticed villagers coming out of their homes as his jeep approached. Perhaps they wanted to observe some drama in their day or just have a small conversation. Either way, the arrival of a British soldier brought news and a diversion to the day. Markham himself had grown up in a small town in England and understood what small village life meant. He cautioned his two aides to remain inside as he waved to Mahmoud, who approached Markham with a slight bow of his head.

"You heard, I'm sure," said Markham.

"Yes. I hope Captain Leicester is all right."

Markham knew the polite response would be to acknowledge Mahmoud's words of concern, but he had lost patience. "Your village is the closest one to the river—to where he was shot," he said abruptly.

"I have good people here," Mahmoud replied. He knew that recently with the arrival of more Jews, although they were not nearby, Arab neighborhoods were becoming more agitated.

Mahmoud also had made peace with his Bedouin brothers, who were upset with him because he could not negotiate with the village elders of the nearby Jewish kibbutz to hire Bedouins to serve as paid guards. He said he would try to speak to the kibbutz leaders, but a voluntary Jewish force, Hashomer, was being organized and had proved to be fierce protectors from Arab marauders. Hashomer was more than the Jewish Mule Corps that the British had reluctantly authorized when the Turks liberated Palestine during the world war, but Hashomer had its roots and history in that first protective organization. They had been protectors once; they could certainly do it now.

"They would rather have their own guards," he had shrugged and told his brothers. "This you should understand." Governmental rules were hard to abide by for anarchic people, and British law had brought many regulations based on their historic preoccupation and experience with governing tribal lands.

"We will have to do a search," said Markham, signaling to his officers to get out of the jeep. By this time, the twenty small homes scattered around the property had families standing in front of doorways, usually with one woman and several children. Men were away constructing other houses or working the fields.

"That is not legal. Don't you need a piece of paper that permits you?"

Markham was surprised. The words came from a grandmother who stood with a woman and four children at the doorway. These villages had such a tradition of operating with tribal law—what the elders said was the law that had been handed down from generation to generation. This is how they learned to live in peace. The land. The tribe. That's what was necessary.

Markham took a chance. "A warrant doesn't apply here. But the men will search each house with respect." He signaled to the three soldiers. "Gentlemen. No disruption or destruction of any piece of property. But search through everything—especially food stored in barrels."

"I will join them and do my duty as well, Mahmoud," said Markham. He had the urge to salute and click his heels but decided it was too militaristic. The British officer was trying to set this up as just a friendly search. He was surprised when he entered the first house to see three men passing around a hookah. The vapors had been recently exhaled; he could smell the distinct odor. The men seemed oblivious to his search and were in no condition to act with deadly opposition.

He had finished searching two houses under the unremitting stares of aproned mothers and barefoot children. He was relieved to finally hear "Over here! Over here!" from an excited officer's voice.

"All right. Keep it down," shouted Markham in return. He was not the only one who heard the cry of "I've found something." Everyone who had been outside their homes watching the drama taking place ran in the direction of the house. Fortunately, two officers stood guard outside protectively. A fresh-faced soldier with barely the hint of stubble on his face emerged from Moussa's house, holding a pistol up with his index finger through the trigger hole.

"Everyone else go home," shouted Markham, stern-faced. This was the home of Khalidi Moussa, and the British had already had interactions with him due to complaints from the nearby kibbutz. He had been identified as the one stealing goats and chickens. He was also caught painting the words "Jews, No" on the kibbutz guardhouse one early morning at 2:00 a.m. The newly installed searchlight at the top of the tower had spotted him, and a siren was sounded. The kibbutz had let him go with a warning and had informed the British authorities. Jews in this kibbutz were uncomfortable taking the law into their own hands. Still, others had developed raiding parties who would reply with a similar deed to the Arab community in some way, citing the Biblical principles "an eye for an eye" phrase from the Bible. Markham knew that both cultures were all too familiar with the passage from Leviticus.

"Where is he?" Markham directed the question to Mahmoud Abati.

Mahmoud shrugged but held the gaze of the questioner. This was not the cast-down look Markham had come to expect.

I'm sure you will find him. He does not have the resources to go very far. Only a small horse. No jeep," said Mahmoud. His English was halting, but the tone was assured and defiant.

Markham knew it would not be that easy. He could be with another tribe who would find means to hide him and get him to another place. They were all connected in some way. They didn't have their central government, their police departments, and they certainly couldn't depend on the British, but they had figured out ways to keep their culture thriving.

Meanwhile, he needed to get the gun to the British police lab. He doubted that Khalidi was sophisticated enough to have wiped away his fingerprints. Markham was an avid crime reader, and Dillinger was one of his favorite criminals to follow. Dillinger would try to have his fingerprints erased from his hands. Not this guy.

He signaled for his men to get into the jeep. He held the gun wrapped in a handkerchief and placed it in a knapsack.

"Well, gentlemen. No field telephone here, so I'm dropping you and the gun off at the base. I'll go on to the hospital." Primitive communication was one of the distinct disadvantages of being in rural areas where field telephones would not work.

When Markham disembarked at the hospital, he thought, *I can't say that no news is good news in this case. There is no way for me to get any information about Leicester's condition.* He was understandably wary about going to the nurses' station. *No,* Markham thought, *I'll go directly to his room and surprise him.* But upon arrival, he saw that the bed was empty and undisturbed. He ignored an uneasy feeling.

"He didn't make it." It was a Hadassah nurse; he recognized her cap's blue and white logo. "He was a captain? Right? He is in a different room where we have people praying over him."

Markham turned and tried to find the entrance. This would not be the place to break down. He would do so back at headquarters in the privacy of his office. And then he would have to think about next steps.

CHAPTER *33*

Chaim Halevi had always been an avid ham radio operator. It excited him to be the first to receive news—good or even depressing, and relay it to friends—primarily other ham radio operators. Halevi started the hobby as a teenager and was devastated when it was prohibited after the World War because it interfered with regular radio transmissions. He had been an eager participant in a resurgence in the 1920s, along with other Englishmen, to create one of the largest populations of ham radio operators globally.

The radio had an honored spot on his bedroom bookshelves. No books or picture frames surrounded it. He had an agreement with his wife that when she heard the static on the radio, she would refrain from starting any discussion, including any question about what he wanted for dinner.

Today, while searching through the stations, he looked at a framed, faded photograph in front of many books. The lens caught his father and his two brothers striking a pose of resistance to the 1903 Kishinev pogrom when gangs managed to kill 49 Jews, rape a number of Jewish women, and damage 1500 homes. The Halevi men were armed with rifles and rounds of ammunition slung across their shoulders. Halevi couldn't decide if the impassive stance disguised fear.

He continued to turn the dial through the staticky sounds, each of which meant different people reporting over the various stations. One report was coming from the official British station, so he listened closely. Over the static, he heard, "Death of British Captain . . . Palestine." The words had dropped off, but he knew they would be repeated. He moved closer. The next time, he heard, "Captain Ben Leicester died of a gunshot wound, probably inflicted by someone from a nearby Arab village." The commentator went on to give some background on Leicester; subsequent sentences were not coming in clearly and didn't seem relevant, but Halevi had heard what was critical. Their British Captain, who was helping with the rowing program for young people, had been killed. He was also the contact for George Grossinger, the young man who had traveled to Palestine and was looking to leave Germany with his family.

Halevi grabbed the phone on his desk.

"Felder," he said, grateful that the party line did not pick up. "Felder?"

"Yes, I hear you. I heard you the first time."

"But you didn't say anything."

Halevi struggled for the words. "Remember this young man, George . . ?"

"Grossinger. Yes, of course. We saw the possibility of a committed Zionist in him."

"We need to get in touch with him." He paused. "Maybe we should get in touch with our Zionist friends in Berlin."

"And the reason for the call?"

"To figure out how we can get them to Palestine. More than ever, this rowing maniac needs to be there. With his family, of course." He paused. "The British army man, Leicester—he's been killed."

While neither Halevi nor Felder were rowers or even rowing enthusiasts, they were committed to anything, anything, that would raise the level of the importance of Palestine to Jews. They adhered to Theodor Herzl's philosophy: assimilation won't make us any more acceptable; we must establish our own country where we can be ourselves without the unpredictable danger of antisemitism rearing its ugly head. Herzl had been a reporter in Paris at the time of the Dreyfus trial. He knew that the Jewish army officer had not received a fair trial because of the antisemitism that dominated the era. The fallout from that case was a factor in the founding of Zionism.

"It's eleven here—it will be twelve in Berlin. Maybe they'll be eating at home. Maybe not. These Germans work a lot. They could be working in their offices."

Felder was impatient with Halevi's musings. "Just call. You don't have to worry. The Berlin office doesn't have a party line. See if they already have the news."

"They won't have the news. They don't have a ham radio," said Halevi.

Halevi knew he was stalling, but he needed to get his thoughts together so a call would result in a plan. Unfortunately, just relaying the news wasn't good enough.

"Maybe they'll have some ideas," said Felder, sensing his friend's hesitation.

"Just tell me before I call if you think we have the money to pay for the escape of six people . . . and maybe, just maybe, more boats?"

"We'll find a way. We'll reach out to rich American friends." Felder tried to hide his impatience. "Get your friend you rely on, the operator, Mildred—to place the call to Isaac Sherman in Berlin." Felder had resisted direct dialing, feeling more secure with people he knew and trusted. He thought direct dialing increased the possibility of some stranger listening to your conversation.

The phone in the Berlin Zionist office rang once. Sherman was not surprised to hear the operator say, "Halevi in London calling." Of course, he thought, London would be calling, and maybe France, and perhaps someone from the United States will be calling later. He understood that this event of a British soldier being shot by an Arab in Palestine allowed more political stars to align with the Zionist goal of Palestine as the true Jewish homeland. The Zionists would seize on anything that could be perceived as an opportunity.

Sherman was glad the phone had a long cord. He picked it up from the desk, the receiver resting on his shoulder, and walked over to the window, looking out over Leipziger Strasse seeing even more flags hanging from windows with the swastika embedded in its circle of white. More flags than yesterday, he thought. I'm not imagining. There are more. I guess what Einstein said is true: "Intelligence is finite, stupidity is infinite."

Sherman always attributed quotes he liked to Einstein even without verification. He connected this one with his belief that people flying the Nazi flag didn't understand that they were losing their individual rights. Individual rights were always at the forefront of Sherman's thoughts, and he wanted Palestine to be the place for Jews where their right to life, liberty, and the pursuit of happiness was always possible.

He continued to look down on the street. He saw a man offer a hand to a woman as she tried to navigate a puddle and an umbrella while crossing the street. Maybe humanity and kindness still prevail, he thought.

"You heard?" Halevi didn't want to repeat unnecessary information. The purpose of the call was to arrive at a solution.

"Yes, Julius Abrahams still has a ham radio. The German authorities have yet to denounce them." Sherman understood this was no time for small talk—no time to ask about families, wives or children, or the situation on the ground as they see it. Casual observations about what was happening in the world were part of the culture in normal times. Tidbits of information were treated with almost Biblical reverence. Schmoozing was considered a positive trait. But not now.

"Can you help George Grossinger and his family leave for Palestine? That's the most important thing." Halevi hoped his voice delivered the urgency he was feeling.

"I know he is working hard with a long boat filled with nine people at the Hebrew Rowing Club," replied Sherman

"Well, that's good, isn't it?" said Halevi, who had no connection with the rowing world despite living all his life in England. He couldn't fathom why training of rowing eight men in a very big, long boat was important to George.

Sherman persisted. "You need to meet with George's family, convince them that the time to leave Germany is now because of the death of Leicester. George is needed even more than ever in Palestine. Maybe George can entice more people to come. And, he would be providing a way out of Germany for those who fear the future. The German authorities here are coming up with more and more restrictive laws." Sherman knew he needed to cut the call short and begin to work. First would come a vital conversation with George and his family. He looked at the ashtray on his desk. He realized he had smoked three cigarettes during the conversation almost without being aware. He squeezed his empty package of Camels and threw it into the trash can.

⁓⁓

George secretly wished that women were allowed to row. Then the boathouse could serve as a convenient and easy place to meet Clara. He never uttered that desire aloud. Nobody would sympathize with him; they would probably think he was a bit crazy. What consoled him was the thought that Clara would not believe that idea so strange. She was always up for adventure, but he was unsure about her reaction to Palestine in his future.

Their meetings took place on walks in neighborhoods where they felt safe from gangs that roamed the streets, now with the tacit support of the police. Tonight, Arthur was going to meet them as well.

What book could he read to figure out how to talk to someone important to you? No book. Talk. Time to set uncertainty aside. A plan would evolve.

Clara was ready, waiting for him outside her apartment building with a book in hand. Unlike his family, who always seemed to want to meet whoever came to the house, her parents were always too busy, she claimed. He hoped it was true, and there was no other reason for the distancing." Besides," she had said, "we can be spending the time together instead of making small talk with my mother and father. They are not interested in the same things we like to talk about."

"We can stop for a soda, yes? I'm thirsty," she said, taking his arm. "Before we pick up Arthur. There's a place right around the corner." He realized how much he liked her directness, as well as the way she tucked herself close to him.

They both ordered Cokes at the counter, watching the server squirt a bit of the syrup concoction along with seltzer water into a glass.

"Would you consider leaving Germany for Palestine?" The few sips of soda must have given him a bit of a jolt. He hadn't intended to be quite so direct. He had planned to tell her his thoughts about Palestine after they talked about the book she was reading. Last time it was Ernest Hemingway; he wasn't sure about this book. Maybe it was about Van Gogh? Clara was aware of his interest in art and attempted to enlighten herself to have something to talk about. She thought that challenging topics of conversation could bring people closer together.

His question about leaving Germany startled her. What was he thinking by asking if she would leave Germany? Did this mean a changing nature to their relationship? Something he was thinking about but hadn't shared with her?

"Let's go find Arthur," she said, evading an answer to the difficult question.

The three sat on the park bench together facing the Dahme River which was only wide enough for a few birds to wade from one side to the other. Arthur got up, pacing along the narrow riverbank. George had a fondness for what he saw as Arthur's natural taciturnity, but he sensed internal agitation in his friend.

"Is there something bothering you, Arthur?" he asked.

"Maybe Arthur just needs to get some exercise." Clara smiled, knowing Arthur's quiet ways.

"I think we need to go to Palestine right away," Arthur exclaimed.

George was startled. He was usually the initiator of the subject of going to Palestine.

"You have not heard. Your friend, Leicester, was killed yesterday." He continued, not wanting to be interrupted by George, who probably had a dozen questions he could not answer. "I had my ham radio on yesterday." He waited for anything George had to say. At this moment, George chose to remain silent and grab Clara's hand, and she responded by interlocking fingers with his and placing a reassuring hand on his arm.

"Immediately," said Arthur.

George found his voice. "Nothing is immediate in Germany, now." His thoughts went to the boat of eight he had been coaching. "But I think there is a way out."

Clara saw that his full attention was focused on the "way out." In a way, she was relieved that Arthur had interrupted the conversation because she could not begin to think about leaving Germany. Nor had she had a clear idea of where their relationship was heading. And headlines in newspapers also contributed to her uncertainty of linking her life closely with George.

CHAPTER *34*

Werner switched on the overhead office light and thought he needed to replace it with a larger bulb because at 6:30 a.m., or even p.m., it did not shed enough illumination to lift the gloom and let him see the words on the page. Writers, editors, proofreaders of articles need sufficient lumens both to read and energize them, he thought, happy that he remembered something from his university engineering class. How did it happen that Germany in the 1920s was so enlightened that a Jew didn't have a hard time entering a university? How did all that change? He had understood from his friends that their best American universities had quotas that limited Jews. Was Germany imitating America?

Werner turned on the desk lamp and pushed aside the green visor one of his writers had recently given him as some sort of—precisely what he wasn't sure. Was it a suggestion that he was on his way out? Were his eyes fading? Did he need to be a better manager of a newspaper? Become a stereotype?

He didn't have much time to ponder his internal questions because the *Der Tagblatt* story editor, Franz Ludwig, walked in, placing two typed sheets on his desk already overflowing with papers. Werner was not surprised because he had organized the day in his head on his motorcycle ride to the newspaper. Ludwig would be the first writer he would see. Naturally, the story of the day needed the most consideration.

"Your office is a fire hazard," said Ludwig.

"One day, I will straighten out all the papers." Werner picked up a pile of papers from one side and transferred it to another.

"It's not just what's on the desk. It's all these papers on the floor and in boxes." Ludwig lifted a box from the floor and placed it on the wide radiator near the window.

"Not there. I need to be able to see outside for my health. Besides, you're distracting me. Do you have a story for me?"

"It's a final draft of a story about a family of Catholics that is unhappy with what they see happening in government."

"You're kidding," said Werner, shutting the lamp on his desk because the sun's appearance now created sufficient light. "You have a family who is willing to expose themselves in this climate?"

"They don't want to be seen as 'dancing alongside the Nazis.'"

"Did they actually say that?" Werner asked, somewhat bemused.

"Something like that."

Werner absentmindedly shuffled some papers on his desk. "My guess is that these Catholics probably believe Nazis will bring war. They want some peace. They understand the Versailles Treaty did not bring us peace."

Ludwig looked up from his notepad where he had his notes. "They said they don't believe that all these parades, fireworks, bands, mass rallies will bring us renewal."

"And you think I can print that?" Werner hoped that question would make Ludwig think twice about the dangers of such an article. Sometimes Ludwig's liberal Catholicism put blinders on him. Did he not see publishing this article as a possible death knell for the newspaper?

It was as though Ludwig had anticipated this argument. "To offset this Catholic story, get Axelrod, the film editor, to do a superb review of the *Morgenrot* movie—you know, where all the Germans are happy to go down with the ship because they are doing this for the fatherland."

Werner had heard about the movie but refused to see it with Frieda because it glorified death. He had never been religious, but he had absorbed the notion that life was precious, and he knew Frieda shared that with him. He understood *Morgenrot* was an effort to rehabilitate the Imperial German Navy and reverse the 1918 High Seas Fleet mutiny when seamen had disobeyed orders and fled from a fight.

"Rewrite it as an anonymous family, and I'll think about it," said Werner. "Get Stein and Walters in." In his ordering of the day, he had planned for news and photography review next. He had not intended to come back to the Catholic family story and was surprised Ludwig had revived it. Usually, Ludwig chose the right topic to avoid the possibility of the newspaper being shut down.

Stein and Walters sat, notebooks in hand, waiting for Werner to return from his stance at the window. They had noted that it was with more and more frequency that this was the way meetings began.

"Well, at least we don't have people selling apples in the street," Werner said, adjusting himself in his wooden chair.

"Not this street," said Stein. "I could take photos—one that I know of is on Wittenbergplatz." He took note of Werner's dispirited air. "But people don't want to see men selling apples unless they're doing it in the United States. They want to see pictures of violence in the street."

"And what's the angle for that?" Werner tried to curb the sarcasm in his voice as he could feel a rush of crimson spread on his neck at the suggestion of the need for photos depicting violence.

"That the SA are doing their job to preserve law and order," said Stein, his voice barely above a whisper. Everybody entering Werner's office knew their jobs were in jeopardy, and the editor's choices significantly influenced the Minister of Propaganda's decisions, often capriciously made, about shutdowns.

"And what do you have for me, Walters?" Werner asked. "A comet, perhaps, that will bring instant destruction to us all instead of a slow death?" God, he thought, I need to quiet my sarcasm.

Walters looked up from his notebook. "We've done the Day of Potsdam about the reopening of the Reichstag after the fire, but maybe we can find another angle. About how the Reichstag is even stronger than ever under Hitler's leadership, and nobody wants to go back to the Weimar past."

"Keep going," said Werner, reaching for a cigarette and offering his pack of Camels to the journalists. They both declined.

"I need a pencil in my hand. Not a cigarette," said Walters. "I have something else. They are limiting the number of Jews who can attend public schools."

"Is there a good side to this story?" asked Werner, this time not even trying to keep his sarcasm in check.

"Well, I guess they can establish their schools. Maybe they would be happier just with themselves in their own schools," Walters said quietly. Werner hoped his face wasn't communicating how hard he was trying to suppress his tongue from saying the wrong thing.

"Oh, I have another good one for you to make into a good photo story," quipped Stein. "Tennis anyone? The German Tennis Lawn Association has just decreed that no Jew can be selected to play for the Davis Cup." Stein had given up any hint of Jewish religious practices but strongly identified as a Jew.

"But the Swedish King has protested. I suppose we could propose they establish their own Davis Cup—an all-Jewish-one—according to your plans." Walters was trying to maintain a measure of decorum. They were all trying to hold on to printing newspapers. These men had been journalists all their lives.

Some said they had ink instead of blood in their veins.

"But you and I both know there are not enough Jewish tennis players to have their own anything, let alone a Davis Cup." Stein attempted a chuckle. "And do you honestly think that Feuchtwanger's column in the esteemed *New York Times* is going to make a difference?"

They were all aware that Lion Feuchtwangner had written a column in a United States newspaper on March 21, 1933, with the headline "Terror in Germany Amazes Novelist." A paragraph boldly stated:

> *Every Jew in Germany, they said, must expect to be assaulted in the street or to be dragged out of bed and arrested. To have his goods and property destroyed, while complaints are met with a shrug from Minister Goering and the remarks. "Where timber is planed, shavings must drop off."*

A more damning paragraph followed:

> *What has, in fact, happened to Germany? Six hundred thousand very young men to whom every characteristic can be acknowledged except moderation have been stirred up by every means against the workmen and the Jew.*

The three sat there impassively after Stein's reminder, waiting in silence for someone to say the words that would lead them to take the right action. They were all gripped by the knowledge that no easy solution was in sight.

"I know what to do," Werner finally said.

"Thank God, you're going to tell us without walking to the window and looking over the goddamn street and seeing Nazi flags every day magnified by the multiple of ten," said Stein.

"That window peering helps me reflect. To slow down the decision-making process." Werner leaned forward on the desk, offering his hands as a weary gesture to his journalists. "But I'm not going to do that today. My mind says, 'enough.' We will run the story on the Catholic family and the *Morgenrot* movie. And we're going to do a translation in German of the Feuchtwanger paragraphs from T*he New York Times*. Walters, that's for you, so get started. Stein, you get a photo of the family."

"And what's the timeline on this?" Stein asked.

"Tomorrow's newspaper. All this needs to be done tonight for tomorrow's newspaper, along with all the ads. Might as well give the companies what they paid for up to now. There might be no more ads after tomorrow's edition." Werner didn't dare add that there might be no newspaper.

The morning edition of *Der Tagblatt* was on newspaper stands by 6:00 a.m. Werner had decided to sprinkle the three stories throughout the newspaper in its various sections. None of them made the front page. He scrapped the tennis player article; tennis was not on the minds of many readers. The story about the Catholic family appeared under Home Life; the review of the movie in the Entertainment segment, and the Feuchtwanger piece was on the continuation page of the news stories, most of which praised the attempts of the Third Reich to bring law, order, and prosperity to a new prouder Germany.

Werner had given longstanding assignments to several journalists to write about the wonders of the new government. He never questioned them about their ideological beliefs. They all came through, understanding that this was the way to hold on to their jobs. These writers had no idea of the other stories that were being printed today, so they, along with the other newspaper workers, barely looked up when three representatives from the office of the Minister of Propaganda, dressed in fresh uniforms and knee-high black boots, boldly marched in and demanded to see the editor.

Werner never asked them to sit down and have a discussion. They handed Werner a piece of paper that read that the newspaper would be shut down. No warning order, but an official-looking document with the Minister of Propaganda seal with the words "Officiell Geschlossen" written in large black letters after *Der Tagblatt*. "Officially Closed."

Werner's jaw tightened as he felt his heart racing. If ever he needed to be a defender of the free press, this was the time, even though these men were only the messengers.

"Gentlemen, we printed nothing but the truth," he told them in a quiet voice.

The shortest and stoutest of the officers spoke first. "There is good truth in telling everyone how important this new government is."

"That's the stupidest argument I ever heard." Werner realized he raised his voice and thought this was not the way to go.

"We thought you might resist," said one officer, who stood closest to the door. Suddenly, he proclaimed, "Heil Hitler," and raised his hand in salute. "He is resisting." The official apparently felt he needed to proclaim those words to the silent observers.

"There's no need to do that here," said Werner, trying to maintain a soothing voice and think about what his following words should be. After all, he had always relied on words to convince, to lead, to change someone's mind. Too late.

Just then, Werner heard a loud banging and crashing of metal against metal or wood against metal. He guessed it was coming from the basement where the printing presses were located.

"My men. They know what to do, and I have been ordered to do what needs to be done when people are stubborn. We will go downstairs to see that everything that needed to be done was done." The officer spoke with precise diction as he turned to leave with the others.

"Please don't click your heels on the way out," said Werner. "I know when I've been beaten." He refrained from telling them that their language was vague and redundant.

Werner surmised that they had ordered a squad of brown-shirted teenagers to storm the floor where the printing presses were located and destroy them. He didn't need to go down there to verify. Nor did any of the employees sitting quietly at their desks when the officers left. No one was typing, writing, or reading. They all heard the same disturbing noise and immediately understood what it was and what it meant. One by one, each picked up a briefcase, grabbed a jacket or sweater, and quietly left. They avoided Werner's office as he quietly wept at his favorite window overlooking the street.

CHAPTER 35

Maps covered the dining room table. Glasses of tea and small plates of biscuits were squeezed in between spaces. Werner, Frieda, George, Arthur, and Clara leaned over maps—Werner and Frieda with magnifying glasses in hand—commenting so quietly they almost seemed to be talking to themselves.

"We could check out Turkey."

"No international competitions in Turkey," George noted. "And we need a race location that's on the way to Palestine."

"England's out of the question. Zionists there could help, but too far."

"Too bad. England has the most exciting regattas."

"We need to prepare Grandmother and Grandfather."

George extricated himself from his hunched-over position, his face pensive as he regarded his mother, who quietly uttered the last comment. She added, "You have to begin to think how we may need to go first and have them come later."

He put his arm around Clara, seated on a chair next to him. "Clara will help them make plans to leave. We will leave them with necessary money for bribes—whatever the damn government asks of Jews who want to leave." She reached for his hand and gently wrapped her fingers around it, and he immediately returned the gesture.

"I will see that they have copies of their passports . . . and their wills," Clara said. "That is a good idea, isn't it?"

"You're not going to ask Clara to take that risk and responsibility," said Werner. He was not sure why he said it. Was he annoyed that his son seemed to be taking on the authority in his household? Or is this the way it's going to be in this crazy world where goons can come in and smash a newspaper office, and no one is accountable? Where all the old norms are suddenly stripped away, and the son is now the head of the household?

Werner threw up his hands. "Besides, who knows how valid a will is going to be in a new country? The Middle East is notorious for its bureaucracy, and I suspect Palestine is no different."

"You don't need to worry about me, Herr Grossinger." She let go of

George's hand and went over to touch Werner gently on his arm. George smiled. Clara, unlike most Germans, was appreciative of touch and somehow understood the value of it. He had found that out on their very first outing to the movies, and it drew her to him even more than her curiosity about and compassion toward the world. "My father has a position in government. Thus far, he's untouchable. I will ensure that they also have letters of transit."

"Well, we want to make sure he . . . and you . . . and your mother, remain untouchable, too," Werner grumbled. "Let's get on with this. We have a burning question here. Where's the best regatta going to be held that will allow a voyage from that regatta to Palestine, never to return to Germany?"

"Someone at the rowing club will have that information. Either Schindler or Wilder keeps a list," said George, not surprised at his father's quick summary of what needed to be done.

Frieda sat up, gesturing with her magnifying glass. "It will be Cyprus," she said.

"How do you know?" said Arthur, who up to this time tried to be quiet, understanding that these complex decisions were made more complicated by family dynamics. He hoped that what he learned here would help inform the decision-making that was coming up for his family.

"Because it's geography, pure and simple. It's the closest to Palestine by water. We find a ship. Look!" On the map nearest her, she pointed to the island of Cyprus off the coast of Greece on the map. She picked up a pencil and drew a line from the southern end of the island of Cyprus to Haifa. Arthur looked closely over her shoulder. He had always had a particular interest in maps.

"I estimate 200 nautical miles. Maybe a half-day by boat."

They all gathered around Frieda to look closely at a map to peer at places that previously they had only considered either to pass a school test, locate a possible vacation spot, or inspire the imagination for stories. Now it was knowledge that could create a new life—with all the trepidations that came from leaving family, friends, important locations, and even special memories.

"No decisions, tonight," said Werner. "We need more time to plan properly."

⸺

The next day, George welcomed the stillness at the boathouse. He arrived a little early, skipping his last class at university because he relished the moments of seeing boats and oars resting quietly in their assigned places at dusk. If the sun continued to shine at the right time of day, light would be reflected in the gleam of the wood. It was a wonder to George that the appearance of wood became better with age, as did a boat's agility. As George looked at the gleaming stacks of eights, he thought of the way rowers washed the boats with soapy water and wiped the boats down meticulously after each row. Sometimes a rower would stand back in admiration when a particular spot began to shine.

He was surprised Arthur wasn't here yet. He knew the crew of eight with the coxswain would be waiting for them. And they were—all dressed in rowing shorts, but with long-sleeved shirts, because there was still an April chill in the air. They were standing next to the eight, just waiting for the instruction to get in proper position, remove the almost nineteen-meter boat from its rack, hoist it overhead, and split to four rowers on each side. George nodded, and the coxswain gave the directions, and they completed the movements in unison and with muscular grace. Just those preliminary motions released the tension George had seen in their bodies in anticipation of the coxswain's instructions. He could identify that feeling of relief almost, knowing you were about to get out on the water and demonstrate your ability to be part of a team and push yourself almost to exhaustion.

Arthur came flying in on his bicycle.

"They're already waiting at the dock," said George. "Take them alone today. Start with warm-ups and push them to a 2K." He knew that to the average person, 2000 meters on water might not seem like a lot, but the exertion required to take even a second off the time was enormous. "But start slowly, "George reminded his friend. "I'm going to find Schindler and Wilder to talk about . . . about the future of rowing for us."

Arthur waved him off, indicating he had the coaching under control.

George was not surprised to find the two older men in the upstairs room drinking tea while standing at the window, observing boats already on the water.

Schindler motioned for George to take a seat next to him, but George went around the room looking at black and white photos of young men standing tall with oars all held in right hands. They wore matching outfits, but some had knee-high socks as part of the uniform, others matching beanie hats. History, George thought. Lots of history here. Also, inspiration.

"I should have a picture of my crew that's out on the river now," George suggested, reaching for the tea kettle.

"In time, you will," said Wilder, who had forsaken his glass of tea for a cigarette. "They have not been together that long. They have not even participated in one regatta together."

George put three sugar cubes in the glass of tea, stirring slowly, then picked up the glass and held it close to his eyes to see if the cubes had dissolved. "Sooner rather than later. I'm going to enter this crew in a regatta—probably Cyprus and they are never coming back to Germany. They and my family are going to Palestine. My father's newspaper was shut down. My mother no longer has her orchestra seat. My grandfather, a university professor, was brought to a police station. Germany is changing for the worse." He decided to stop his declaration. I've said enough, he thought and sat back in the chair, sipping the tea, waiting for a reaction from the men who had been so supportive in his effort to row in helping him organize this group of nine men.

"Cyprus won't work," Schindler said abruptly. He removed a giant book from a shelf and ran his finger down what appeared to be a ledger sheet, but not with money amounts—names, places, and dates of regattas. "We are coming out of a depression. There haven't been too many regattas. People just didn't have the money for travel. But there's one coming up in Naples." He pointed and taped a finger almost defiantly to a place on the page.

"I can't believe you're offering words of wisdom," said Wilder.

Schindler waved a dismissive hand. "You look at the world through rose-colored glasses. You are blind to the worms that have crawled out of the woodwork. You think that because you still have your jewelry store, and nothing has happened at the boathouse, everything's all right? Trust me. If I could figure out an easy way to leave with a wife sick with cancer, I would leave, too." He paused. "I would, at least, be thinking of a way to leave."

George pulled a dog-eared map off the wall, held in place with just two thumbtacks at the top. He pushed aside the glasses of tea, ashtrays, biscuits, set the map on the large coffee table, and started to draw a pencil line from Naples to Palestine in the Mediterranean Sea. Then, he erased it. Next, he redrew the line from Naples to Cyprus and then from Cyprus to Palestine. "That's the more likely route. We are more likely to get a boat to take us from Naples to Cyprus and then Cyprus to Palestine." George straightened up and practically shouted, "Yes, that's it. Just set us up to participate in that regatta—whatever it takes."

"Not me," said Wilder. "I want no part of this. It's too dangerous. You have to think of what will happen to those remaining here, and the government finds out we were complicit in a plot to escape."

"You need to get it through your thick head that the government doesn't want us here. They will find some way to get rid of us," protested Schindler. "This way, George and these rowers, they're doing it on their own. These dedicated Zionists are doing it on the pretext of rowing for Germany. What could be better to evade these addled-brained bigots now running the Reichstag? If the plan works and Jews have departed Germany with their bodies and wealth intact, they deserve some sort of medal. I'm going to do whatever I can to help."

George realized that he was damp with anxious perspiration. A plan was coming to fruition. Now the challenge would be in the details. Registering for the regatta. Making sure there was space available on the boats that would take them and the family from Naples to Cyprus to Haifa in Palestine. The biggest challenge was reaffirming the commitment from this crew of nine. And there was no easy formula for that. His hope was somehow they all had come to understand that the policies of the Third Reich were there to destroy those that rowed at the Hebrew Rowing Club.

CHAPTER 36

George stood on the dock watching Arthur in his launch while rowers in the eight glided home, oars in position, just as the fading blue sky, with hints of pink clouds, indicated dusk was approaching. A light on the boathouse wall illuminated the dock's edge so George could see rowers execute "the bringing in of the boat" with ease. Yes, he thought, they are ready. Gordon, the coxswain, had called the directions clearly, and each rower had obeyed with perfect timing. They even stood, placed a foot on the dock, pulled in their port oars simultaneously in one uniform motion. It was as though external discipline had finally translated into synchronized internal discipline, and George thought his musical mother would appreciate its demonstration of lyrical timing.

"Ten seconds," Arthur called. The rowers understood that this was the time allotted to get out and lay hands on the boat to lift it out of the water, swing it overhead, bring it down to shoulders and start the walk back to the boathouse.

"Well done," said George, opening the extra-wide metal door that allowed them to bring the sixty-foot boat into the boathouse. He looked at their relaxed faces, muscles taut, and eyes brimming with excitement. This is what rowing does, George thought. It excites. Although the young men had just expended a mountain of energy, rowing six thousand meters, some at an extraordinary pace, they still appeared spirited.

Arthur grabbed towels and threw them to two rowers, who proceeded to wipe down the boat. "Do a thorough job. Tomorrow, we'll wash it. Tonight. we have an important discussion . . . in the locker room."

Eric, Walter, Robert, Emil, Carl, Oscar, Claude, Paul, and Gordon, the coxswain, waited expectantly. They knew they were preparing for a regatta. Which one? Where? When?

Some wrapped towels around their shoulders as the heat their bodies had generated subsided, and a chill had settled in. They all took seats on the narrow locker room benches and focused their attention on George, their frames still holding a certain amount of tension. This was usually the time when they received a critique of what they had done well and where they needed to improve. Their competitive souls thrived on such information.

"Yes, we are going to compete in a regatta in Naples in a week." George waited for a bit until the subdued smiles they shared with one another subsided. He knew they all—each one of them had the yearning of a champion in their genes. He captured this moment in his mind's eye with the idea that some painter needed to illustrate rowers in anticipation of competition. Eakins' paintings of rowers on water were exceptionally beautiful, but this was another dimension. His team's contained eagerness was palpable. Could he ever capture that special feeling of anticipation in paint on canvas? And what would happen to that tension when he needed to share hard truth?

He looked over at Arthur, and he could see by his friend's furrowed brow and a slight hunch of shoulders, he shared his apprehension about the rowers' reactions. George focused on each of the rowers as he spoke, his eyes going from one to the other as the words came forth. He had rehearsed these thoughts in sentences many times, especially before falling asleep.

"We are not going to come back to Germany after the regatta in Naples. By 'we,' I mean my family and Arthur's. Instead, we are planning to continue by sea to Cyprus, pick up a boat there, and go to Palestine where we plan to remain."

The joy that had been so evident before in their expectant faces and eager bodies diminished gradually. Robert and Oscar stepped away to a locker, grabbed a sweatshirt, and returned. George could tell that everyone seemed to be waiting for someone else to make a move—to say something to relieve the jumbled thoughts. Their anxiety was palpable.

"You will arrange for transportation back to Germany?" The first comment came from Claude Silberberg and was what George and Arthur had expected. Claude had recently been given a full scholarship for the rest of his university career to continue to do some research on splitting of the atom.

"What if we want to come with you?" asked Walter Fuchs, who sat in the four-seat usually with Eric Cohen in the five-seat because they were two of the strongest rowers.

"Yes, what if we want to go with you to Palestine?" a few others also asked.

George had prepared for this possibility. "We can arrange for you to join us, but we cannot arrange for your families. It would be too risky at this point. You need to get your papers and passports in order, and most of all, prepare your families." He paused. "I have a good friend who can work on a letter of transit. I think that may be required as well."

Arthur indicated with a nod that it was time to share other thoughts. His clean-cut face became even more somber; his eyes narrowed, and the creases in his forehead deepened.

"There is a tremendous danger to us and to you if this plan leaks out and what was discussed here falls into treacherous hands. There are already 50,000 in Dachau prison for so-called nefarious crimes against the state. It is not an easy time to leave Germany."

"Why didn't you give us more time?" The pained question came from Eric Cohen, who had recently been chastised by a university professor for asking about the need for so much government propaganda on radios. His family had recently purchased one and greatly enjoyed the funny Jack Benny show produced in America. Eric noted it improved his English as he tried to listen and translate for his family, who also appeared to appreciate the window onto America. He and his family wanted more entertainment and less propaganda.

"More time means more chances that people would let something slip, or talk to God knows, to declare us enemies of the State . . . and we may wind up in Dachau," said Arthur.

"So, go home. We have been preparing you to win a regatta, but also for a different life. The rowing club is arranging for your flight to Naples so everyone will have their passport. But for those who wish to go with us to Palestine, your small suitcase should be filled with enough possessions and money to get you through a regatta and a month in a new country, and maybe your new home. An undisciplined place, I might add. Nothing like Germany, but your safety as a Jew will be guaranteed," said George.

Neither George nor Arthur had seen Wilder or Sherman enter the locker room, but they were not surprised to hear a clearing of the throat. It was Wilder's way of saying, as politely as possible, that he wanted to be part of the conversation. George broke the silence.

"Yes, please come in, Herr Wilder and Herr Sherman. We know you understand the situation," said George, indicating to his rowers to make room on the bench for the two gentlemen.

"No, we'll stand," said Wilder. Both had an unusual pallor—almost powdery white as though they had been drained of color. "We just need a minute." Wilder took in all the expectant faces and thought, so young, so much promise, and yet threatened. "It pains me even to tell you this. Perhaps you know this history from your books, but we were here in 1923 when you were mere children and this man, this man Hitler—tried to take over the government in Bavaria with a Beer Hall Putsch." Wilder's voice rose. "He had no respect for Weimar Germany—my Germany." Tears began to well up, and he looked to Schindler to continue.

"That nogoodnik went to prison, and we thought that would be the end of anarchy, revolution, but he wrote a book, *Mein Kampf* and his party gradually gained seats in the Reichstag. That is the short of it, gentlemen. That's where we are today. And what has that turned into? The country wants to be judenfrei—free of Jews." Schindler practically spit out the last words before he continued. "In case you didn't know it, they are building judenlager—camps for Jews." Schindler caught his breath. "So now it is up to you—you young people—to find us a new home. Maybe it is too late for my wife and me, but not for you."

Wilder placed a hand on his friend's arm. "We need to tell them their plan is safe with us. As far as we know, you have worked with us to perhaps win a medal in Naples and are planning to bring honor to Germany." He paused. "And for those of you who come back to Germany, who decide to remain, we will try to protect you. He turned to his friend, blinking away tears. "Come, it's time to play a game of chess. Upstairs in the boathouse. It quiets the nerves."

Arthur wasn't sure, but he thought he heard a surge of pride in the words of the older men. Pride in others for actions they wished they were taking.

Arthur looked to reassure the group. "But we also know that this is a tough decision—it's not just a regatta—not just a race—it's about freedom, resistance. You need to think about your families and whether you should come back and fight. But right now, we have Palestine, and we will always have Palestine even when Germany will not have us." With that, Arthur sat down amidst the rowers and put his arms around Carl Klitzing and Oscar Rathenau, who were closest to him. Neither returned the gesture; they weren't sure.

George raised his hand slightly. "I think they have heard enough. Two days to decide. Whatever you decide is okay. We know this is a difficult decision, and we are talking about lives and futures here. Just compete at your best level."

"I am sure we are all committed to Naples. I'm not sure about the rest of the plan," said Carl on his way out.

~~~

That evening George was grateful for the tea and kugel Frieda had set out on the table. He was even more pleased when Frieda and Werner sat down to join him, quietly sipping and adding cubes of unnecessary sugar.

"So, what do you think?" Werner thought he needed to start the conversation.

"I think we will place in the top five," said George, taking the last bite of his kugel.

He was startled when Frieda banged her hand on the table. "Not that," she said. "What do you think they will decide? Will they leave Germany for good for some unpredictable piece of geography?"

"They will go home, talk to their families, listen to radios, and read newspapers," Werner interjected. "I think your mother knows this, but she is a bit anxious."

"And Clara?" she asked. "What about Clara?"

"It is too much to ask that of her now. When we are secure in Palestine, I will write to her, tell her what life is like there. The distance and the time away should be helpful to us both. The unpredictability of Germany's future will make many people think about their own."

Frieda and Werner took silent sips of tea, each thinking about the maturity of a son who was quietly deciding to confront the precariousness of the world. How did that maturity happen?

~~~

In Naples, the driver of the large van who picked them up at the airport was determined to share with them some of the history. He told them that the body of Parthenope, who had committed suicide mourning Ulysses' departure, had reached where "Castel dell'Ovo" is located today. "And," he added. "You will think about all that while you are rowing in the Gulf of Naples."

"No," said Arthur, delighted that his guide spoke German and at the same time, happy to be away from the gray of Berlin. The sunshine of Naples and the even sunnier disposition of the driver seemed to lift the spirits of all, considering the difficult decisions that many of them were facing. For a brief half-hour during the ride from the airport to the hotel near the bay of

Naples, the mood of the young men was high as they observed pine and palm trees thriving in the strong sunlight. The immediate challenge of competing and winning for themselves and Germany was before them, as well as the much more fateful decision whether to leave Germany and go on to Cyprus and then Palestine. They all came with passports and letters of transit, but both George and Arthur knew that decisions would be made hours after the competition. They knew the adrenalin rush would need to subside so that serious commitments could be made.

Fortunately, the competition for the eights was the next day, and George and Arthur wanted this to be the rowers' sole focus. "Represent your club to make it proud but mostly make yourselves proud."

As the boats lined up in the Gulf of Naples waiting for the signal to start, George and Arthur took to the bike path along the water. After waiting for the "Ready! All! Row!" boats from Germany, Italy, Austria, Sweden, and Norway with eight rowers and a coxswain sprinted their starts and steadied their splits at the coxswain's call. Spectators could see the boats through the mist with only seconds marking distances between them. Launches with referees in jackets and smart caps followed, and not once did they have to shout out to boats to maintain distance. Calls from coxswains sailed over the air. "More on port." "Push to forty strokes." "We're almost there." "Forget the other boats."

When coxswain Gordon Tornow shouted, "Germany's got it," the crew put on a final power ten and sailed into the finish line five seconds ahead of the Swedish crew and seven seconds behind England.

After a brief respite at the finish line, either leaning back in the boat or relaxing over the oar, they rowed back to the starting dock and gathered so that Werner could quickly take a photo. Each rower and the coxswain stood with a wooden oar in hand, held straight up at his right side—smiles on every face.

"Not sure if I'll send it back to the newspaper. Depends on what everyone decides to do," Werner said. Smiles suddenly disappeared. The young men bent to retrieve the boat from the water to place it on the slings on the nearby grass, out of the way of the next race.

"Well," said George. Eric Cohen nearly shouted, "To Palestine."

From that point on, George couldn't quite associate the comments with the person, but he was sure he heard nine of them. They all wanted to go. Their combined effort in a boat for eight men and a coxswain and coaches who taught them to excel had given them both direction and courage. They understood the dangers of Germany and would take their chances on Palestine.

They would be going to a different place to row and grow into adulthood, but it would become home, and they would be there together to help build a nation and continue the possibilities of the human spirit overcoming and excelling.

ACKNOWLEDGMENTS

This novel was inspired by my trip to Israel in December 2019 when I rowed at the Tel Aviv Rowing Club founded in 1935 on the Yarkon River. Jewish and an avid rower myself, I thought that a rowing club that began in 1935 in what was then Palestine must have had a history. I gathered some bare facts from *Wikipedia*. From Berlin, in 1933, a Jewish rowing team seeing what was happening in Germany, was supposed to be heading to a regatta in Barcelona. Instead, they arrived in Haifa with their boats, where they founded the Haifa Rowing Club, which moved to Tel Aviv in 1935. These actual events inspired the novel—but what interested me most was not the escape itself but what led up to it.

"We continue to circle around the events of 1933 because the rise of the Nazis exposed so many conflicting motivations about political and social behavior. . . . In the flash of a moment Adolf Hitler became, and remains one of the most recognizable figures of world history." This is from Peter Fritzsche's book Hitler's *First Hundred Days*, which became the source of much of my material. The events of 1933 occurred two years before I was born, yet they remain etched in my psyche. They remind me of how vulnerable we are to despots and authoritarians.

The characters I created to explore this with me are imagined. In writing this book of historical fiction, I wanted to explore the motivations of a family deciding to leave Germany in a time of profound uncertainty to start life in a new country with a geography and a culture completely different from their usual circumstances. What allows us to know when it is time to leave everything we know and love? What allows us to leave soon enough?

I leave to the reader's imagination what happened to these intrepid German rowers after their arrival to Palestine in 1933—a life that would undoubtedly involve another set of intense challenges.

I read many books to understand this topic, including Fritzsche's. I also received crucial help from rowers Susan E. Cohen and Moshe Deutsch, who introduced me to the Tel-Aviv Rowing Club. I am grateful for the years of friendship and support from my Israeli friend, Dr. Tamar Ariav, whom I met in graduate school at the University of Pennsylvania over forty years ago. I appreciate the support of Yad Vashem in Israel permitting me to use the photo of rowers from its archives. There's so much history in that photo alone.

My writing group—Susan Chamberlain, Reba Parker, Lori Vogt, and Judith Zalesne—who hunkered down with me virtually from coast to coast during the pandemic and provided the most marvelous critiques and advice on how to tell this story. A special thanks to Carolyn Daffron whose critiques were superb.

Thanks as well to Keith Woebeser for the wonderful author photo.

I hope for wisdom from our leaders and an effort not to repeat the mistakes of the past.

AUTHOR

Sybil Terres Gilmar is the author of two other novels of historical fiction, *The Jew and the Pope* and *Chasing Stolen Art*, both also based on the Jewish experience. Her short stories, essays, and articles have appeared in *The Philadelphia Inquirer*, *Main Line Magazine*, *Reconstructionist Journal*, and the Wising Up anthologies *Love After Seventy* and *View from the Bed: View from the Bedside*.

Rowing Home was inspired by a visit to Israel in December of 2019, when she was privileged to row on the Yarkon River in Tel Aviv with a club that had been founded in 1935. As a rower and a child of immigrants, she knew there was a story there.

Her own fascination for rowing began at the age of sixty-nine. Returning to Philadelphia after a ten-year sojourn in Costa Rica, she was so fascinated by the sculls on the Schuylkill as she walked along Boathouse Row that she decided to take lessons. At eighty-seven, she is still rowing her single Arca de Noe at Whitemarsh Boat Club in Conshohocken, PA.

Her work as an educator in public schools for thirty years—as well as her volunteering as a docent at the Weitzman National Museum of American Jewish History and as a guide at Independence Hall in Philadelphia—inspired her to be truly grateful that her parents made the decision to leave the Pale of Settlement and come to America in 1922. It informs her focus on how and when decisions to emigrate are made.

www.ingramcontent.com/pod-product-compliance
Lightning Source LLC
Chambersburg PA
CBHW031947010726
47493CB00007B/2117